ASHLEY MACK

The Feel of You

CONTENT WARNING: mental health, suicidal ideation and self-harm, apathy, child abuse, sibling abuse, graphic sex and sexual situations, sexual assault, kidnapping, murder, mayhem, parent death, sibling death, fire, captivity, degradation

First edition

ISBN: 978-1-960161-02-4

This book was professionally typeset on Reedsy.
Find out more at reedsy.com

Kim, because this story is totally your vibe and you read things I wrote before I knew how to write well.

"I see us giving love to each other in a time of quiet between storms. It's what we were meant to do."

- FROM FRANK HERBERT'S DUNE

Contents

III   Falling

IV   Fractured

V   Determined

VI Whole

Where Were We...

Happily ever after was within reach. After death and loss, the sisters had found their life partners and were ready to fight whoever wanted to hurt their family. Anora was about to walk down the aisle and fulfill her dream of marrying Owen.

Life's never that easy, is it? The oldest and most secretive Sorrelle has been taken by their enemy, revealed to be former high school friend Elton Forrester.

Now they have to do everything they can to find Anora. While some questions will be answered, new ones will be asked. This isn't the end of the story.

Prologue - Owen

PRESENT

There's blood staining my wedding tux. It belongs to me, to Rafe, and to Alonzo who tried to stop me so I punched him in the goddamn face. The police are here but I don't care. They'll be less than useless. We won't tell them what really happened and we'll pay them off to make this go away because they'll be more of a hindrance than a help anyway.

I stalk toward the parking lot. Voices call out behind me but I don't care. I need to get to the house, get my shit, and hunt down the motherfucker who took Anora. The visions of how I will make him writhe, bleed, and burn have me salivating. This is what it looks like when I lose control. It's never happened like this before. I don't know how to stop it.

Something smacks into me from behind just as I reach for the door, smashing my body into the SUV. Strong hands grab my wrists and pull my hands behind my back, while a third hand presses between my shoulder blades. My face is smashed against the hot window as I try to fight.

I fight until all of the air is gone from my lungs and I'm suffocating while continuing to keep fighting my way to her. Death would be better than feeling this way. It would be what I deserve for not protecting her, for losing her. I've worked to keep her safe her entire life and at the moment where I could finally make her mine, I failed. No one is safe from me. From my rage.

"This isn't going to help anything," Isaac yells at me, momentarily snapping me out of my haze. "Calm the fuck down so we can do this the right way."

I still, his words and the logic of them permeating into my brain. He loosens up enough to let me take a breath. I cannot be fire in order to find her. I have to be made of ice and stone.

"Let me go," I growl. Isaac takes a step back, and after a second, the grip on my wrists releases too. I turn to see Harp, and I'm a little surprised. Aro said he's all in with helping us, but it's a brave asshole who would try and catch me in a rage.

"Gailen followed the van. Let's get back to the house and regroup."

"What about the girls?" I turn back, my instinct falling back into place and my logic taking over. Keep the Sorrelles safe. That's been my second priority for so long that it centers me. Isaac puts a hand on my chest.

"Derick has them. They want to be with Alina."

I nod, remembering my pregnant almost sister-in-law, and terror clenches in my gut. "Is she okay?"

"She's fine. Everyone is with EMTs. To the house, fucker." Just as Isaac says that, Alonzo runs up to us. He's got blood smeared from his nose, over his lips, and down his chin.

"There was a second van. They hit Gailen. She's gone." Alonzo braces himself like I'm going to hit him again. Instead, the fight goes out of me for a moment and I fall into the car, agony and ferocity at war inside me. Fuck.

"Get everyone who doesn't need medical attention to the house. Call everyone," I focus on Alonzo. "Every favor owed us, every person you can think of, and you find my wife." It doesn't matter that we haven't gone through with the ceremony. She's my wife and I am her husband because that is the demand of our souls.

I walk around the SUV and get in the passenger seat. Isaac gets in to drive, taking the keys from Alonzo who is already talking rapidly and quietly on his phone. We are going to war and there are no limits until Anora is safely back where she belongs.

Anora has been mine since the day she was born. The first time I held her, I loved her. I can't tell if it's my earliest memory or a story I heard so many times it became one. My parents and I visited Don and Arianna in the hospital. I was 2, and the adults thought it would be cute to take a picture of us together - the eldest, the heirs, the sign that their legacies would continue. I sat on the tacky, uncomfortable couch, and a minuscule Anora, only 7 hours old, was put in my chubby, clumsy arms.

In my mind, I can see her scrunched up red face and her fluff of dark brown hair. I remember her opening up her strange newborn eyes and looking right into my own. The picture they took is her and I looking into each other's eyes. A soft smile on my round little face.

"Love you," I garbled to her, a phrase that I had barely mastered at home. Then I poked her cheek and she opened her mouth. The adults all fawned, she was taken from my arms and given to Arianna to eat. It felt wrong to have her taken away from me but instead of saying so I cried, because I was 2, and that's how I knew how to communicate.

My mother slapped my hand to shock me out of it and then covered the action with a hug. It wasn't the first time she'd hit me that day but she had to be careful when it happened in public.

We grew up with our lives intertwined. No matter how we fought it, ran from it, tried to resist, or tried to hide it. We were meant for each other. Anora had finally accepted our fate and her own feelings, only for it to be ripped away. We'd already lost so much time. I refuse to let any more be stolen from us.

Our story is epic, and this is our grand fucking finale.

I

Friends

1

Owen

PAST

Sundays when I was really young were spent at the Sorrelle's house. The parents would chat, drink, eat, and leave me and Anora to amuse each other. Before she could crawl was boring, and I mostly sat by her side and watched Sesame Street. I learned my letters, numbers, and colors sitting on the floor of their living room.

Once Anora was mobile, we had a lot more fun. We got into things we weren't supposed to, moved as fast as we could to find hiding spots, or get to the kitchen and sucker the staff into giving us a snack. We played stupid games involving hiding objects, we played rescue with her dolls, and when she could finally run we spent hours in the immense yard of the Sorrelle compound making it our own. The world that we knew was ours to share.

For a time, it felt like I knew every tree, bush, and patch of clover. I knew how to follow Anora's dainty footprints through the grass, through the dirt in the woods, and the wet prints on the concrete of the back porch. I could find her anywhere. A tug in my chest would always guide me in the right direction even when I had no hints to follow. The world would arrange itself to bring us together.

Even when Alina came along, it was still Anora and I in our own little world. The one that we built and imagined for ourselves. I was always the prince and she was the princess, the king and the queen, Peter Pan and Wendy, Beauty and her Beast, and on dramatic days, the Ken to her Barbie.

Sundays were when I was safe. I dreamed and wished for Sundays.

"Can I stay?" I asked my parents. "We can play and sleep and then I can come home." I bounced with excitement, my hands clasped together in front of me, pleading. The first and only time I asked that question.

Mother laughed but it wasn't real, her teeth showed but her neck was tight. Father ignored the question, talking quietly to Don. No one even looked at Arianna to ask if it was alright. Mother put her hand on my shoulder, digging her thumb into the soft space below my collarbone. It was one of her favorite places because it was hard to bruise.

"No, sweetheart, we want you at home." I heard the message and I nodded.

"Okay, mommy," I agreed with her and turned to Anora. She raced forward and wrapped her arms around me. I didn't hug her back, I never did. I never hugged anyone. It was frowned upon in my house to seek comfort or affection. I couldn't even recall the last time I'd hugged mother. But I didn't fight her. I leaned into her tiny arms, giving back what I could.

That was a Sunday that stood out. When we got home, father slapped my back and knocked me to the ground. He held me down and smacked my backside 8 times. I counted.

"Never ask to stay there. As if our house isn't good enough. As if what we give you isn't enough. You ungrateful child."

"How dare you," mother chimed in, watching father with nothing but disappointment on her face. When father was done they didn't say anything to me. They went about their evening and had a drink together while watching the news. Eventually, I walked upstairs and put myself to bed. It was only when I heard their door close that I felt it was safe enough to cry. I was 6.

Then, I wasn't hit often, but the Sorrelles were the trigger most of the time. Something I said or did that made them think I was ungrateful to them for feeding and clothing me. That I thought the Sorrelles were better than us. If I talked too much about Anora, if I called her my best friend, when I said I liked something we had for dinner when we were there. If I was too happy when I said goodnight to them.

Tension was building between father and his supposed best friend. Things he felt were not dealt with fairly. He didn't get enough for what he did, but I didn't understand what that meant.

I'd hear mother and father talking about Don and Arianna, about Designation, which I knew was where father worked. They talked about owing people. Their voices were a nervous hiss when they did. They talked about wanting more and that they needed to handle Don in order to get it. I didn't understand anything. Not only what they were saying but why I paid a price for saying nice things about father's friend and his family.

I didn't understand their anger or their hatred, and that made me the perfect target. I couldn't tell anyone because there was no one to tell, and no one to explain it to that would understand. I was shamed into questioning Don, so I couldn't trust him either.

I learned to be quiet. I learned to keep it in, to feel nothing.

The only person who could make me feel anything was Anora.

2

Anora

I was born anxious. It's the thing that taints every memory that I have, unless I was with Owen. He made me see things differently, let go when I wanted to hold on, to run when I was frozen in place. Owen always made me feel like I had someone to watch over me and make me see what was real, and remind me what I had control over.

Like the first time he put a wet toad in my hands and showed me that while it might be wet and weird feeling, it wasn't scary. That I could laugh when the toad leapt out of my hands and away instead of scream. Owen showed me that worms ate dirt and wanted nothing to do with me. That I could scrape my knees doing something fun and I didn't have to worry that anyone would get mad at me as long as I sucked it up and didn't cry. Owen made me feel like there wouldn't be a price for being brave.

We had Sundays, and we explored the world around us like I'd never felt fear before.

On Sundays I'd forget that I woke up screaming in the night, afraid of something I couldn't describe. That I didn't think about not being alive, even when I didn't understand what it meant to be dead.

I could pretend I didn't shake myself into vomiting from anxiety about going to pre-school, interacting with other kids, talking to adults I didn't know. That crowds didn't make me panic and cry.

When I was with Owen, I wasn't the little girl who told her mom that sometimes being alive hurt but I couldn't show her where the owie was. There was so much to pay attention to and so much to be careful of, and it got even worse when Alina came along and I had to worry about everything for her, too. I was her big sister. It was my job.

The older I got, the more there was to worry about. The more things I took on my shoulders, that I had to deal with, and it didn't matter how many times my parents told me that wasn't true. How many times my therapist assured me that the grown ups could worry about these things for me, that it was my parents job to consider all these things, and keep an eye out with their grown-up senses.

I didn't have the words to explain that I couldn't turn the fear off. I didn't have the understanding to learn how.

Unless I was with Owen.

Maybe it's because he let me be afraid and found another way to do things, or that instead of dismissing my fears he either validated them, or showed me why I didn't have to worry. Owen's gift was to change my perspective.

I loved him with every fiber of my tiny, disastrous being.

I wanted to tell him how bad it was without him, but I knew something was weighing on him too. Maybe that's why we worked so well together - we were both pulled into a hell we couldn't talk about, and all the things we didn't say made sense to one another. I was born with a broken mind, and he was always on alert, vigilant, and sharp. I'd watch the mask fall over his face when we were with his parents.

Uncle Roman was fine, he gave us good candy, but something was always creepy about Aunt Elaine. It reminded me of the Other Mother in *Coraline*, like behind her smile was a spider waiting to suffocate me in her web. She hated my mom, but I don't think mom saw it. Not the way she should have.

Sometimes I'd think about asking Owen why we were both afraid, but even if we had an answer there was nothing we could do about it.

The summer I was 8, mom caught me curled in a ball banging my head against the wall. It hurt but the pain kept me from being afraid. The pain gave me clarity. No one was coming to get me. No one was going to die. Everything was fine, everything was fine, everything was fine.

They sent me to a specialized pediatric inpatient program. As far as everyone else in our life knew, they'd sent me to a summer camp for gifted children. It wasn't a stretch - I was good at school. I excelled because I focused on only that because it was easier to do what was asked of me than navigate the murky waters of interacting with other people. I didn't have friends.

I'd learned to smile, it wasn't hard to blush, so it was easy to be labeled as shy, and no one pushed me too hard.

The program was scary at first, but it gave my little mind coping skills. It gave me masks to wear, disguises to hide behind that would put distance between myself and my fear. Boxes and traps for my anxiety. They also toyed with medicating me, but decided they could wait until I was older.

I missed three Sundays. I cried during every single one because it wasn't just that I needed Owen, I also knew that he needed me and I wasn't there. Even if this was helping me, I wanted to be helping him.

The first Sunday after I got back, I ran through the yard looking for Owen. He was deep in the back by the trees, the spot he liked best where only I could find him. When he saw me, he lit up from the inside in a way I rarely saw, and when I threw my arms around him, he hugged me back for the first time. That moment was burned into my mind, one I returned to for comfort over and over. He smelled like the hot sunshine and the wet grass. His body was warm, and I felt his cheek squish against the top of my head as he pressed me into him.

"I love you," I told him. Owen didn't say anything but he squeezed me, and that said everything.

Owen asked about camp and I told him the truth, but pinky swore him to secrecy. I even lied to Alina, but I couldn't lie to him. It felt like he needed to know in order to protect me, even if he was protecting me from myself.

3

Owen

I was 12 when things got worse.

Shouting woke me up in the middle of the night. The clock said it was after 11:00 P.M. and I'd been sleeping for hours already. My body ached and throbbed as I quietly made my way out of bed. That night's beating had been particularly brutal, and there was going to be bruising all over my back. I'd have to change carefully for gym class the next day so no one would notice. I'd gotten good at that.

I crept down the hallway and stayed close to the wall in order to avoid the places in the hallway that creaked under my weight. I made it to the balcony that overlooked the living room. Father, mother, and Don were all standing close to one another, hissing in each other's faces, forgetting themselves and yelling. I picked up what I could.

"What the fuck were you thinking?!" Don roared. He never swore, so whatever father did, it was really, really bad.

"It's a way to make money and open doors. This is how the world works, Don." The expression on father's face made me uncomfortable. In hindsight, it was derision, but at the time it just made me sick to my stomach. Something was breaking and I was watching it happen.

"The hell it does," Don jabbed father in the chest and mother slapped his hand away. Don glared at her. "This isn't who we are, or what we wanted Designation to be. I don't *have* to do anything."

"You do, or they'll kill us. All of us. The girls, Owen, wiped off the fucking planet."

I covered my mouth in horror because I had a grasp on killing and dying and knew that one led to the other. Someone out there wanted to kill us if Don didn't do whatever father wanted him to do. I wasn't worried about me or my parents, but the Sorrelles didn't deserve this. Don would do anything to keep them safe. I knew that instinctively.

"It's protection. You'll fucking do it. It's easy for you. A program here, a line of code there, it'll be barely anything, and it will change the whole game for us." Father had the weird smile on his face like he was trying to convince himself as much as Don. Don frowned and shook his head, disappointment and anger radiating from him. I knew those emotions, and I wondered if Don was going to hit father.

"We're already millionaires you son of a bitch. You fucked up, Roman. This will come back to bite you in the ass."

"Don't be such a snob, Don," Mother chimed in. "This is the cost of doing business."

"That's all we are now. This is just business," Don sneered as he gestured between himself and my parents. Without another word, he walked away from them and toward the front door.

For some reason, his eyes strayed upward and he saw me. Sadness flashed in his eyes as he kept going, not saying a word that I was up and listening to everything. I was relieved when he didn't say anything. The front door slammed and I flinched. The break had happened and I didn't know what it would mean for any of us.

There were no more Sundays at the Sorrelles after that.

Except when it came to Anora and I, life would always find a way. With whatever father had gotten them caught up in, it meant longer days and weekends at Designation for both him and Don. They needed to be in the office when everyone else wasn't.

The first time father brought me with, I was there by myself, running through the Tower, the atrium, and down the dark, muffled hallways by myself. It was fine. I got away from him, I read books, I played video games, and I stayed off his radar. I'd gotten good at it because I could read him. He was never actively angry with me, just consistently, passively annoyed.

Father was rarely the one who initiated my punishments. Mother would demand them, father would enact them. It was like he went to someplace else inside himself, or a monster came out that obeyed her and existed to please her, no matter what she wanted. I knew mother was beautiful, but I knew something messed up lived under her skin. Mother stopped hurting me herself as I got older; she wanted to know that she could get father to do it. No matter the reason. It was control over me and over him.

The next time I went to work with him on a weekend, Don brought Anora. I hadn't seen her like this in almost a year. We were all trotted out at the company parties and holiday gatherings, but then we were sent away without having a chance to play together. Mother kept us separated.

Anora had never been to the Designation campus before. I held her hand, which I should have felt weird about but I didn't, and took her through everything I'd found in my last exploration. It didn't matter how much time we had been apart, we fell back into the pattern of our existence: I led, she followed. I kept her safe. I made her happy.

Anora listened with rapt attention. Speaking to her that day was the most I'd said to anyone in months. Our hands were sweaty but neither of us let go, we communicated through that connection in a way only we understood. When we touched, something opened inside me that was closed to anyone but her.

"So what do you do?" she asked.

"Last week I played video games, mostly," I shrugged. "There's a game room, though. Want to play?"

Anora shrugged back. "Sure. What kind of games?"

And that's how Anora Sorrelle became a secret pool shark.

We both sucked at first because the cues were too long for our bodies, but we kept trying.

We would compare each other's stance and hold, we even tried to understand the physics, but it came down to practicing over and over. It was more than a year's worth of playing pool once a week until we could do it and do it well. Until it was a true fight to see who would win the game. A year of getting close to each other, and being the one who was always there for the other.

"8 ball. Corner pocket," Anora called. At first, we just tried to sink the balls. Then we looked up the rules and started playing actual games. Her body moved so smoothly as she drew the cue back and forth, one eye squinted shut as she checked her shot. The sharp jolt of her arm was quick, she hit the cue ball, and the clack of it hitting the remaining black solid was loud in the quiet space. It landed in the corner pocket without touching green.

Anora stood up and stared. Usually when she won she would do a little dance or rub it in my face. It took a few weeks for her to believe that I wasn't letting her win. Something in her expression put me on alert.

"I think my mom is dying."

I dropped my cue and went around the table to take her cue from her before I took her hands in mine and grounded her to me.

"Why do you think that?" I was familiar with Anora's fatalistic thoughts, her constant fears, and that she would need patience from me to talk about what was on her mind. Anora's default setting was afraid, and it was my job to fix every fear, and protect her from what I couldn't fix.

"They told us she has cancer, and she's really sick. Alina asked if she was going to die and they didn't answer." Anora's voice cracked and I pulled her into me. The only person allowed to touch me, and that I was willing to touch. Her tears soaked my shirt and into my skin, burning me because I could do nothing.

I didn't say anything. I let her cry. I took her tears straight into my heart because this was something that I couldn't protect her from, and something I couldn't fix. Don found us like that, and I saw the strain on his face. He knew why Anora cried, and it was a burden on him, too. It only took a glance at his face to know that Anora was right. Arianna was dying, and there was nothing that could be done other than wait and watch her die.

Don had to drag Anora out of my arms, and even though she was a big kid and not a baby, he still picked her up and carried her. Her eyes peered at me over his shoulder, and I reached my hand out to her. I didn't know why, but she nodded like I'd said something. We understood each other even when it didn't make sense.

Father beat the ever loving fuck out of me that night. He wailed on me with his belt so hard that the whistle of it haunted my dreams for the rest of the week. There were welts everywhere on my body except my face. Mother had sat in her usual chair in the living room, watching impassively.

"If you were a better son, we wouldn't have to do this." Mother's voice sounded like she was soothing me, but I heard the venom underneath. "Such a beautiful boy with such a black heart." She shook her head while she looked into my eyes, then focused on father and nodded. He resumed his task, saying nothing.

I don't know why he beat me that night. I don't know if Don told him what was happening and he took out his guilt on me. If mother punished father by making him punish me. I was their whipping boy.

This was how they stopped themselves from hurting each other. This was the worst beating I'd ever taken.

The fact that I was growing up to be good looking, and how much I favored her side of the family, seemed to bother my mother, and resulted in increased violence against me. I had her blonde hair, blue eyes, and the same light spattering of freckles on my nose and across my shoulders. I'd seen photos of my uncles and grandfather, whom I'd never met, and could see myself reflected in them. I was very clearly my mother's son, and she hated that fact.

The next week at Designation, I couldn't hold my cue. My back still hurt so badly that I couldn't flex the muscles needed without shaking or flinching. Anora watched me with confusion, and when she came toward me, I backed away. It was early in spring and warm, but I wore long pants and long sleeves to hide the marks that were livid on my skin.

It was my fault I hadn't been paying attention and backed myself into a corner.

"Owen," Anora reached for me, her hand landing benignly on my arm but right over a welt. I hissed in pain and jerked away from her. Her brow furrowed in confusion, and a strength I didn't know she possessed came over her as she grabbed my hand and pulled up the sleeve of my shirt.

"Owen," she said again but this time her voice was barely a whisper. Her eyes flickered as if everything occurred to her all at once. They flashed to mine, and the fury inside them provided me with a comfort I didn't know I needed. There had been genuine fear inside me that she'd think I deserved this. That she'd ask me what I'd done to set them off. Instead, she was angry for me.

"You have to tell my dad."

"No." I flipped my arm around so she would let go of my sleeve and took her hand. Even though we'd spent all this time together, we didn't talk about anything deep unless it was really important. We needed an outlet where we could be normal, and talk about surface things that were fun. I knew Anora was in therapy and talked about her shit a lot - I wouldn't ask unless I thought she wanted to tell. There was nothing for me to talk to her about except school, and that would've been boring. I was starting high school and wanted to play sports, but I'd have to find a way to explain the injuries I had that wouldn't come from the game. I had been so careful to keep this from her. To leave her untainted by my secret.

"Please, Owen, this is wrong. It's a crime."

"Don't, Anora. Promise me." I let go of her hand and grabbed her shoulders, pulling her close so she knew how serious I was. It was the first time it occurred to me how staggeringly beautiful Anora was - smooth, tan skin, glowing brown eyes, soft pink lips. I'd kissed a few girls at parties but I'd never paid attention to their mouths like I did with Anora's right then. I started getting the most awkward semi of all time. She was still a kid, but her eyes dropped to my mouth too. I kept my hands on her shoulders but took a step back.

"Promise me," I begged, my forehead dropping to hers. I held it there for too long, comforted by the contact, and then let her go to offer her my pinkie. "Please?"

"No," she shook her head, and tears of fear pricked at my eyes. "I won't tell, but I'm not promising. I'll tell if I have to."

That was the best I was going to get from her. I nodded in agreement and let her go so I could lean gingerly against the wall. Everything hurt, and the tension of my fear made it worse. I wanted to close my eyes and make it all go away.

"You're my best friend," she told me, her voice thick as she tried not to cry. "I have to take care of you."

I shook my head at her and forced a laugh, trying to break the tension. "I don't think so, Button, that's my job."

As I intended, Anora blushed when I called her Button. As a baby, everyone had always said she was "cute as a button" and since I was a kid with little cognitive ability yet, I'd always called her Button. I'd grown out of it, but every once in a while I threw it out there. It distracted us both. I liked making her blush.

"Let's go watch a movie," Anora offered, knowing I couldn't play pool like this. I nodded, and we left the game room, and a piece of our innocence, behind.

4

Anora

The house shut down while we waited for mom to die. It was the darkest time of our lives.

The end was coming and everyone knew it, even her. I was the oldest, so I went in to see her last. I got the most time with her and it was going to be hardest on Aro and Aster; they wouldn't remember her. We all knew it. She knew it. I had to remember her for them. Alina would remember her for them. My heart cracked more every day.

Dad was a wreck. It was hard to even look at him because pain and sorrow radiated from him like a heat wave. One glance and you wanted to step back and away. It wasn't until now that I truly understood the depth of my parents love for one another. I simultaneously wanted it, and was terrified of it. I wanted someone who would love me so unconditionally they would be radically altered if they lost me. I was afraid of experiencing that same alteration, and in a way, afraid of love; I didn't know yet that I was already in a love I would never escape from.

I waited in the hall until Alina came out. Our eyes met, she nodded, and we both understood what we needed to do after this. Shut down our emotions, push aside our own needs, and take care of everyone else. Even dad. At least I had her. The older she was the less I had seen her as someone to take care of, and more as an ally in taking care of everyone else.

Mom sat in her bed, surrounded by machines. I'd heard dad talking to her home care nurse that they were going to start increasing her pain medication and it would make her sleep most of the time. This was the last thing she wanted to do before letting herself fade away. I didn't want to lose her but I didn't want her to suffer either.

Arianna Sorrelle was still beautiful, even on the brink of death. I looked the most like her, even though we'd all gotten dad's dark hair and dark eyes. Our features were similar, the same shapes even if they were different sizes. I was built like her as well - what people referred to as "delicate." For me, that had always meant I was breakable. That it would be easy to destroy me, that's why I had to be afraid of everything. I wasn't built to take on the world.

She smiled when she saw me, and it highlighted the hollows that had developed in her face, but the smile was real. I sat down next to her on the bed and took her hand. It was dry but still warm. It still felt like my mother's hand.

"Do you know what's happening?" she asked.

"You're saying goodbye." My voice was hollow, my feelings distant.

Mom nodded. "I love you."

"I love you, too."

"Someday, when you're older, you need to be more honest with your sisters." She looks down at our joined hands, and I feel shame burn in my chest. "You're not alone in this world. They will never abandon you or judge you, even though I know that's what you fear. You feel so much, Anora, that it overwhelms you, but you don't need to do that alone. Trust them." My parents had agreed to keep my secret when it came to my mental health even though they didn't entirely agree with me. They wanted me to be more open and reduce my shame. I wasn't ready yet.

"I'll try." It was the best I could give her.

We sat in silence for a time.

"I'm sorry," she said, and this time it was her that broke and cried.

"Me too," I answered, and hugged her. It wasn't the last time. I would hug her every night that they would let me, even when she was asleep from the medication. I wanted her to know that I loved her and forgave her for leaving us. If there was anything I could read in another person it was misplaced guilt. This wasn't her fault. She didn't want to leave us.

The four of us were in my room on my bed when it happened. The TV was playing reruns of some sitcom we liked but weren't capable of laughing at because somehow we knew it was today. It was a feeling in the house that had worked it's way into our marrow, becoming the fundamental alteration that would occur from losing our mom.

The sound came.

Dad's cry of horror, of pain. A shout that served no one and did nothing, but was like a lock clicking in a door. It had happened. She was gone.

Alina and I took care of our sisters. Aster was crying silently, so still it was like she was a statue in a fountain. Aro was trying hard to be brave, to be big like me and Alina, but she was still too little to regulate herself like that. Too innocent to have learned how to shut off her pain.

We got the little kids into bed. Then I turned to Alina and held her until she broke, before tucking her in too.

I was dazed and tired as I walked to my own room. Footsteps sounded in the hall behind me and when I turned he was there. Owen stared at me, cautious and sad, waiting for me to let him know what I needed. I shook my head because I didn't know.

He stalked down the hall to me and didn't stop, picking me up by my thighs so my legs wrapped his waist. I threw my arms around him and buried my face in his neck, holding on for dear life until we were alone. Owen closed the door to my room, sat down on my bed, and held me while I finally had the safety to fall apart.

I sobbed into his neck as he rubbed my back, murmuring soothing nonsense to me.

The only one I heard, the one that mattered. "I'm here, Button. I'll always be here." Finally safe because I was with him, I let my grief shatter me into pieces because I knew he'd put me back together.

I woke up in my bed, and when I sat up Owen was there. He was sitting at the end, playing a game on his phone, keeping vigil over me. My face was sore and my eyes swollen from my tears, but I couldn't cry anymore.

He looked over, his cool eyes assessing me. "You have a phone call with your therapist in 15 minutes. Don't argue."

Why would I? I nodded and went to the bathroom, cleaning myself up and trying to get rid of the heavy feeling that surrounded me. I splashed cold water in my face and took a quick drink to relieve my aching throat.

Owen handed me my phone, kissed my forehead, and told me he'd be in the hall when I was done. He'd never kissed me before. I was stunned for a second.

I didn't know what else was going on, but if Owen was at the house, it meant the Carvers were too. Despite how much I hated them for what they did to him, I kept my promise, and I knew they'd get business taken care of for dad. That was all they cared about: that business got done. I hated that dad had to rely on them for anything but there was no one else to help. In his pain dad reverted to seeking out the person he once trusted.

Most things had been decided and prepared in advance. There wasn't much to do except make sure dad didn't lose it. Uncle Roman could handle that, I hoped.

I got comfortable on my bed, even though I felt like something was wrong with my body. Even though I'd been working through my grief and fear with Dr. Landry for months, the reality of mom being dead felt different than I expected. The phone rang and I answered. I talked and I listened. I tried to believe that we would heal, and I would keep trying to believe it until I actually did.

Dr. Landry knew me well, but she also reminded me that grief was a process. There was no talking my way through it like some of my anxieties. Losing someone you loved would demand to be felt, so all I could do was hold on and feel it. She reminded me that I wasn't alone, that I needed to reach out. I agreed but didn't know if that was the truth. I said it with conviction because I wanted it to be true.

When we ended the session, I couldn't move.

"Owen!" I called for him because I couldn't leave the bed. I couldn't breathe. My vision tunneled. "Owen," that time it was a whisper but it didn't matter. He was coming.

He walked into my room, took me in his arms, and demanded that I breathe. I breathed for him.

Other than to feed me, Owen didn't leave my side for three days.

Not until we needed to fulfill our obligations and have a funeral. One I barely remembered, and wasn't present for. Not really.

While we'd been hiding, something had happened to Aster. She was more silent than ever, almost terrifyingly so. Whatever it was, it had dad more caught up in worrying about her than dwelling on the loss of his wife, so in one sense I was grateful. I wanted to ask, but dad kept us distant from her. It worried me, but for the first time in my life a different feeling overwhelmed my ability to worry.

We all returned to the house, and Owen and I retreated to my room.

We sat side by side, leaning against the headboard of my bed. I held his hand and leaned my head on his shoulder. I had needed him, called out to him with my heart, and he'd appeared to hold me together.

"I love you," I whispered, afraid how he'd respond. I knew I loved him in a way that was more than friendship, but also a way I didn't quite understand yet. A way that I wasn't ready to understand. Still, he needed to know. Life was short and I had to say it.

Owen kissed the top of my head for the second time. "I love you too, Anora."

5

Anora

I barely saw him for the next few years. It was only at parties where family attendance was mandatory. Even then, we'd be kept apart from each other. It was us sharing looks heavy with meaning across crowded rooms.

The gulf between our dads expanded, the darkness invaded Designation. We all knew something was going on that made dad nervous. That when once the Carvers had been Uncle Roman and Aunt Elaine, they were now Mr. and Mrs. Carver. I would ask dad about Owen but he would only smile sadly and tell me he hadn't seen him.

Dad hired more security, our lives got smaller and less normal. We couldn't go anywhere without a bodyguard. We didn't ride in the same car as dad when we went places as a family because there was a risk I didn't understand. I knew dad was making more money. Designation was in the news all the time for expanding and creating new things. I was proud of it and what dad was doing, but I didn't know why he wasn't as proud. I was afraid to ask.

The summer before I started high school, I finally got to be alone with Owen again. It had been two years without mom and so it had been two years since we'd really seen each other. Since we'd spoken more than hellos and goodbyes.

It was the annual Designation picnic. Owen and I had made eye contact across the lawn and I tipped my head in a question. Owen looked around and then nodded. He stepped away immediately, and I followed. We entered the familiar atrium of the building and walked casually beside one another until we reached the elevator.

When the doors closed on us, I flung my arms around him. He was so much taller than he'd been. I had to jump to get my arms around his neck and my feet didn't reach the ground. I dangled from his neck without shame until he wrapped his arms around me and held me in return. Kept me close. Dug his nose into my hair and inhaled me.

When we parted, we didn't really let each other go. I slid down his body, pressed against him, and looked into his face. He had aged. Grown into himself.

My heart and stomach fluttered because I could now recognize that Owen was gorgeous. He was the most handsome boy I'd ever seen. I knew I loved him, but now a full blown crush blossomed. I blushed as our eyes met, and the icy heat in his made everything flutter again.

"I miss you." I whispered. "Are you okay?"

"No," he shook his head. "I wasn't. I am now."

When the elevator doors opened, we stepped apart but he grabbed my hand. Owen kept my fingers entwined with his and we walked to the game room. As expected, it was empty. We set up the pool table and he let me break. We played for a few minutes before I broke the silence, feeling the need to fill it.

I started chattering to him about everything that had happened since I saw him last. I interrogated him about high school because I was nervous. He asked about therapy and for the first time I gave honest answers.

We didn't talk about his parents, but I asked if he still wanted me to keep his secret.

"I'm almost out, Anora. Two more years. Don't worry about me."

"I'll always worry about you." I smiled at him.

He stepped close to me. "I don't want to be a burden to you."

I shook my head fiercely. "You aren't. Worrying about you is thinking about you and I want to think about you." It came out before I could stop it, and I blushed fiercely as a slow, dangerous smirk spread across Owen's face. He smiled so rarely that even one that was so teasing was treasured in my heart.

"I think about you, too." He reached up and held my chin. My eyes fluttered shut when his thumb trailed down my lower lip. The touch was an electric tingle through my body. We stood there in a bubble of tension, then he stepped back to break it.

We resumed our game, I kicked his ass, and we snuck back to the party before anyone knew that we had left.

In the elevator back up, I looked at him and steeled myself. "I love you."

Owen looked at me out of the corner of his eye and a hint of the smirk returned. "And I love you, Anora Sorrelle. Never forget."

That aside, one of the most important exchanges happened that night: we finally had each other's contact information. Owen was no longer out of my reach at any time.

Every night, by 9:00 P.M. without fail, I would get the same text:

Owen: *Goodnight. I love you.*

6

Owen

By the time Anora joined me in high school, my reputation was solid. I was smart, and I took absolutely no shit. I had zero interest in friendships, but I didn't mind mutually beneficial arrangements. People knew not to expect anything of me outside of what we owed each other. Guys who had my back because I had theirs, but not anyone that I could truly trust or let in. They weren't bad guys, they just weren't people who would understand my life.

I hadn't figured out a way to play sports and still hide what my parents did to me, so instead I helped the jocks get their work done and they made sure I was respected.

What my father had done, getting in bed with the criminal elements of Chicago, became a well-known thing. Even though it was all him, the bullshit of the movies convinced everyone that this had always been some "Family" connection of Don's. There was an air of criminality and danger attached to him and the girls now. No matter what they were actually like as people, the idea that their dad was a criminal who was getting away with it preceded them. It made people intrigued but it also made them afraid.

That worked to my advantage to protect Anora.

I couldn't claim her yet, not the way I wanted. She was only 14, and needed to live more of life on her own before it became a life with me. Plus, I knew it would delight my parents and they'd see it as another way to manipulate Don. I'd wait until we were both 18, free of their influence, and then I'd make her mine. I wanted to keep what she and I had untainted. It was the thing that burned in my chest and gave me the strength to put up with bullshit every day. I was working toward the life I could have with her.

It was common knowledge that our dads worked together, and people still believed that our families were close. I insinuated that it was my job to protect her; that Anora needed to be kept untouched because she was going to be a mafia bride. That if anything happened to her, the violent man she was supposed to marry one day would torture and kill them for touching what was his.

They believed me. They just didn't know that man was me.

I hadn't killed anyone, but I knew without a doubt that I would take any life if it meant protecting hers. Anora made me abandon any morals I had.

Anora and I weren't friends in school, but I made sure people saw us together. I made sure they remembered that she was always under protection. Because of her struggles with anxiety, she kept to herself and while she was friendly she didn't make friends. It was like watching a female version of myself adjust to the catty, petty halls of the institution of teenage education. Except I wanted to be alone, and she felt she had to be. It was something I didn't know how to fix for her, and I hated it.

Anora struggled to trust anyone, and didn't let them in. She was afraid to make friends, so she made acquaintances. It was easy to keep things shallow and pleasant.

With everyone but me.

Our friendship, our everything, bloomed in the conversations we had at night. Thousands of messages, serious, benign, academic, idiotic, private, even sexy a few times, although I shut those down. Yes, I wanted her and could recognize that she was fucking stunning, but she was a kid still. She was my only friend, and we needed to stay just friends for awhile longer. We had shut ourselves off from a lot of the world and the only door we kept open was to each other.

By the time I was 16, I was taller and stronger than father.

It didn't matter though. When mother started talking, and he started listening, all the fight that I worked hard to develop would dissipate from my body. They'd programmed my brain to break when they wanted to punish me, and I hoped that if I took it, it would make me stronger when I finally got away. Two more years and I'd be free. It was harder to hurt me now, but that didn't mean he didn't try.

"You're a stupid, useless child, Owen," mother sneered. "Harder." That was her favorite attack now, but her opinion of me had never mattered. I never let them see me react anymore.

Father's belt whipped through the air. It wasn't even one he wore anymore. The leather had been broken in on my back, and it snapped across my skin over and over. Sometimes she'd make him go so hard for so long that I'd pass out, and I'd wake up on the floor hours later. They'd have gone to bed, and I'd pick myself up, take care of it, and go to sleep.

I never missed my nightly text to Anora though. She needed to hear that I loved her, that she was loved, and I needed to be consistent about it so she knew she could rely on me. That I'd be there, no matter what.

Things were getting bad at home in a way that was new. A way that scared me enough that I told Anora things had changed.

A: *You have to tell my dad.*

O: *No. I don't know what's going on, and he has no reason to believe me.*

A: *I think your body is evidence.*

O: *Not until I know more. Something bad is happening.*

A: *Come stay with us.*

O: *You know I can't.*

A: *I'd keep you safe.*

I smiled at the message because Anora didn't know she already kept the most important parts of me safe - my mind, my heart, and my soul. Without her, I would have lost them all a long time ago. She was the refuge I hid in while they tried to break me. The memories, the fact of her existence, the way she knew my darkest secret and still trusted me, cared for me, regardless. That was how she kept me safe.

She kept me whole as they broke my body.

Mother joined in sometimes because she knew it didn't work the same as it used to. The opening salvo was an insult and multiple slaps across my face, but she didn't have the strength to leave a mark. I'd pull inside myself, give her a dead-eyed stare, and she'd shove me to my knees and demand father get to work.

When I'd fall, she'd kick me before using her foot to turn me over. Sometimes she'd wear heels and bury the point of the stiletto into my thighs and biceps, leaving deep, incredibly painful bruises that made it hard to move.

Those took the longest to heal but were the easiest to hide.

It was happening almost every night. The tension when I would get home from school would be so thick I couldn't escape it in my room.

Change was coming, and I started to fear I might actually be in danger from them. Whatever was going on it felt like they'd take it out on me until they killed me.

They would whisper in the office. Even behind locked doors I could hear their frantic hissing. Something bad was happening. They were nervous.

I knew a bad beating was coming when there was only silence in the house. Before going downstairs the night that changed my life, I'd messaged Anora that I loved her, that something was happening, and that if she didn't hear from me by midnight she needed to tell her dad that something was wrong at our house. I debated telling her to call the police but whatever father had done, he'd dragged Don in with him, and I didn't want to give law enforcement an opening to fuck around with their lives.

I waited for her to say she loved me too, and to promise to go to her dad. I pocketed my phone and went downstairs, dread and fear pooling in my stomach. If I could find the will to fight back, I would, but there was also the fear that once I started I'd never stop and I'd kill them both. I didn't want their blood on my hands. I wouldn't let them drag me down to their level.

When I stepped into the front room, mother was sitting in her chair, but I didn't see father. Then he shoved me from behind and I crashed to my hands and knees. The whistle of the belt was my only warning. The beating was fast and ruthless. Sometimes I tried to count the hits as a distraction but this was so quick and hard I lost count. I grunted with each hit, bracing myself as I tried to retreat inside my mind. Mother kicked me over so she could see my face as he whipped me across my back and side.

There was no expression, but a glimmer of glee in her eyes. Watching him hurt me was what kept her madness at bay. I met her eyes and wished she was dead.

Father grabbed my shirt and yanked me up to face him. I was surprised the old man had the strength in him to do it, and I glared at him with all the energy I could muster. I hadn't looked at him in so long I was startled to notice how gaunt he was, how faded and aged he'd become. Still gripping my shirt, he slammed me down onto the floor. My head smacked the wood, pain radiating through it, and across my face. He did it three more times before I lost consciousness.

The last thought I had was that I hoped Anora stayed awake. I needed her to save me.

7

Owen

When I woke up in the hospital, the first face I saw belonged to Don Sorrelle. I knew he'd be concerned, but there was something else in his expression that caused fear to wave through my body. With a quick check, I could still move all my limbs, so it wasn't that I was paralyzed or something. He was worried, and it wasn't only about me.

My head ached as I moved to sit up. He turned to me, and I prepared myself for bad news. Was I being arrested? Had my parents told some lie that would end up with me incarcerated? Did something else happen while I was under?

"Is Anora okay?" I didn't have the control to stop myself from openly focusing on her. Don almost smiled and nodded.

"She's fine."

"How long have I been here?"

Don sighed. "Three days. There was some bleeding, they kept you under until it resolved." Fuck. Three fucking days. He'd never hurt me that badly before.

"Am I going to be okay?"

Don nodded. He looked away from me and out the window, and I wanted to tell him to get on with it, rip off the band-aid, spill whatever the fuck is so upsetting.

"What happened." It wasn't a question but it was at the same time.

"Your parents are dead." His voice was gentle even though his words were a knife.

Okay, band-aid ripped. The air left my lungs, but a huge burden also lifted off my shoulders. I stared down at my hands, trying to navigate my emotions. They were dead. They couldn't punish me anymore. In the three days that I'd been in the hospital, something had happened to take their lives. I was free in a way that I'd never experienced before.

Had anyone ever been so relieved to be an orphan as I was right then? What the fuck did it say about me that I could only feel good about the fact that they were gone?

"Because of me?"

"No," Don rushed to me and awkwardly patted my arm. "How much do you know about what's been happening at Designation?"

"Enough," I answered, cagey. Don nodded in approval, and glanced around the room as if there was a chance that someone was listening to our conversation. For all I knew, there could've been; I'd listened to father talking to mother, to conversations he had when he didn't know I was around. I'd gathered enough information on what he was doing to destroy him if needed.

"Roman made an enemy, and that enemy took them out. If you had been there, you'd probably be dead too."

I snorted in derision and it hurt like a fucking bitch. "Thanks, dad."

Don paled at my acknowledgment of who did this to me. He opened his mouth to ask a question, but shook it off.

"I've resolved the issue. You're safe. As far as the world knows, they were killed in a mugging while out to dinner for their anniversary."

"That's some Batman shit, Mr. S. And no one questioned it?"

"No." He cleared his throat. "You'll be coming to live with us."

I shot up from the bed, nearly roared in pain, and collapsed back on the mattress. Alerts and bells started going off around me and Don was shuffled away as nurses came in to poke at me and try to calm me down. My head throbbed and I was sweating profusely because of it, but adrenaline was racing through my body and I couldn't stop it.

I was afraid that I was hallucinating. Or that I'd died, and this was some kind of strange heaven.

My parents, my tormentors, were dead. Murdered, hopefully painfully, and I was going to be in one of the only places that had ever felt safe to me. When the ruckus died down, Don approached again. I wanted this, but I also needed to know that it was the right thing to do.

"Is it safe to have me there? Are you safe? Are the girls?" It wouldn't be worth it to live with them if the shadow of my father put them at risk. My presence tainted them enough, I wouldn't let the specter of his bad choices do it too. If the deals he'd gotten them involved in put a target on their backs, I would run. I would give up the future I had wanted with Anora as long as I was keeping her safe. I could love her from afar, just like I'd been doing.

I'd missed three days of telling her I loved her. I needed to find my phone.

"It's safe. As I said, it's been resolved. To everyone's satisfaction. We'll need to be more cautious with security but that's true regardless. We're safest when we're all together." Don sounded confident, and I knew he'd never put his family at risk, not for me. I believed him that it would be safe.

"Right," I nodded.

Silence fell between us; I knew he had a million questions, and I didn't want to answer most of them. Did he feel guilty for not knowing the monster that lurked beneath his former best friend? Did he have any idea what Roman had been doing to me? I decided in that moment I'd only ever call them by their first names. My parents were dead, and

I was disowning them, disavowing our relationship, because they'd never cared for me the way they should. They were Roman and Elaine Carver, and they meant nothing to me.

There was still something in the back of my brain that squirmed, wondering if I'd deserved what they did to me. That I might have deserved to die with them for the complication and danger that Roman had brought to Designation, and to the Sorrelles. The world might have been better off if all the Carvers had been wiped off the map.

"They're releasing you tomorrow if observation goes well today. Your things are already packed and at our house, in your room." Don hedged before asking his next question. "Your home is currently not available for entry, but is there anything you'd like?"

"No. And when it's all done, get rid of everything. Sell it, trash it, burn it. I want nothing. Sell the house, too."

Don nodded. "And services?"

"A private burial. Me and you. No one else." They didn't deserve to be grieved. To have people pretend they knew them or lost them. For the weird transition to occur after anyone dies that they were saintly, special, amazing. Roman and Elaine were none of those things. They were selfish, greedy, violent monsters. They and their memory will be buried. The fact that the lie about their death was so brutal would work in my favor.

"I think that's for the best," Don agreed. "Everything is yours, although some won't be accessible until you're 18. Did Roman ever talk to you about Designation?"

"What about it?"

"He and I were joint owners. His ownership passes to you."

I owned Designation now. Holy fuck.

I don't care what an asshole it makes me, but I wish they'd died a long time ago.

"In the earlier days when things were better, we had agreed to a succession plan. The oldest child, of either family, would get the first offer to take over."

My head spun and it had nothing to do with my injury. This was information overload. The other shoe had to fucking drop. "Take over Designation?"

"Yes. Is that something you'd want?"

"Yes," I nodded and regretted it as pain stabbed my skull. I swallowed around my nausea. "I'm not bad with computers."

"I know," Don smiled, and it was his real smile, for the first time since he'd been in this room with me. I had a feeling he wouldn't grieve Roman and Elaine either. His concerned state was about me, and it was gratifying and frightening. I didn't deserve care from the Sorrelles.

"I'd like us to work toward that then, but right now, get some rest. Do you need anything? Do you want me to stay?"

The kid in me that Roman and Elaine hadn't destroyed wanted to ask him to stay. Wanted someone to parent me through my fucking brain injury. But I'd hidden that little kid away for a reason. I was alone now, and I needed to keep standing on my own two feet.

"You don't have to stay, thank you. Is my phone here?"

Don stepped to the table next to the hospital bed and slid it across my lap. My phone sat there, ominous and untouched. It had been in my pocket when Roman attacked.

"I charged it. Do what you need to do."

I forced a smile, and after wavering for a few minutes, Don left the room.

When I was sure he was gone, I turned on the phone. After it fully turned on, notification after notification filled the room with buzzing. They were all from Anora on multiple platforms. If Don had turned on my phone or looked at it, he would've seen that we were talking. He didn't ask about it, and I doubted he ever would.

The thing is, Anora had followed through on what I'd asked her to do; she and Don were the reason I was in this hospital and alive. I didn't even think to ask him about it, and it was too late now. My friendship with Anora had been revealed, and I had no idea how Don was interpreting it.

I read through Anora's messages, and my heart cracked at how desperate and scared she sounded. How scared I'd made her. She filled me in on my own situation, telling me that Don had gone to the house and then called her and said I was being taken to the hospital. She told me I needed to report my parents. There was silence for a few days when she knew I was okay, then a lone message: *I'm not sorry they're gone.*

Neither am I, Button. I loved that she hated them so fiercely on my behalf.

I opened up our chat thread where I had every message saved automatically.

I looked to check how many nights I'd missed, and typed.

O: *I love you. I love you. I love you. Had to catch up.*

The phone rang and I answered. All I could hear on the other side of the call was gasping. My heart hurt worse than my head in that moment.

"Don't cry, Button. I'm okay."

"This is all so fucked up," she barely whispered.

"It is. I'm sorry."

"What are you sorry for?" she snapped, the feisty Anora only I got to know coming out. "They hurt you, they're dead, and they're not even paying for their worst crime."

"I love you," I couldn't think of anything else to say to that.

She let out a watery laugh. Then we talked, and my body loosened. The pain decreased, and the burden lifted a little. I'd get to see her every day, but it was going to be more important than ever that I kept boundaries between us. Anora needed to grow up. I'd protect her innocence, every aspect of it, for as long as I could. When I protected hers, I protected my own, too.

8

Anora

The four of us were in the library when the front door opened, heralding the arrival of the next big change. I heard the sound of dad's footsteps, followed by the slower, softer footsteps that I knew belonged to Owen. I could hear the pain in them. He didn't want to take a step, but he had to keep moving forward.

We left the library and waited as they walked closer. Owen looked pale and closed off, even a little green because I'm sure he was nauseous. He told me that the pain was rough, and that sometimes he still had weird side effects. I'd made sure we added blackout curtains to his bedroom to help with the headaches and his reactions to light.

I stepped in to take over and make sure he knew he was home.

"Welcome," I smiled at him, polite and distant, unsure how we navigated our relationship in front of people who didn't know it existed. "Let's get you to your room."

I started to walk toward the stairs, keeping a slower paced so that he could follow. Owen trailed after me, and to save his pride I didn't walk with him. I waited at the top, just out of view. As soon as Owen turned into the hall, I darted forward to take his arm and lead him. When it was just us he wouldn't care.

His bedroom would be across from mine. It was an accident of availability, but I liked it regardless. I liked knowing he would be right there if I needed him, regardless of the circumstances that put him there.

He was in enough pain that he gripped onto me without hesitation and we walked down the hall. There was so much I wanted to say and ask but I didn't think it was the time, and I didn't think it was my business. Not until he wanted to talk, which might never happen. We talked about everything except what happened with his parents. I didn't think them dying was going to change that.

The door was open, and I walked him straight to the bed, sitting him down on the edge while I fluffed and stacked the pillows so he could sit back and rest.

One corner of his mouth lifted. "I could get used to this."

"You should. I'll take care of you."

"No, Button. I'll take care of you, this is just a temporary setback."

I shook my head at him. "We take care of each other."

"Okay," he said as he patted my hand. I went to his en suite and got him a glass of water and set it next to the bed. I wrung my hands because I didn't know what else to do, I just knew I needed to do something. I had to fix this. I could've fixed this earlier but I'd kept my promise. I kept his secret because it was him and he asked me to.

The anxiety that I'd failed him welled inside me, strangling my breath.

"Do you want to talk about it?" I forced the words out. I figured it wouldn't hurt to offer.

"Not yet. Tonight."

I gulped. "You want me to come back tonight?"

The corner of his mouth lifted again. "Yeah. That okay?"

I nodded, and the tightness loosened a little bit. He wasn't upset with me. My Owen was here, and he would be whole again soon. I hadn't failed him.

Pulling in a hard breath, I couldn't fight the impulse anymore. I stepped forward and cupped his face, tilting his head up just a bit so that my lips could press to his. It was quick and soft, but it was what I needed to do and feel so that I didn't freak out.

I needed to feel Owen in exactly that way because I needed to be closer to him than I'd ever been before. I needed to feel that he was real and safe. I could imagine everything else, but not this, because we'd never kissed before.

It was tame in comparison to the things other people our age did, but it was crossing a line for us that he'd been very careful to keep well drawn.

I stepped back but he grabbed my wrist. I could only look where his hand grabbed mine, then he tugged me closer. When I looked up to meet his eyes, he was amused more than anything.

"Come here," he rasped. I leaned over him again, and Owen lifted a hand to dive into my hair and hold me. He pulled my mouth back to his. The kiss was deeper this time, our mouths still closed, but it communicated something regardless. That I hadn't stolen that kiss because he'd wanted to give it to me. The butterflies rioted from my stomach up to my heart, and I breathed out sharply when he pulled away.

"I'll see you tonight," he said against my lips, looking into my eyes. "Now I need to rest." He tilted my head down so he could kiss my forehead, and I inhaled again. Owen didn't smell like himself right now, but that was okay. I could feel his warmth and maybe I would stop having the nightmare that he'd died. That dad hadn't gotten there in time, and I'd been responsible for his death.

Owen was alive. His horrible parents were dead. He was with us where he belonged.

Owen was home.

The light on Owen's bedside table cast a golden line under his door, and I didn't bother to knock. Everyone else had gone to bed. I'd listened to my sisters chatter about Owen's presence, speculate about his parents, and I'd seen the suspicion grow in Alina's eyes. She didn't trust Owen, and she blamed his parents for what we'd gotten pulled into.

My closest sister already spent most of her free time learning various martial arts, and I knew she'd been itching for a real fight. At some point she'd confront him, and I hoped that Owen would handle it well. They needed to trust each other. We all did. Owen rarely showed what he was thinking or feeling, so at best Alina would send her rage at him and it would break like a wave against a wall.

When dad had come home from the hospital after Owen had woken up, he'd laid it all out for Alina and me. He'd decided we were old enough to know, and believed we had learned from recent events how imperative it was to keep secrets. He'd been honest that they were involved with criminals, and that Roman was killed for getting out of line. The situation had been fixed. He also told us that Owen inherited Designation from Roman, and that based on how they'd structured things, Owen would inherit it all if he wanted. Someday Designation would belong to him and that Owen had said he wanted it.

That wasn't news to me, but I had to keep a straight face. Owen had often talked about wanting to work for Designation, and he'd started working with computers more to learn about programming and what they did. He'd even told me about how he wanted to work his way up, although I had a feeling that wasn't going to be possible anymore. He was the next in line.

We had to protect him. Whether he wanted it or not, Owen wasn't just Designation's future, he was ours too. Dad made that clear without directly saying it. He made it clear that Owen was family, and he expected us to treat him like family.

Whenever my sisters asked me about Owen, I demurred. I lied. It made me think about my last full conversation with mom, and that I lied to them so much more than I ever expected. I told myself it was to protect them, but the truth was it protected me. I didn't want them to doubt me if they knew about the medication that kept me from falling down the rabbit hole in my own head, or hurting myself.

I didn't want to let them into my relationship with Owen. They would tease, they would interfere, and sometimes he was the only solid ground I had. He didn't seem to want anyone to know either. There was a secret world that was only Owen and me, and that was the way I wanted it to stay.

So I walked in to his room when I knew there was no one to see, and climbed onto his bed right next to him.

Owen had showered and changed into flannel pajama pants and a long-sleeved t-shirt. He was covering in bruises. I felt the phantom pain of them in my own skin, and I would have taken that pain from him in a second. I would have born his pain if I could.

I leaned back against the headboard and took his hand, pulling it onto my thigh.

"Tell me," I demanded.

He did.

I couldn't stop myself from crying even though I tried. The years of harm that he endured right under our noses. It had been going on for years before the first time I discovered it. Owen's voice was dead as he talked about it, like it happened to someone else, like he didn't feel the pain of any of it.

At some point he took away his hand to lift his arm and tuck me under it. I cried tears for him into his shoulder, and clung to him as if he'd died. Some part of him was dead, and he'd never get it back. I hated them more than I thought possible. I hated myself for crying for him because I knew it hurt him when I did, but I couldn't help it.

"You're safe now," I promised him. "We have you. I have you."

"I know." He sighed and then extricated himself from me. "But we need to be careful, Anora."

"Careful how?" My heart thumped wildly, painfully, in my chest.

"We're friends. That's all we can be right now."

I nodded, trying to school my face into something I had control of, that didn't show him how much that hurt. I failed. I was so head over heels for him that it was like my heartbeat said his name. He was the first and last thing I thought about every day.

"Hey." He tucked his hand under my chin, tilting my face up until I met his eyes. *"Right now,* Button. I need to focus on getting through what happened to me. We might want more, but we're not ready for it. Do you understand?"

I nodded. "But…" I looked to the side, unable to meet his eyes as a blush crept across my face. "Will you - with -"

"No," Owen said sharply, and my stomach fluttered. "And you won't either."

I glared at him then but couldn't hold it. "You don't own me."

"Yes, I do," his voice dropped, deeper than I'd ever heard it before. "And you own me. I'm waiting for you. Will you wait for me?"

"Of course," I answered. It wasn't even a question. There was no one else. There never would be. While that might be the naive thought of a 14 year old girl, I had no doubt it was also absolutely true.

"Good."

He kissed my forehead, and kicked me out of his room to go to bed.

He didn't need to text me anymore. Every night, before we went off to our respective rooms, we stood at our doors and looked at each other.

"I love you," Owen would whisper. He always said it first.

"I love you, too. Goodnight." Then I'd smile and he'd smile back. He only smiled for me those days, and I saved every single one in my memory.

It was agony. It was heaven.

9

Anora

The morning of my 16th birthday, Owen woke me up when he crawled into my bed. We faced each other on our sides, and I didn't feel self-conscious even though my hair was a mess and I had morning breath. Owen came to me so I was happy. In the year and a half that at the house, he almost never went in my room. It was one of his lines and I respected it. Even when I didn't want to.

He slid a small box across the space between us. "Happy birthday, Button."

I shifted so that I could take the box and open it. Inside was a bright chain, probably platinum, and a tiny charm in the same metal. At first, it looked like a simple hoop, but then I noticed it was slightly ovular in shape and realized it was an O. It was a discreet way to mark me as his, in a way that was known only to us.

"Thank you," I blushed, and maneuvered it out of the box. I rolled onto my back to put it over my head. The chain was long, and the charm rested deep between my breasts. When I looked at Owen he was looking there, and I remembered that I wasn't wearing a bra. My body reacted to his attention, so I rolled back onto my side to hide myself.

"I love it," I told him.

"I love you," he answered. "I'll see you at the party." He slid out of the bed and walked backward toward the door, his gaze admiring as he looked at me. Owen still kept his physical distance, but he was nearly 18. I could feel him looking at me like a man looks at a woman, and I'd started to want him the way a woman wants a man. I understood now what that meant and how it felt.

He wasn't wrong that we were young, but he made me want to jump ahead to the good part of being older.

My birthday party was an obnoxious, lavish affair in a hotel ballroom downtown. The entire school was invited even though I didn't know, and wouldn't consider myself friends, with most of them. We moved in the same circles and had to be nice to each other, but I didn't trust any of them. I didn't let them know me.

When I had three built in best friends in my sisters, and Owen in my corner, I didn't need anybody else. They laughed at me and with me, protected me, pushed me, and knocked me down a peg when I needed it. We spent all our free time together and I felt like the odd one out with other people when I said I genuinely liked my sisters.

Aro and I could talk books for hours, even though I had read far less than her. When she was littler she'd let me do her hair and I'd be the queen when she ran off to play princess. Alina and I did everything together, even when she didn't want to, like making her buy new clothes. Or when I didn't want to, like going to a million tournaments for her to compete in. Aster was the harder nut to crack, but Aster was who I sought out when I needed quiet, or sarcasm. She could provide both.

She was brilliant too. Aster was on track to start high school early and could already program and code better than some of the people at Designation. Even though the darkness inside her was obvious, I loved her and was proud of her. I was the one who'd convinced dad to let her fast track school. He wanted her to try and be "normal" but she wasn't, and it wouldn't be fair to force her into a box where she didn't belong.

He'd had an expression close to pity when I said it, and I wondered if he thought I'd done that to myself. If I'd anxietied myself into pretending everything was fine, into demanding polite perfection and stuffing myself into a box I didn't fit. If I'd cut off and mangled parts of me to make it work. He wouldn't be wrong, but my not normal was tame compared to Aster.

I was mentally ill. Aster was dangerous. They were not the same.

She sat at a table in the back, typing away on her phone. No one approached her. In fact, they gave her a wide berth. Instead of being offended, I found it funny. I envied her for being able to shut out the world so thoroughly. Even at her age, people feared her. They felt they were in danger in her presence. Even I did, but I also knew without a doubt that she would never hurt me. She had walls so strong they were almost visible.

People constantly ignored mine.

After the dinner, it was time for dancing, and even though I'd say no thank you, I'd be dragged out and whirled around. It was my party. Everyone wanted to be able to say they danced with me. I knew about the mafia bride rumors, and that meant people treated tonight like some sort of free pass to touch me. I had no doubt come Monday there would be some rumor going around that I'd fallen for one of the boys I danced with and my mafia fiance was pissed.

The only person I wanted to dance with was sitting at a table on the edge of the dance floor looking sinful and decadent. He was wearing a tuxedo with a white jacket and black lined lapels. There was a deep purple rose pinned to it, matching the purple rose in my hair, and the roses on the tables.

He'd done his hair, the swoop of blonde pushed back from his sharp, angular face. There was enough of a smile on his face to be a smirk and some of the girls looked at him and approached, but he didn't acknowledge them with more than a brief word of rejection. Owen never took his eyes off me, seeming to be more and more amused as each partner whirled me around.

We were rich kids, we knew how to dance to this shit. It's like we were playing dress up as our parents at a party like this. It would end early, and everyone would go find a real party. I would get to go curl up at home, hopefully with Owen.

"What do you think?" The person I was dancing with leaned too close, his breath on my cheek. I snapped my gaze away from Owen, flinching a little to find someone else's face so close to mine. Elton Forrester was nice in a bland way. It made him hard to describe, like he was so normal he was unnoticeable. We had a lot of classes together and I considered us friendly.

"I'm sorry, what?"

Elton pulled me tighter against him. "I think we should go on a date next weekend."

"Oh, Elton, I," I stumbled as I tried to kindly reject him. "I don't date."

"Okay," he nodded. "Then we can hang out."

I shook my head. "My dad wouldn't let me."

Elton straightened, and I relaxed slightly because it put space between us. "I'll talk to your dad. He can trust me. I'm a Forrester. I'll take care of you."

"That's very sweet Elton, but please don't. I respect his rules, and I wish you would too." Dad had no such rules, but he wouldn't mind me hiding behind him either.

"You're such a good person, Anora," his voice was reverent, and I gave him a weak smile.

"Pardon me," Owen's voice cut in, and I almost sagged in relief. "It's my turn with the birthday girl."

Fury flashed on Elton's face for a second but then he smiled and nodded. "Of course. She should dance with her brother."

Owen turned to Elton with a feral grin on his face. "Not her brother. Not even close." Then he winked at a flabbergasted Elton, and whirled me around. This was exactly where I belonged, and my real smiled peeked out for the first time tonight.

"You're stunning." Owen stared down at me, mesmerized.

"Thank you. You clean up nice," I glanced appreciatively down at his tux.

We danced more, enjoying being in each other's arms, and no one interrupted us. The advantage to Owen having made it clear he protected me is that no one got between us either. I wanted Owen to own me, truly own me.

"I need some air," I murmured as my need for him took me over. Owen tucked my hand in the crook of his elbow and led me out of the ballroom and down the hall and out onto a small balcony. It was just the two of us, and I snuggled into him. I was surprised when he let me.

"Anora," his voice was pained, and I looked up to see his eyes were dark and dilated. Only a small rim of blue remained. "I don't know if I can keep my distance anymore."

"I never wanted you to," I answered.

Owen opened his mouth to speak, closed it, and something settled in his expression.

He bridged the gap between us and took my mouth with his. This was not the same as those emotional, brief kisses we shared years ago. This was something feral and destructive, that reached into every aching, needy part of me and satisfied it.

Owen's tongue swept into my mouth, devouring and tasting, and I opened for him like a flower at first bloom. I touched his tongue with my own, and ran the tip along his bottom lip. His hands flexed on my hips and then yanked me closer. I felt something against my stomach and it took me a second to realize that it was his erection. Kissing me made Owen hard.

The idea sent a flutter through me so powerful that I whimpered.

Owen broke the kiss, his eyes pressed closed. "That was…"

"Hot," I finished for him and he opened his eyes. We laughed, and things felt good between us.

I pushed up and kissed him again, drawing his mouth back down and diving in to taste him again. My body and mind wanted so many things, but I had to be careful with myself. I knew that. Not because I couldn't trust Owen to be careful with me, I could, but I had a tendency to overthink and beat myself up, to the point of wanting to hurt myself sometimes, and a big change like this always opened me up to spiraling.

This was what I wanted, and there was no reason for me to rush it.

"I still want to be careful," Owen broke away from me.

"So do I," I agreed. "But I'm glad you broke first."

Owen laughed and dropped his forehead to mine. We stood on that balcony with our arms wrapped around each other and swayed to music only we could hear.

"Someday, Button, you and I are going to rule the fucking world."

I smiled but said nothing. If I had Owen, I had my world.

10

Anora

The day after my party, I was on cloud nine. Owen wanted to figure things out, and I'd spent hours with him in my pretty dress. When we returned to the ballroom he didn't leave my side and he didn't let anyone dance with me. We sat with my sisters and he helped me relax just by being there, while I got to spend time with them.

That night we stood in the hallway like usual, only this time he kissed me before telling me he loved me. Owen didn't even wait for me to say it back, just nudged me in the direction of my door. I dreamed about him all night and woke up with a smile on my face.

Every year it got easier to keep control of my thoughts. Therapy was consistent, I took my medication, I communicated what I needed. I worked so hard to stay in control that sometimes I didn't give myself a chance to experience or feel things because I was afraid they'd throw everything off. It had been a long time since I let myself feel this kind of unrestrained happiness.

It was so powerful it dimmed some of my more persistent intrusive thoughts. Owen understood me, and knew about the things I struggled with, and having him still love and want me anyway was powerful. That kind of acceptance is rare, and I wouldn't waste it.

Dad wanted to talk to me first thing, so I got dressed as soon as my alarm went off and headed to the library. I knocked and then opened the door, automatically glancing to the left to see if Aro ended up here or in her room. The green velvet chair was empty.

At my footsteps, Dad looked up and smiled at me.

"How did time go so fast?" His eyes filled with tears and I laughed him off. "You look like your mother." He said it with happiness, so I never felt bad about how true it was. More and more every year. Dad was truly happy that an obvious piece of her still existed in the world.

"What did you need to talk to me about?" I flopped into the soft chair across from his desk, curling my feet beneath me. I didn't like this room, I never had, but I couldn't deny that the chairs were comfortable. The serious things happened in here. The conversations in this place usually meant bad news or big changes. The only person who seemed to love it like dad did was Aro, but I think she would love wherever the books lived.

"Ah," Dad's face fell and he cleared his throat. "This is going to be awkward, but I've always been as honest with all of you as I could be. At the end of the day, this is a family business, and while I might be the patriarch, and the CEO, I don't make unilateral decisions."

I had zero idea where he was going with this. "Of course, Dad."

He frowned and looked down at his hands. It was odd to see that expression on his face. Dad could be serious, and often he was sad, but a straight up frown felt wrong.

"You know that I came from a regular, middle class background." I nod and he continues. "We're in a different stratosphere, and there are things that happen in the circles we run in now that I never could have imagined. That are expected, even normalized, and there are reasons those things exist."

"Like what?" I'm even more confused than when he started.

"Arranged marriages. Strategic marriages." I must look as confused

53

as I feel because he fumbled his words, trying to figure out what to say. "People in this world treat marriages as alliances. Opportunities to strengthen what they have, or build new relationships. More than one person has mentioned to me lately that you've reached an age where decisions like that are made about your future."

My heart stopped in my chest, but I held the panic down hard. "You want to promise me to someone?"

"No," Dad waved his hands, like he needed to dispel that it was put out into the universe. "I'm asking if that's something that you want. It could be beneficial to us, to Designation, I understand why it still happens in the worlds of immense wealth. I wanted to give you the option, and I'd respect whatever decision you made."

"Would I have a say in who?"

"Of course."

"But I'd marry someone because it would be useful to the family?"

"In short." Dad looked confused too, and I wondered what these people said to him that he took it seriously enough to ask me about it. They must have really believed in the value of allying me with someone. Of building a marriage into any contract or agreements we'd make in the future.

I'd be useful.

That's what I wanted, right? I worked hard to keep the Sorrelle name clean in the public and get involved with philanthropy and a light dabble in politics when necessary. I researched and directed where we spent our donations, and even though I wasn't old enough to attend the parties, I kept myself apprised of what was going on. I wanted my family to succeed. I wanted to secure the legacy of what dad created. If this was how I could do it, was there any choice but to agree?

Owen was going to hate it, but he'd understand. We were kids. I mean who ended up with the person they loved at 16? He would understand that we needed to put security and taking care of everyone else ahead of ourselves. I needed to know that I was taking care of my family. I loved Owen. He understood my needs. He would understand this choice.

I was lying to myself, but I also couldn't come out and tell dad that I wanted the ward who lived in our house, who kissed my breath away yards from his bedroom door last night. The feelings that sometimes controlled me, the ones that hurt me and ripped me apart, that kept me in therapy once a week for almost a decade now, those feelings wanted me to be useful. They demanded that I find a purpose because that voice in my head was always telling me how worthless I was, how I was a pretty face and nothing more, and that I'd never bring anything to the family.

Even my happiness from last night couldn't overshadow the certainty of knowing that I'd be useful to my family. That this was an action that might finally silence that voice that told me I was useless and didn't need to be here.

This was something I could do, and dad wouldn't force me to be with someone I hated. I'd do something good and I'd still have a choice.

"I think we should do it. I want to be useful."

Dad's eyebrows flew up in surprise. "Really?"

"Really." My answer was firm, and Dad nodded, working past his confusion.

"Well, you know the local players, anyone we should keep in mind?"

I almost rolled my eyes. He laid this on me minutes ago. That would take a lot of careful thought and analysis.

"We've been approached by the Forresters. In the past."

My stomach clenched. "No. Elton is nice but I could never see him that way, or learn to; I know too much already."

Dad's shoulders dropped like he was relieved. "The Forresters are powerful, but I think we'd be getting into bed with trouble if you went that route." He sighed. "Anyone else? Someone you're close to?" He sounded like he was hedging, but I didn't understand where he was going with that. I shook my head. Awkward silence fell, so I excused myself and then raced up the stairs to Alina's room.

I didn't knock, I knew she'd still be sleeping. I busted into her room and something came flying at my head, smacking hard into the wall next to me. When I looked down at the floor it was a pointed black shoe. I turned back to Alina.

"Don't fucking surprise me like that," she snarled and flopped back in her bed. I ignored her attitude and went over to her. I crawled under the covers next to her and I explained everything that Dad had told me.

"Why would you do that? I'm not fucking doing that." For some reason Alina had gotten really into swearing recently. I thought it was because she'd started training with the security guys and wanted them to think she was tough. I'd seen her kick their asses or get close; I'm pretty sure they knew without the foul mouth, but it wasn't my place to say anything.

"I want to be useful. This sets us up to make a strategic alliance. To be safe."

"Who knew that mafia bride shit would be a self-fulfilling prophecy. It got willed into existence with that dumbass rumor." I winced at her words because Owen was the one who started that rumor, and he was the one that would be hurt by it coming true. I had to believe he'd be okay though; we hadn't even started, not really, and we'd still be friends.

He'd go on to find a woman that would make him better; where he wouldn't need to babysit her emotions like he had to do with mine. Someone who wouldn't break down over the terrible voice in her head. It would be fine.

I would hate her, then I'd learn to love her. She would be family, the same as him. I sighed. Owen was better off without me. It was easy to believe that. Almost easier to believe it than that he loved me and wanted to be with me. The voice in my head was stronger than him a lot of the time.

Alina shook her head and ended the conversation. She held my hand because even if I didn't say it, she knew there was something going on inside me. We watched TV together like that until Aro barged in to tell us that lunch was ready. We made our way downstairs to the dining room, which was laid out with the usual Sunday spread for build your own sub sandwiches.

"Is this what you're going to do when you're some rando's little wifey? God you're nuts." Alina stacked her sub with roast beef and tomatoes.

"What rando?" Aro asked.

Alina snorted. "Dad asked Anora if she'd be cool with an arranged marriage, and she said yes. Dad's gonna marry her off like some medieval princess."

We all jumped at the sharp clang of a plate hitting the table, and I knew before I looked up that it was Owen. "You what?" he asked, dazed and confused. I watched him put the mask back in place so my sisters wouldn't see. Even upset he protected our secret. "That's archaic. He can't do that."

"I agreed to it. Dad said it would make me useful." My voice was small and weak, even to my own ears. Something dark passed over Owen's face. The words I used were specific, and he knew what they meant to me.

"Well in that case, maybe he should find someone for me, too," Owen said as he picked up his plate and resumed making his sandwich. "I'm the heir after all, and the legacy has to be preserved."

"Anyone would think you were a catch Owen," Aro said as she patted his hand. She always picked up on Owen's insecurity but never the reason for it, and would reassure him at the oddest moments.

Owen stared at me, then turned and left the room without another word.

"He needs to pull the stick out of his butt," Aster intoned. "I'm worried he's going to have a heart attack before he turns 20."

"Be nice," I scolded, as my own heart was plummeting to shatter at my feet.

11

Owen

On my way to my room, I ran into Don. I couldn't keep the stress inside, I had to ask him about it even though I had no legitimate reason.

"Anora wants an arranged marriage?"

Don gave me a sharp, piercing look. "She agreed to the possibility."

"Interesting," I responded. "Well, whatever helps the family, right?" I barely kept the fury and derision out of my voice, but I think he heard it anyway. How could he not know that she'd agree to it even if it would hurt her? There had to have been conversations over the years with her and her therapist about the root of her struggles. Don had to know he was walking her right into a trap that fed into her vulnerabilities.

For the first time in my life I was disappointed in him.

"I'd let her change her mind, any time." I'd always wondered how much Don knew about how close Anora and I really were, especially after the night I ended up in the hospital. He had to know we were communicating with each other, but it's unlikely he knew how often. Still, sometimes he'd ask me things with a tone that made me believe he knew how I felt about her and how she felt about me. He was waiting for us to get it together and trying not to force it.

Maybe that was a fool's fucking hope.

"Do you think it's the right thing?" The stupid teenage boy inside me asked.

He looked off into the distance, as if he could see the future and mine it for answers. "I don't know. I know that our world is precarious, dangerous, and competitive. I know that we need friends and alliances, and that sometimes there's a cost."

"Right." Maybe I'd been selfish, thinking only of her and of myself. Unfortunately for us, our lives and what we were connected to were bigger than ourselves. Still, I wanted her. I knew that there would never be anyone else for me. Unless it was her, I didn't think I'd ever marry. I'd pass Designation on to one of their children, give it back to the Sorrelles. After everything Roman and Elaine had done, it was the least I could do.

It was weird, at 18, to accept that I would have a loveless and childless existence. That I was okay with it, in a weird way. It would come close to killing me to see Anora marry someone else, but if I understood her reasons, if I thought it would take some of that imaginary weight off her shoulders, I'd stand by and let it happen.

But I could never do that to her. I could never, even for strategic reasons, declare myself for someone else in front of her. Even if she stood by her decision, I know what seeing me with someone else would do to her. Even when she hurt me, I was incapable of hurting her.

Would I be a monk for the rest of my life? Probably not. But I had a feeling I'd come damn close until her power over me dimmed. If it ever did.

Nearly an hour, and only half a sandwich eaten later, Anora knocked on my door.

"Yes?" I asked, feigning boredom. I'd spent that hour rebuilding the paths in my head and the promises to myself to keep distance between us. I would have to build a mask where she was concerned that hid my feelings and thoughts from her. It was just me now. I was alone again.

"Can we talk?" She stepped further into the room, standing next to my bed.

"The moment to talk has passed, Anora. You made your decision. I'm trying to respect it." She flinched at the cold tone in my voice, and I hid my reaction from her. It wouldn't help her to see that I was both hurting, and hurting for her. If she wanted to make adult decisions, I'd have to try treating her like one.

"Owen," she tried again. "We're still kids. We might think and feel differently when we're adults. This was an adult decision." Her words echoed my thoughts. It hurt to always be so in sync even as we were about to start moving in different directions.

To cover my pain, I sneered at her, the first time I'd ever looked at her with anything nearing derision. I stood from my seat at my desk and stalked to her. I loomed over her tiny frame and made myself do what I'd thought was impossible: I pushed her away.

"Fine, let's talk about adult decisions, seeing as I have two years on you. Adults think about the people their decisions might impact, and adults have open conversations about the potential fallout. Adults make decisions together." I stepped closer and couldn't recognize myself when I wrapped my hand around her throat so I could hold her in place as I forced her to look nowhere but my eyes. "An adult would have realized that the most useful, strategic person for you to marry…is me."

I let her go and stepped back, watching as she processed what I'd said. It hadn't actually occurred to me until that came out of my mouth. Then it all clicked clearly into place. This all could have gone down so differently if she'd just fucking talked to me.

"Connecting the Sorrelles and the Carvers, unifying Designation ownership into a single entity, a single family, and securing the legacy for your family."

"Owen," she tried, but I waved a hand at her.

"This is done, Anora." I couldn't look at her as I crushed her, even though she's the one that did it first. "I will always be there for you if you need me, and honestly, I will always fucking love you, but I know now that I'll never be before your family, and I don't want to get in the way of that. I understand why you'll always choose them over me. I wish I knew what that felt like. No hard feelings, okay?" Half of what I said was a lie. The other half was letting her in on my most vulnerable truth. I wasn't her family. She would never choose me. Not really.

Tears spilled down her cheeks but she nodded, retreating deep inside herself. I knew she'd beat herself up about it all for…ever. Anora would agonize over this decision for the rest of her life, and to be honest, so would I. It wouldn't matter who she married or how useful they were or what she tied to the Sorrelles or Designation. Anora would always be left wondering if throwing me away was the right decision.

I'd wonder it too.

I turned away from her, sat back at my desk, and pretended to focus on my homework until I heard her close the door and leave the room.

12

Anora

Owen moved out a week later. He was in his final semester of high school and technically his requirements were all done. We had talked about an opportunity he had to join an early academic program at Northwestern. He left and the only person who knew was dad, until he was already gone. I'd known about the program but not when it started or that he'd decided to go. I wasn't allowed to know his plans anymore.

I found out he'd left because not speaking to him was getting to me and I broke and went looking for him. I went to his room and found it beyond the usual bare, stripped of almost everything. His closet was empty, and only a few stray toiletries were still in the bathroom. He'd kept his life light and it had made it easy for him to run. Dad had been under the impression he'd said goodbye to us separately.

Later, I found out that he'd said goodbye to everyone but me. If I were him, I wouldn't have wanted to face me either. Even though I still felt like I was doing the right thing, it didn't make it hurt any less. It made me believe the pain would pass because my decision was justified.

The best and worst part was that he still texted me every night.

The day after my marriage bomb dropped, he sent the text and told me why he'd keep going, even with everything that now stood between us. He was still better than I deserved.

O: *I love you. I know your mind is good at saying you aren't worthy of it, so I'll remind you every day anyway, until you ask me to stop.*

Then he'd done everything he could to avoid me and he'd succeeded. Even when I tried to pop in on him in his room, catch him after school, his routine had changed so significantly and immediately that I couldn't find him. Then he was gone.

The day he moved out, the text was late, and the pain nearly knocked me out.

O: *Goodbye, Anora. I love you.*

I was doing the right thing. I had to be.

II

Distance

13

Owen

It was weird to leave the Sorrelle house on such short notice, but it was what I needed to do to survive. Now that I'd had a real taste of Anora, I needed to get away from her once I couldn't have her. Not after I knew what she felt like in my arms, finally, and then she'd thrashed my fucking heart.

So I lived in a dorm room by myself and did a pre-college program. It got me ahead in general education credits so I could focus more on my dual degrees: computer science and business management. It seemed like the right route to go to lead Designation.

Once summer came, I enrolled in a summer class so I could keep living on campus, and I started interning at Designation, like I promised Don I would.

The first day he had me come to his office and tried to fill me in on the girls, how things were at the house, but I didn't want to hear it. I couldn't. I loved them with all that I was capable of, but I had to tell myself they weren't my family. As much as Aro and even Anora tried to change that, I didn't want to taint them with my own familial experience. I didn't want to put them in danger because of Roman's real legacy, and lose them.

So I loved them distantly, like a fond cousin rather than the brother Aro wanted. I protected them even when they didn't know it - like keeping an eye on them in school even though I was gone. I had contacts everywhere, and it was never too early to become the kind of businessman who exploited them. I would keep them all safe.

Don looked sad when he realized how uncomfortable talking about his family made me.

"I want to remind you that you are not obligated to do this. I need to know that working here, dedicating your college career to working here, is what you really want. I'd help you succeed anywhere, you know that."

I did know. But I realized that I really did want Designation. I'd been excited for days leading up to this, knowing that I'd be making my own mark here. That I could erase or counter Roman's damage. This place deserved all of me to make up for what he'd done.

"I want this," I confirmed. Don clapped his hands and became all bouncing joy again. He spent the day personally giving me a tour of the campus, showing me everything we did, what was being developed, and introducing me to staff. It was weird seeing it from the professional side during the day, rather than the childlike exploration I'd engaged in when here on the weekends.

It was impossible to escape my memories of Anora, but I had to learn to embrace them. I had to learn how to think of those weekends fondly instead of with excruciating pain. Being here almost every day would be like exposure therapy. If I could face our memories and survive, someday I'd be able to face her again too.

Don had decided I was going to be his personal intern, so I'd actually get to be with him for meetings and see his decision making process as the man in charge. It was a heady feeling to be given that much trust. It felt kind of insane that he was willing to give it to me.

I started finding my way that summer. The more I loved being at Designation, the more comfortable I felt asking Don for new experiences because I was excited to learn everything. I shadowed managers in different units and tried to understand why they did the things they did. I wanted to know what leadership in this context looked like, and what it was about Don that inspired such fierce loyalty. The employee turnover rate at Designation was well below industry comparison.

It wasn't that he was nice, it was that he listened. He communicated. He valued every person as an individual and did his best to understand their motivations. It helped him figure how to leverage the best work out of an employee. Show them that he valued what they valued, and it made the work great.

I could never be as friendly as he was, but I made a point of remembering names and tried to show everyone that I took this seriously. It had taken half a second for it to get around that "THE HEIR," as it was written in emails, was an intern now, and that I'd be learning the ropes to take over someday. I think they expected someone like my father, which I wasn't, but I wasn't like Don either.

Some of the more disgruntled employees called me the Orphan.

They weren't wrong. I was a young man adrift, and I was looking for somewhere to belong. It was the weirdest notion to realize that what I wanted in that moment was a friend. Someone to share my excitement with who would be excited for me. A person to take up my downtime with and possibly someone whose ass I could kick at video games. It had been a long time since I'd let myself feel lonely, but I couldn't deny that's what I felt now.

I missed Anora. I grieved for the future I'd dreamed up with her, and what I'd imagined things would be like between us while I experienced this.

When my official freshman year started and I moved into my residence hall, I found my friend. Rafael Montaigne was my opposite in personality, but somehow my kindred spirit. We both came from big money with big expectations, and we understood each other.

Rafe looked like a fucking pirate, with long red hair that he kept tied back in a knot, a crooked smile with a dimple on the higher side, and a twinkle of mischief in his eye. We were both tall, broad guys, and I knew he was going to be my friend when he ignored the looks of the women on campus the same way I did. I was sure there was a story there.

From day one, Rafe dragged me out of the pit of losing Anora. He made me join intramural sports teams and go to the gym with him. He made me go to football games, and even a few parties, although he rarely drank and we always left together. Rafe lit up every room he walked into, making people laugh and watch him, while I was the shadow by his side that got him out before he started a fight, or had his back when it couldn't be avoided.

Somehow, Rafe crawled under my skin.

We were both a little drunk the first time I told him about Anora, because he asked why I never hooked up. I wondered the same thing about him.

"You're a decent looking motherfucker, yeah? So what's your type?"

I sighed, staring up the blank ceiling of our room. "My type is a tiny brunette that I've known since the day she was born who needs to get her head out of her ass."

"A one and done guy, got it. I've become one myself," he grunted and rolled over. "A girl was promised to me, and I didn't want it, until I met her. Like the world fucking stopped, you know? I wanted her more than I'd ever wanted anything in my life and she felt the same. My Sophie. Then some shit went down and she's - she's gone." He finished in a way that hinted there was more to that.

"What happened?"

Rafe was silent for so long I thought he'd fallen asleep. "I gotta ask ya something."

"Yeah?"

"The Sorrelles - your company - there's some crime shit going on with that, right?"

"Yeah," I answered, deciding to trust him. He'd earned it.

"I've got some crime shit too." That was a fucking understatement. I knew who the Montaignes were. It wasn't some vague dipping into criminality like Designation. They were a straight up criminal dynasty.

"Her family is part of a crew in Eastern Europe. The marriage agreement was part of an alliance. It's still in place, but once they realized I actually wanted her, they've used her as a bargaining chip. Took her overseas even though she's lived in the States her whole damn life."

The pain in his voice got to me, because I understood it. "How long?"

"About a year. They let her call me sometimes."

"Fuck."

"Pretty much."

"What are you going to do?" If there was anything I learned about Rafe, it's that he wasn't going to let this stand. They'd taken what belonged to him and he would get her back, but he'd be careful about it. The asshole ran his mouth at parties but was smart as fuck when it really counted.

"Working on it." Rafe's voice was the lowest I'd ever heard it. This fucked with him more than he let on. "You gonna get your girl back?"

"Someday. She needs to grow up, and I have to give her the space to do that. I've been fucked up over her my whole life." I rolled over onto my stomach and looked at him across the room. "She agreed to an arranged marriage. With someone else."

"What?" Rafe turned on his side, and the entire story poured out of me. I even told him about Roman and Elaine, and how much it had messed me up when it came to trusting people. How I'd attached to her like my single thread of life, survival, and family. Maybe I did put an unfair burden on her. Maybe she didn't feel the same as I did, or feel it with the same intensity. Maybe it would fade for her and I'd have to live with that.

"And I thought my family was dramatic." Rafe chuckled and his lack of judgment made me feel better than I had in a long time.

"Isn't that just a thing that happens when you make enough money? We don't have to put our energy into survival, so in our outrageous privilege we fuck everything up?"

"I see no error in that."

"So what about you and Sophie?" I asked, because I was not the kind of person who didn't realize I'd just cemented his position as my best friend. The first person I'd genuinely considered one since I was a little kid. There was something about him that made sense to me, and I was thin on connections. I'd always be there for him. Do anything he asked of me. I knew it right then.

So Rafe told me. The summer he met Sophie, he had gone in thinking he didn't want to be married to someone he didn't choose and he was going to find any reason to break the engagement. Instead, he fell in love the second he saw her. And it was mutual. He told me all the shit about the deal with their families, the infighting, backstabbing, and the way they'd made a deal her family thought they could fuck his family over with. It was sad as hell.

"I know she's not safe where she is. I know they're hurting her, even if she won't admit it to me. They listen when she calls, they want to keep me on the hook."

"If I can do anything, you tell me."

"Know any good hackers?"

I snorted. "Is that a serious question? Of course I fucking do." And that was the moment I became his best friend in return, because I had his back when his family couldn't.

I also found him a hacker.

14

Owen

Over the next four years, Rafe turned me into what he called "a gentleman criminal." I'd finally found the world where I belonged, straddling the law but pursuing what I felt was true right and true wrong. I also learned I had a talent, if discovered late for that world, in cyber-crime and digital manipulation. I learned that from school and my own explorations. Rafe and his brothers taught me how to fight, shoot, intimidate, blackmail, and have a good time.

To an extent. I never could move on with another woman, and even drunk and wild, it was only Anora for me. It helped that Rafe wasn't interested in women either. We intervened for one another when necessary, and still lived the life we could while our hearts were locked away.

His brothers never teased us about it, although we did get looks of wonder and pity on a regular basis. They accepted me as one of them, and I gained brothers when I thought I'd be isolated forever.

It also took four fucking years for us to find where they kept Sophie.

Six weeks after graduation, the hacker I'd been working with, one of the few willing to take on the kind of criminals we were watching, found the compound where Sophie was. Her family had hackers of their own, and it was a death sentence if they realized you were looking into them. Their hackers were good, mine was better. Or maybe we just got lucky.

I didn't officially start with Designation for a few weeks, and I convinced Don I needed some time off before settling in, as I'd done very little except study and train with the Montaignes. He approved it without question. Even though what I learned from my best friend would be infinitely useful with my future there, I guarded the kind of person I'd become. I didn't want him to associate my choices with the things Roman had done. I didn't want Don to paint us with the same brush. Roman had been a criminal, but never a gentleman.

I jumped through some mental hoops to see us as different, but I know I'd never do the things Roman did. I'd never put people in the positions that he did. I would only ever make moves to protect, never exploit. And no decision I ever made would be motivated by money.

"Everything is under my name or a false name," I told Rafe and his three older brothers: Michel, Thierry, and Lothaire. "It can't be associated with you. They'll be watching. Even the money only traces back to me."

"You didn't have to do that," Rafe said.

"Yes, I did. One of us should get our girl." We exchanged a look and finally he nodded. I meant every fucking word.

We left for Ukraine that night. It was the first time I killed anyone, and it didn't bother me as much as I expected it to. I blended in with the Montaignes and their men as we worked our way from the guarded forest to the nondescript concrete building where they were currently holding Sophie.

We'd gotten even luckier that after some threatening from Michel Montaigne Sr. to follow through on the deal, her family said that if the Montaignes could find her, they could have her. So we fucking found her. We were going to make them regret everything they had done. Every minute they had kept Sophie and Rafe apart.

A part of myself I'd never felt before came to the surface, and I went to work. I walked up quietly behind the first guard I saw and moved swiftly and silently as I slashed my knife along his throat. I caught him before he could make too much noise, and waited until he bled out before moving on.

Even though the only prisoner here was Sophie, they had a lot of bodies standing guard.

I moved through the segment of woods assigned to me, and I killed without remorse.

I slashed throats, I fought, I stabbed a man in the chest while he was looking straight in my eyes. He swore at me and spit in my face. I twisted the knife and waited for him to die. Lothaire approached as I was standing over him.

"Nice. You get everyone?"

"I think so."

He patted me on the shoulder and looked in my face, checking that I was okay with what we had done. They'd trained me, but I'd never done anything like this before. Whatever Lothaire saw, it confirmed I was fine. We met up with the others at the door to the building.

Thierry liked to blow shit up, so after we confirmed all external guards were handled, he blew open the door. We weren't going to bother with breaking into the coded locks. Rafe was the first through the door and we took out the rest of the men as he raced from room to room, like a complete lovesick idiot, until he found her.

Sophie was frighteningly thin compared to the photos I'd seen of her from the summer they met. Her red hair was super short, almost as if they shaved it from time to time so they didn't have to deal with it. There were bruises on her wrists and ankles. I was a few steps behind him when he came into the room, and I knew that we'd done the right thing the second I saw her see him.

76

She lit up. It felt like she literally glowed from the inside when her eyes met Rafe's.

"You came," her voice was raw and raspy, as if ravaged by years of crying.

"You're mine," he answered before picking her up in his arms. We raced out of there and got as deep into the woods as we could. Thierry had wired the entire place to blow just in case we missed anyone. We couldn't leave any witnesses, and Michel was a believer in the total devastation of his enemies. They had disrespected his family and tried to fuck them over in a deal, a signed contract. If they weren't thoroughly punished, it would make the Montaignes look weak.

While we'd flown commercial there, I booked a private jet for the return flight. I didn't want Sophie going through security and I wasn't sure how she'd do around large crowds of strangers.

Other than to go to the bathroom, Rafe and Sophie hadn't let each other go. Even when the doctor I hired to examine her came, Rafe was there holding her hand. Listening to every word of what had happened to her. I admired his control, because I didn't know if I could've done the same. Sophie clung to him like she didn't believe he was real yet.

It was awkward for me and his brothers to sit in the outer room of our hotel, listening to their muffled sobs in the bedroom. They'd been apart for so long, and she'd been through more than any person should have to endure. I loved Anora, but I don't think what I felt for her had anything on what Rafe had been through and how much his love for Sophie withstood. I didn't know what I would do if I was ever in that position.

My hacker had found more than just this location. While Rafe, Sophie, and I were headed back to the States, the brothers were staying behind to exact some punishment. We couldn't be involved in that, and Sophie needed to get somewhere safe to heal. I hoped they had a good time. I hoped they punished the people who would do this to an innocent girl.

When we got back to Chicago, I was more drained than I had been in a long time. I didn't think I'd felt this low since recovering from Roman's last beating. A weird mix of relief and sadness that I could easily drown in. I only lasted a few hours alone in the apartment I shared with Rafe before I cracked.

I called Don and asked if I could come over to talk. He knew it wasn't business, even though I'd worked very hard to keep our relationship strictly professional the last few years. It didn't matter to him. I was welcome, and he was there for me.

Anora was still away at school, so there was no chance I'd run into her when I walked into the Sorrelle house. Don waited for me and we went into the library. The center of operations for everything that was the family business.

He poured me a drink, and we sat in dim silence for a long time. Don's face was relaxed and open, waiting for me to be ready.

"What would you have done if I'd told you sooner?" He knew what I was referring to. We'd never spoken about it before.

"I would have killed them myself." My head snapped up because Don was serious. "No one should ever do that to their child. There was nothing you would ever have done to deserve that. I'm sorry to say it, but I'm not sorry their dead."

"Neither am I," I said lowly. "That's what worries me."

"What does?"

"That I'm tainted. Who doesn't grieve their parent's murder? What kind of monster doesn't care?"

"One who never really had parents. There is nothing wrong with you." The adamant tone of his voice should have reassured me, but it didn't.

"I'm not a good person, Don. The things I've done…"

He cuts me off with a sharp sound. "No one is all good or bad, Owen. Would you ever intentionally hurt someone who didn't deserve it? Would you hurt someone for your own amusement or gain? Hurt them just because you could?" I shook my head in the negative to all those questions. "You would protect people who needed it, and only hurt people who were trying to hurt someone you cared about. Things anyone with a heart and a conscience would do."

"I know you're obligated to give me an opportunity at Designation, but am I really who you want? I can step down. I'd be okay."

Don smiled and it surprised me. "I know you'd be okay. I've seen your grades, kid. I know how good you are. You're exactly who we need. I'd choose you if choosing was an option. You're a great leader, Owen. You might be young, but I know our staff respects you. I know they'll follow you because you'll earn it."

It took everything in me not to cry. If a heart could break from feeling overwhelmed in a good way, mine would.

"Your last name might be Carver, but you're mine, too. You're as much a Sorrelle, because the person you needed to become, that happened in my house. I've always been proud of you."

"Fuck," I barked before my emotions took over. I finished my drink, trying to pull everything back inside myself. When I'd come over, I hadn't realized how much I needed to hear the things he said. How much I needed to be reassured that I wasn't a monster by someone who'd known me all my life.

"I'd really like it if you moved back home," Don continued. "Things aren't…safe. It would be more efficient to protect everyone from here."

It snapped me out my emotions to know that he was worried. "I can do that. Anything I need to know?" I didn't want to be back here, and I'd have to learn to survive it, but I guessed I'd take a page from Anora's book. I'd do what was best for the family even when it hurt.

"Not yet, but I'd rather be cautious."

"Our lease ends in a few weeks."

"Good." Don got up and took my glass, then refilled both our drinks. He handed me mine and held his up. "To family. It'll be good to have you home."

I clinked my glass to his and drank. I felt more concerned than relieved, but I had two years before she'd be back here all the time. I had to decide if I was going to truly let her go, or remind her that she belonged to me.

I took another drink and sighed because there was only one choice. She belonged to me. I'd tried fighting my feelings. I'd tried getting over her. The way I felt hadn't dimmed at all. If anything, the experiences of the last few years had made me more certain that I would never love anyone but her. There would never be anyone else for either of us. I'd fight her tooth and nail if she tried to marry anyone else. I'd find a way to break it. Anora was mine, and I'd take my time, lay the groundwork for our future, and claim her.

15

Anora

Owen didn't come home. I knew he was alive and doing well because dad would keep us updated. He still texted every night, but never responded to any of my other outreach. He'd built a wall between us and I tried really hard not to blame him. I did this to myself.

Things were hard. Sometimes I'd get so caught up in anxiety that I'd lose time. Hours spent in my room sitting on my bed staring at nothing, paralyzed by the idea that I was useless. That I don't need to be here. That everyone would be better without me. I never self-harmed, but I would stop eating sometimes, unconsciously, until finally it went too far and I fainted at school.

I confessed to dad how I'd been feeling, and it got me a day 10 "retreat" to in-patient care during junior year holiday break. It had been a long time since I'd needed that kind of intense care, but I came out feeling better. Stronger. Convinced I would work harder to find a purpose with my family. That I would let go of Owen like I told myself I would.

To keep moving forward, I threw myself into philanthropy and charity projects. I started raising money and running half-marathons, then marathons. It was finally something I could bond with Aster over.

She had no interest in running in races, but she gave me good tips since she'd been running for so long, and once in a while we'd do road runs when the weather was nice. Aster wouldn't run outside alone and didn't like when I did. I didn't ask why. There was no way she'd tell me.

Elton Forrester asked me to Prom and I said yes because I couldn't think of a reason to say no in the moment. To save myself, I attached us to a huge group of people and didn't have to dance with him more than once. I found a way to disappear during the slow songs. His infatuation with me seemed to drop after that, and he went back to being purely friendly. I was so relieved.

I decided that I needed to go away for college. I needed to escape who we were here, and figure out who I was without my family. Without the ghost of Owen haunting every decision I made, and because, if he was never going to be there, why was I staying? Why was I waiting for him to come home?

I applied to the four corners of the country, that was far enough away. I had good grades, a good track record with my charity work, and I wouldn't require financial aid. I thought I was a good candidate.

I spiraled again when the first letter I got was a rejection. It wasn't a daze this time, I went full on catatonic. I lost three days before I came back to myself in the hospital. They changed my medication after that, and things got better.

I got accepted. I went to the East Coast.

I didn't make friends, but I learned a lot. I joined things. On the surface I had a solid network of people. Other people like me who came from a certain kind of family and lived under the burden of expectations.

I let myself go out and be cautiously social. I had a drink or two, I maintained control. I put in an appearance when people asked me to; I was a good time without being a burden.

For the most part I held myself together until my final semester. I had high expectations for myself and had been assigned a notoriously difficult professor for my capstone project. I'd already been struggling with senioritis and desperately wanting to go home; I was done with East Coast vibes. I was done not being part of the Sorrelle presence in Chicago. When I got home, I had a lot of work to do to get more respect for our name, and I wanted to do it.

When I got my first draft of my capstone back, it had been eviscerated. He questioned how I even made it this far in my degree, if I was capable of forming a coherent or original thought, and told me I would be better off as a society wife and leave the thinking to the men. It was brutal, unethical, would probably get him in trouble as an employee, but I couldn't see that at the time.

All I could see was that he repeated every terrible thought that went through my head. It was someone outside of me saying everything I thought about myself. It proved me right. Someone else saw it. They saw that I was inadequate, a waste of space, a waste of brain power. I was not worth the air I breathed.

My limbs had started to go numb. I wanted to die. I wanted to jump out the window of my apartment and I wanted to hurt. I wanted to punish myself for existing. These weren't good or rational thoughts, and I had enough left inside me to know that.

Instead of calling my therapist, or 911, I called Owen.

I hadn't called him in six years.

He answered in one ring. "What's wrong?" I wouldn't call unless something was wrong.

"I want to die." My mouth said it and I felt it, but I also felt outside myself. "I don't deserve to be here."

"Yes you do, Button," Owen answered. His voice was soft and soothing. Familiar and foreign at the same time. It hurt. My fingers toyed with the necklace he'd given me, trying to seek comfort and distract myself.

The sound of a male voice in the background jolted me. I heard Owen move away from the phone and say something that sounded like "call 911" and "the address is on the fridge, you know" and the person agreeing.

"I don't even know why I bothered going to college. I'm not smart enough. I'm never enough, Owen."

"You're in your last semester, Button. You've done so well. Your dad tells me about it all the time. Listen, I need you to go to your front door and unlock it. Can you do that?"

"I don't know. I can't - I can't feel my body."

"Did you take anything?"

"No."

"Do you have a plan?"

"Yes."

Owen let out a shuddered breath and I hated that my pain was causing him pain. "What?"

"The window. The screen is broken. It's high enough."

"Anora, get up and leave your bedroom. Unlock the front door and then sit on the couch." The command in his voice had me moving without thinking, and that was exactly what I needed.

I did what he said, and told him so. "I need to talk on the other phone. I want you to meet my friend Rafe. I'll be right back."

Before I could say anything, a different voice came on. "Hey, beautiful. I've heard so much about you."

"Like what a horrible person I am? That he wasted his time on me, and I broke his heart?"

"No. I heard you're a hell of a pool player. That you love your family very much. That they love you." Rafe was being so nice and he'd never even met me. I also realized how much Owen had told him if he knew about us playing pool. This big important person in Owen's life and I didn't know him at all.

I started to cry, but Rafe kept talking to me. "Some people might tell you not to cry, but not me. Crying is good for you. You have to let it out. I'm always down for a good cry. When you come home after graduation, me and you, we'll have a full on sob fest, okay?"

"Okay." He made me commit to plans for the future. There was a scramble and then Owen was back on the phone.

"The EMTs are almost there. You go with them. I'll call your dad."

"Okay."

"Anora." The pain in that single word blasted down the line and straight into my heart. "I love you. You are worth loving, and I need you to remember that. Even if it's the only thing you can remember."

"Okay," my whispered sob was all I could get out, and then my front door opened and a man and a woman in uniform stepped inside. "Thank you, Owen."

"Always, Button." We ended the call, and I went to the hospital.

There was a huge fallout with the professor that graded my paper and his commentary. I was assigned a different mentor to finish the capstone.

I survived for now, and that would have to be enough. It was time to go home.

16

Anora

After I graduated, I fled the empty world I'd built for myself to come back to the complicated one I'd left behind.

Dad had thrown out a few possibilities for a marriage alliance, and I had turned them all down. Owen and I avoided each other. I'd know when the right one came along. I wasn't sure why I felt that way, it was just a gut feeling that there was a connection out there that would do us the most good.

It wouldn't only be about money and status. It had to be something of more value.

I was a commodity and I wanted to be in a place of high demand. I wasn't going to take the early opportunities, I was going to take the right one.

As soon as I settled, I started joining committees and organizations. I was immediately added to the board of an organization that set up races for multiple charities. I said yes to everything. I stretched myself thin, but I raised the Sorrelle name to one that was respected for our presence as much as for our wealth. I had made us look so good people wouldn't talk about the rumors about our criminal connections openly. That's all I wanted.

The invites started rolling in. I became an in-demand attendee at fundraisers, banquets, and benefits. My wardrobe of formal wear quadrupled. I started up relationships with designers because I wanted to look different from everyone else. I wanted to command the spaces I walked into on a visual level, because sometimes it took me a bit to click my mask into place and stuff down my fear.

I kept a journal I wrote in when I got home from every event, venting everything that I'd done wrong, that stressed me out, that I needed to change. My therapist was not a fan of it, but sometimes when I let it out it didn't haunt me or build up inside me. Sometimes I realized immediately that I was being stupid about certain things. It helped me let go of some of my insecurities when I looked at them on the page.

I'd done so good at keeping everything to myself. All my secrets buried inside my heart so no one ever saw a version of me that wasn't perfect.

I served my purpose; I made us look good. I made myself look like a queen - respected and mostly untouchable. The boundaries I kept between myself and others were firmly intact. I didn't date, I didn't flirt, I danced because I was obligated to, and I made everyone think that I thought the world of them.

It was exhausting, but it kept me out of the house.

I had finally convinced Dad to come with me to a benefit dinner. It was for city schools, and if everything went according to my plan, it would result in a massive donation to the district and cover much-needed funding. If the city and state wouldn't give them the money they deserved, I'd drain it from the rich assholes who only made a donation to make themselves feel better.

My dress was from a local designer I'd forged a connection with. Daphne was classy and ridiculous, the perfect combination for me. The dress was a deep, dark purple, and it revealed flashes of skin without really revealing anything at all. I loved the material, the cut, the color. I wanted to drown in it.

I walked downstairs while I double-checked I had everything I needed in my clutch, and carrying my shoes because I'd put them on in the car. With this dress and my complete disregard for how much shorter I was than everybody else, I'd decided to wear more comfortable, short heels. I wanted to spend tonight on my feet wooing as much money as possible out of everyone. I wanted to drain their pockets dry.

I looked up to see if Dad was ready, but it was Owen waiting by the door. He was in a classic black tux and he had a purple flower on his lapel. I'd given it to Dad to wear to match my dress.

"What are you doing here?" I asked, struck. Owen and I had barely spoken in the last year since I'd moved home. It was cursory greetings or asking to pass the salt at the dinner table. Brief thank yous when we exchanged gifts at the holidays or our birthdays. He still texted me every night, but I'd stopped responding, and never tried to talk about anything else. The way he'd completely shut down on me still hurt, even if I knew he'd be there for me if I really needed it.

I didn't want to need him.

I didn't want to lose my breath every time I saw him. I wanted to become more numb to his presence. I wanted to get over him.

I hadn't. Not even a little bit.

"I've been assigned escort duty," he smiled at me, a small one, but more than he'd given me in a long time.

I opened my mouth but nothing came out. I was mad at Dad for backing out, and I was afraid of being with Owen all night. Of having to be in a small, enclosed space with him. Of eating next to him. What it would feel like for the two of us to arrive together, as if we were truly there together. My heart raced.

"Hey, I...I can not go," Owen stepped closer to me, holding out his hand and then taking it back. "If it's that hard for you."

Public Anora took over and I snapped into the mask. "No, of course not. It's important that you be at things too, for the future."

After analyzing me, Owen stepped back and opened the front door for me. The black town car waited in the driveway. I slid inside and tried to make myself comfortable even though every inch of my skin was ablaze with awareness. I looked out the window, trying to burrow inside the deepest parts of myself, to hide so thoroughly behind the mask I was unshakable.

When Owen's hand dropped next to mine on the seat I flinched, unable to stop myself. He didn't move his hand away.

I looked over at him, so handsome in the flickering light that it hurt. He'd always been gorgeous, pulling off his blonde hair and light eyes in a way that still made him terrifying to people that didn't know him. The years, college, being away from me, had all been good to him. He knew I was watching him but didn't look at me. Not because he didn't want to, I could tell he did in the way his jaw flexed and his pulse throbbed. I wanted to believe he was still as drawn to me as I was to him.

There was more muscle packed onto his frame, and I knew he worked out and trained with our security staff regularly. He'd lost all the last bit of softness in his face that was still there the last time I'd seen him; now he was all man. He had been mysterious and intriguing as a teenage boy, and I was just as intrigued by the man and the hardness that appeared from every angle. The desire to burrow beneath it burned in my chest.

"How've you been?" I asked. It was going to be on me to repair anything about us. I wanted a friendship with him again because if that's all I could get, I wanted it. Maybe if we were friends again the dull, constant ache in my chest would dim. Maybe I would feel less like I betrayed him.

"Good. Designation keeps me busy."

"Do you like it?"

"More than I expected. I love it." He's looking forward now, but still not at me. "What about you?"

"I keep busy."

"Have you…are things good?" Owen meant with my head.

"About the same." I tried to lighten the mood. "I still haven't met Rafe."

"You will," he laughed and it hit me in the chest with a thud. How long since I'd heard him laugh? I couldn't believe he was still so free with me. "When I can trust him."

"Trust him to what?"

Owen shook his head, declining to answer. We pulled up to the hotel where the benefit was being held. There was a short red carpet and some media present. When we stepped out of the car, Owen took my hand to help me out and then didn't let me go. The cameras flashed as we walked to the door, and it was very clear that Owen took his role as my escort seriously.

I tried to break away from him when we got inside but he didn't let me. Everywhere I went, he went with me. In the end it was probably a good idea for him. I introduced him to every person I talked to, I got to talk him up as the future CEO, and he always complimented me on the work that I did.

It was frustrating to I think he got some of the donations to be higher because what I was doing was being validated by a man, but whatever.

And he wouldn't stop touching me. A hand on my arm, my lower back, taking my hand when the moment called for it, his body brushing against my body. My panties were a flood zone and I hated myself for it.

We hadn't touched each other in 6 years, and I was more aroused from incidental contact with him than I'd been when trying to get myself off. I couldn't even remember the last time I'd successfully had an orgasm. I was wound so tight he could probably have broken me with a finger trailing down my arm. I was still an untouched, inexperienced virgin, but he awoke something in me that I didn't understand. His mere existence set me on fire.

As the night drew to a close, I stepped away to take a break before having to be in a car with him, but he wouldn't let me go then either. I'd hid myself away in a corner behind some plants and decorations.

I'd thought I was alone as Owen stepped to my back and I felt him speak across the sensitive skin of my neck. His fingers toyed with the chain of my necklace, and the place where the O pendant rested between my breasts burned. I wondered if he knew I was wearing it.

"You look beautiful, I didn't tell you that." His knuckle brushed down the back of my bare arm and I gasped at the feeling that moved through my whole body. "Even more beautiful when you're passionate. Like you are about this. Even behind the mask, I can see the light. See you shining."

My eyes fluttered closed. He felt so good.

"Are you happy, Anora?"

"It doesn't matter," I answered. "I'm doing what needs to be done."

"Is that enough?" He stepped closer, his body now lined up with mine. We were off in a corner of the room, in a shadowed space where I hoped no one could see me. "I want you to be happy, Button. I'll do anything for you to be happy."

My breath hitched and I was on the verge of tears. "Owen." I missed him so much.

"Anything." Owen's lips pressed against my neck and if I'd thought I was wet before, I had no idea. My entire body stood at attention, my nipples hardened, and my core clenched around nothing. I was more aroused than I'd ever been in my life. I was on the edge of coming over nothing.

We stood close like that and I had no idea what to do or say. He'd stayed away from me for years. I had dreaded the moment he would move on. The second I would have to accept that he didn't love me the way he used to anymore. He'd always love me, there was too much history between us, but someday that love would change from a burning flame to a glowing, nostalgic ember of what used to be.

"I love you," he nearly growled it. I hadn't heard him say it out loud in so long that a whimper escaped before I could stop it. Owen trailed a hand up my back until he could wrap it around my nape, and then he slid it around to the front. He grasped me by the throat and pulled me back into his body. The softness of my curves pressed into the hardness I'd noticed in him. Including his erection, pressed against my back.

"I thought I could let you go, but I lied. You belong to me. I own every breath you take, every blink of your eyes, every lick of your lips. I know you never stopped thinking of me. I know your feelings haven't changed, even if your decision stands. I'm going to make you change your mind. I'm going to remind you every fucking day," the harsh tone of his voice exploded across my skin, "that you love me."

"You can try." I don't know how I managed to say it, or even where that kind of sass came from, but I meant it. I wanted him to try, because maybe I would change my mind. Maybe he could convince me that the right thing to do was to be with him. I wanted it to be, I just couldn't see it.

With another angry sound, Owen turned me around and pulled me close. His blue eyes were a blaze of want and fury. My eyes dropped from his down to his mouth. His soft, perfect mouth.

Then it was on mine. He pressed his lips against mine for only a second before parting them with his tongue and owning me.

Owen was right, he owned me. Down to the deepest parts of my soul, I belonged to him.

I couldn't be with him forever, but I could be with him right now. I would take what I could because there was no resisting him. After a moment of hesitation, I kissed him back.

III

Falling

17

Owen

Anora stepped back a little after I made my first move and didn't let me kiss her again, but she also invited me to every single thing she went to as her escort. We started talking again, and breaking the tension between us. We started fixing the foundation we had shaken.

I could not have imagined the sheer amount of things Anora attended. When her assistant gave me access to her calendar, it was terrifying how much she showed up for things. Doing work she wasn't getting paid for was more hours than I spent on work that I was. She made a lot of money for a lot of people who really needed it.

It drove me crazy when her sisters teased her for it, like all she was doing was going to fancy parties instead of hustling rich pricks. Anora never corrected them or challenged that view, so I didn't either. People loved her at those things, and the people she worked with appreciated her, so if that was enough for her it was enough for me. I wanted to stand by her, but I didn't want to make waves.

Finally, there was a break in her schedule.

I blocked off a Saturday night and sent her an itinerary including dress code and locations. It was time for her to meet my friends, and time for her to finally relax and have an actual good time at a party she wasn't throwing.

I waited with a serious amount of anxiety in the foyer. Anora had only responded to my text with an "okay" so it was kind of 50-50 if she'd even show. I knew her fear would eat her up, but I was hoping she still trusted me enough to take a chance. I hoped she knew I would never put her in a situation she couldn't handle, or where I didn't have her back.

I heard her footsteps on the stairs and turned around. In that moment, I was sure she was trying to kill me.

Anora wore a black faux leather dress with a corset top. It hugged every beautiful curve of her body and made her look like temptation incarnate. My devil and my angel all wrapped up in one.

When she reached me she looked down at herself. "Is this too much?"

"No," I reassured her immediately. "It just puts every man who looks at you too long at risk of being punched in the face." I grabbed her and pulled her into the darkness by the front door, away from where anyone could see us. "Mine," I groaned into her neck and my hands rested low on her back. It took all my self-control not to grab her ass.

"Fucking gorgeous." I kissed her racing pulse, happy I affected her so easily. "Let's go."

We stepped outside and into the car. I texted Rafe that we were on our way, and reminded him again that he needed to keep his mouth shut and his thoughts to himself. I did not need Anora hearing what a worthless, heartbroken shell I was for a long time over her. It'd be just like him to make some offhand or seemingly benign comment that will hurt her, even if that's not his intention. He doesn't know how easy it is for her to self-destruct with blame and guilt.

In the car, I didn't let her sit away from me. I crowded her against me and kept my arm around her and rested it on her hip.

"What do I need to know?" she asked, a little shy but I heard the excitement too.

"Rafe Montaigne was my roommate in college, and we're going out with his wife and his brothers."

"Like...the Montaignes the..."

"Criminals? Yeah. But they aren't what you think. They're good guys. And you're going to love Sophie, Rafe's wife." If I could have built a best friend for Anora, it would be Sophie. It felt like fate that Rafe, who was my platonic goddamn soulmate, would be with a woman who was perfect for Anora, too. Despite everything she'd been through, Sophie was a gentle, relaxed soul. The kind of person who picked up on what other people were feeling and could soothe them with reassurance. They both believed in putting others before themselves, sometimes to their detriment, and cared about being productive and useful. I knew they'd get along.

"I've never been out like this," Anora admitted. "I mean, I showed up at parties in college, but this is another level."

"I know," I laughed. "It took a while for me to get used to it too. I've got you." I leaned in and placed a lingering kiss on her throat. Anora melted into me. "It's going to be fine."

Anora could only nod, and I spent the rest of the drive teasing her with soft touches and more unexpected kisses to everywhere except her lips.

The club was already going when we arrived, and I pulled Anora close as we approached the door. Out of the corner of my eye I saw her look at the line, confused why we weren't waiting. This place belonged to the Montaignes, they knew me here. I'd never waited.

I gave a nod to the two guys working the door and they let us in.

I moved Anora in front of me so I could watch her reaction. The large open space was dominated on two walls by a bar, the rest of the building was all dance floor, and then there were VIP platforms and booths all around. The music was loud, people were packed on the floor, and the bar was busy. It was always like this. Some nights I liked to be able to hide in the midst of the chaos and watch people.

I led Anora through the space and didn't rush her as she observed everything. I kept her close and glared at everyone who stared at her for too long. She was mine.

Finally, we made it around to the VIP area for the Montaignes themselves. As we walked up the few steps, cheers rose from the couches.

"Owen!" All the voices shouted. We were then descended on by four large men and one woman. While Rafe was happily married, and the youngest of his family, his older brothers hadn't gotten "trapped" yet, as they said. They were all very careful about women, and I almost never saw them with anyone up here. Thierry said it was because they liked discretion at their clubs and didn't want to appear available.

Anora got wrapped up in the greeting, her little body squished against mine, and I held her close. I was relieved that she was laughing when they stepped back and introduced themselves to her. Lothaire dared to kiss her hand, and only laughed when I glared at him. She slid deeper into my side as a result as if to reassure me she knew she was mine, so I couldn't be too upset with him.

Sophie didn't let that stand for long, and took Anora's hand and pulled her away from us. They stood at the balcony overlooking the dance floor. Anora was in safe hands, but I couldn't keep my gaze away for long.

The guys continued talking and I spoke up occasionally, but all I could do was watch her. Watch as her body gradually relaxed, as she started talking more and engaging in the conversation with Sophie, as her hips started to move to the music and she felt comfortable enough to have a drink. This was the right thing to do. She needed a night out.

Sophie walked back to the table and signaled the waiter. "Shots!"

Anora perched on the arm of my chair, but I pulled her over until she was on my lap. She looked at me and her eyes were conflicted.

"What is it, love?"

"What changed?"

I wrapped a possessive hand around her thigh. "I did. You're mine and it's time I proved it to you." I moved forward and gently sunk my teeth into her neck, wishing I could mark her.

"Owen," she whimpered.

Before I had to worry about my reaction to that, the shots arrived. Sophie made sure we all took one. She held her shot up.

"To the family we choose."

We all cheered, and took our shots. I watched as Anora's throat worked, swallowing the vodka. She made a bit of a face but overall did better than I expected. I knew her experience with drinking was limited, both because of her need for control, as well as being careful about her medication. That would probably be her last drink of the night, but it would be enough to make her feel like she engaged with the group.

"You good?" I asked her.

"I want to dance."

"Then let's go." I stood her up and followed, but she was frozen and staring at me in shock.

"You dance?"

I pulled her to my side. "With you I do." I made eye contact with Sophie and tilted my head. She smiled and grabbed Rafe, and the four of us moved away from our VIP area and into the crush of bodies.

I held Anora to me, her back to my front, and moved to the beat of the music with her. The longer we moved, the more she got into it. I stepped back when she moved away from me to dance with Sophie, and Rafe and I both stood and barely moved, watching our women get close and move together. It was hot as fuck.

When they leaned in and touched noses, singing at each other, I heard Rafe let out a groan next to me.

"Why is that so damn sexy?"

"Because they're letting go." I answered him. Seeing our careful, closed women make a connection and be free like that was unbelievably arousing. Like a bright light exploded across our vision, watching the people we loved take off their shields and lower their walls to be themselves. I loved it. I loved that they connected.

Anora moved over to me and wrapped her arms around my neck. "Water."

I led her back to where the rest of the Montaigne's were seated, leaving Sophie and Rafe to dance together. They'd probably be leaving to get naked soon anyway; they didn't last long once she started dancing. I didn't blame him, not after seeing what Anora looked like letting loose.

I wanted more of this for her. More of her being relaxed and free instead of carrying the burden she placed on herself. Everything she did, every choice she made, revolved around the Sorrelles looking good and making sure she never did anything to appear less than perfect. I wanted her to get messy, I wanted her to feel unencumbered.

Without prompting, Anora perched on my lap as she chugged a bottle of water. There was a sheen of sweat on her tanned skin and it made her glow even brighter in the dim lighting. I was so caught up in looking at her that I didn't pay attention when she talked to Thierry and Michel, something about another benefit she was working on. I wanted to pay attention but between her stunning beauty and the drinks I'd had, I was in a daze.

Anora looked down at me as if expecting me to say something.

"What?"

"Nothing," she laughed and leaned onto me more. She wrapped her arm around my neck and relaxed. This was how it should be, how it always should've been. I was going to win her over, and when she was ready we would tell Don that there was never going to be any arrangement except her and me. Together we'd cement the future of Designation, and secure it for the Sorrelle line forever. Despite my last name, we'd be effectively cutting out the Carver involvement.

It served two purposes that would give my heart peace: getting the love of my fucking life, and destroying the legacy of my piece of shit parents.

The rest of the night we relaxed and danced more, and she tortured me with her body in that tight dress pressed up against mine. Every time she laughed and whispered with Sophie, when I watched them exchange phone numbers, the fact that she trusted someone who was important to me, felt amazing. I'd risked my life to save Sophie for Rafe, and in the years between she'd become one of my best friends too. They were a unit in my head, and I wanted the four of us to be close. I wanted Anora to know about the things that mattered to me the most.

We called it a night just after 1:00 A.M. and Anora surprised me again when she crawled into my lap once we got into the car.

She laid her head on my shoulder and I held her close, taking in every second of this closeness until we had to go back home and pretend like we weren't. We were so good at playing that game and I hated it.

"I missed you." The pain in her voice hit me hard, but the break between us hadn't been one-sided. She stepped away too.

"I know, Button." I kissed the top of her head. "Since we haven't gone to bed yet, this still counts for yesterday, but I love you." I whispered it, but I know she heard.

"I don't know what to do, Owen."

"What do you mean?"

She moved so that she could look at me while we talked. "I want you so much but I…I'm afraid. I don't know what the right thing to do is anymore."

"When was the last time you did what you wanted instead of what you thought was right?"

Anora leaned in and kissed me, her tongue sliding between my lips until it touched mine. I let her lead the kiss, taking what she needed from me. When she pulled back her eyes were dark and dilated.

"Just then," she answered my question.

"I'm what you want, but I'm also right for you."

Anora looked away for a moment and then flashed her gaze back to mine. "Show me."

That was all the invitation I needed. I cradled her face in my hand, staring at her and memorizing this moment before crashing my lips down on hers. Anora opened for me, so giving and generous even with her kisses. We stayed wrapped up in each other, mouths connected and breath shared, until we got back to the Sorrelle compound.

The house was dark except the lights where the guards were, and no one paid us much attention when we walked inside. I kept Anora's hand in mine and didn't let her break away from me at the end of the hall. She followed me into my room. We both knew where this was going, and neither of us had any motivation to stop it.

I was nervous, but I'd talked to Rafe a lot. He listened and gave advise without judgment or condescension, and I wanted this to be the best it could for her.

Anora turned to me in the dim light of my desk lamp, and I could see the same nerves playing out across her face.

"I don't know what I'm doing," she admitted and started wringing her hands.

I stepped toward her and pulled her to me. "I don't either."

Anora's mouth dropped open in shock, and then tightened in doubt. "What?"

"I've never done…anything," I admitted. "I never wanted anyone, even for the experience. Since the night of your 16th birthday I've never even kissed anyone else." I slid a hand up her back until I had it wrapped around her nape, keeping her in my control. "Even when I was so furious with you I wished I could fuck my feelings away. Even when I wanted to punish you, I could never be with anyone else. I couldn't even try. You have owned me my entire life. I don't know how to get away, and I know now that I don't want to. You are mine and I am yours, and even if you tell me to stop, leave, never speak to you again, I will still be yours."

I didn't give her a chance to say anything, I pressed her close and kissed her. Things happened naturally after that, and I loved the feeling of Anora's hands on me as she took off my jacket, unbuttoned my shirt, and ran her hands over my body. It was going to be the most difficult exercise in self-control I'd ever faced, but I could handle it for her.

Anora gasped when I unzipped her dress and tugged it off her body. I watched her skin prickle with goosebumps and the way she swallowed nervously, but didn't cover herself from my eyes. She was wearing a black strapless bra that lifted her breasts, and a small black thong that perfectly framed her ass. She wore a single necklace on a long chain, and it took me a second to recognize it.

The necklace I gave her.

The possession that rocketed through me made me impossibly harder. She still wore it. Anora knew she had never stopped being mine.

"Get on the bed."

I was surprised when she didn't protest or hesitate, but turned and walked to my bed, giving me a perfect view of her. She slid on and laid down, raising her hands above her head and lifting her tits even higher. I walked to the bed and climbed over her, sliding one of my legs between hers, but not pressing against her body.

When Anora's eyes met mine I saw that we were on the same, heated, page. I didn't know how far tonight would go, but I knew that I needed to touch her. Needed to start learning everything she needed to feel good.

"If you say stop, I'll stop."

"I trust you," Anora answered. She moved her hands behind her back and unclasped her bra, pulling the cups away from her breasts and revealing her sweet, dark nipples to me. When I looked at her for permission she nodded, and I took them in my hands. I squeezed the soft flesh, then trailed my fingertips around the underside, noting the way she arched her back.

When I grazed her hardened nipples she exhaled sharply, so I did it again. I leaned forward and took one of her nipples into my mouth and sucked. Her hands flew to my head as she moaned, pressing me into her body and keeping me there. I let her reactions guide me, and moved to the other nipple to do the same. I moved up and bit the soft skin below her clavicle, leaving a small mark.

Anora gasped and laughed. "I didn't think I'd like that, but it felt really good."

"Do you want me to bite you, Button? Mark your pretty skin?"

She looked down her body to where my head rested, her hands still buried in my hair. "Yes. Please."

I did as she asked, biting and sucking on the skin of her stomach, her breasts, the juncture of her neck and shoulder, and she laughed as I turned her over and bit into the swell of her ass. That quickly turned to a moan, and I groaned because I could smell her pussy. She was turned on, and I understood now the desire to taste someone. The feel of her skin, feeling the way her muscles jerked and relaxed as I touched her, hearing her heartbeat in her chest, I wanted to devour everything about her.

"I want to see you."

Anora fluttered her eyes open and looked at me. I watched with my breath held as she slid the thong over her hips and down her thighs. I stared at the line of dark hair leading to the slit of her smooth pussy, and my mouth watered. The tiny panties dropped to the floor, and Anora let her legs relax open, revealing herself to me. Her pussy was pretty, pink, and glistening, and I wanted it in my mouth.

"Tell me what feels good," I asked, before moving between her legs. First, I wanted to taste, so I licked from her entrance up to the little hood around her clit. She was sweet and salty and I liked it. I stopped thinking for a moment and savored, licking her over and over to get my tongue coated in her.

Then I spread her lips open and looked at the bead of her clit. I lifted my eyes and looked up her body as I moved to focus on it, licking, sucking, even biting gently, and waiting for her reactions. It shouldn't have surprised me that she liked when I bit it.

"That feels good," she whimpered. "Like that, please."

I did what she asked, over and over. I don't know how long I was buried in her pussy, but I groaned when she pressed hard against my face, grinding herself into me, and then covered her mouth to hold in a scream as she came. Her pussy got wetter, her come on my lower lip and my chin, and when she started to relax I let her clit go and licked her more. I could've kept going, but she tugged my hair until I stopped.

"I want...more," she looked a little scared, but still aroused. "I want all of you."

I didn't expect that, but I also didn't think I had the power to say no.

18

Anora

I wanted tonight to go this way. I wanted to give in. If I followed through on an arranged marriage, there were so many things I might never get to experience the way I'd dreamed. In this moment, I could be with Owen, and I could have what I wanted. I'd always wanted him, and I would regret so much in my life if I didn't do this. If I didn't let myself be with him, even if it's only for now. The moment matters more.

I was tired of fighting.

"Please," I asked.

Owen nodded, and looked nervous too. It was a bit of a revelation that he had never been with anyone, that in this moment we would be each other's only. I loved it and it terrified me at the same time. What if I wasn't good? What if it hurt too much and I never wanted to do it again?

Coming from Owen's mouth on me was incredible, I wanted to feel like that all the time, and I could still feel the aftershocks of the pleasure throughout my lower half. There was still an ache in me for something more.

Owen moved off the bed and I crawled after him. Brushing his hands aside, I used my shaking ones to start removing his belt and his pants. I hesitated for a second before I pulled his boxer briefs down too, and jumped as his cock sprang free. It was thicker and longer than I was expecting, and my hand reached out and grasped him before I could ask him if that was okay.

I looked up at him and his head was thrown back, his neck and jaw tense. My hand grazed up and down and he groaned, wrapping one of his hands around mine to stop me.

"If you keep doing that I'm going to come all over your face, or shove my dick in your mouth."

I clenched at the thought, surprised I was turned on by the idea of Owen holding my head as he slid in and out of my mouth, making me gag and drool. I'd watched it in porn before but didn't understand the appeal. Now I did.

"Do you…want to do that?"

Owen's gaze heated and I felt his cock flex in our hands. "Not tonight."

He moved away from me and went to his nightstand. I watched with some amusement as he took out a box of condoms, but then my eyes strayed to his perfect tight ass. I moved fast, before he could stop me, and smacked it. Owen whipped his head around to look at me.

"What was that for?"

I reached out and squeezed it, amazed at how solid it was. "Because I wanted to." I leaned in before he could realize what I wanted, and bit him. He flinched but didn't stop me, and I sucked the skin between my teeth. It felt good to bite him. I pulled away and grinned at the mark I'd left at the top of his ass cheek, a mix of teeth marks and a bruise.

"Don't use a condom," I blurted. Owen froze. "I want to feel you and I'm on the shot. Please. I want this, us."

He put the box down and climbed onto the bed until he could reach my mouth with his. We kissed ferociously, rubbing and grinding on each other until I was so worked up I couldn't take it anymore. The desire to be filled was overwhelming. I pushed him back and straddled him, sliding down until the heat of his cock pressed against me.

"Is it...okay, like this?" I asked, shamelessly sliding on him, the sounds of my arousal obvious.

"You should," he grunted as I pressed harder. "This will let you keep control. I need you to do that. I don't want to hurt you."

"Maybe I'd like it," I joked, but there was part of me that thought I might. I moved around until I felt comfortable and then lifted, pressing the head of Owen's cock against me. It was tight but I kept bearing down, gasping at the foreign but not unpleasant sensation of being spread open.

It got to a point where it burned and I slowed. "Play with my nipples," I commanded him. Owen cupped my breasts and started to tease the hard tips. Without warning he pinched them, and I felt my pussy flex and my body push down. The burn intensified so I lifted myself, and then slid back down again. It was easier. I repeated the motion, focusing on how good it felt when Owen played with me until I felt my hips touch his.

I looked down and his cock was buried inside me. I wasn't a virgin anymore. Neither was he. Our eyes met and his hands dropped from my breasts to my hips.

"You good?"

"I'm amazing," I whispered, tears welling in my eyes. I never thought I'd have this with him. I never thought he'd find a way to forgive me and come back to me. Even if this was temporary, I would make sure that in whatever time we had, Owen would be my first everything. Just like he had been my whole life.

I started to slide my hips back and forth, adjusting to the feeling. I shifted and opened my legs wider, and I felt the pressure of his hips against my clit. I liked that. I braced my hands on his chest and kept sliding, chasing that good feeling.

"Does this feel good for you?" I asked.

"God don't worry about me," Owen groaned. "Anything feels good. Fuck it's amazing."

I continued to move, my muscles tensed and my breath got shallow as the pleasure built inside me.

"You're so beautiful, Anora," Owen spoke quietly. "A goddess. An angel. I want this moment to last forever."

"You don't want to orgasm?"

"I could give a fuck," he answered, shifting his hips under me in a way that made me cry out. "I want to live in this pussy, orgasm or not."

"Keep doing that," I moaned, and we started moving against each other, hips pressing and grinding until I felt myself break. I cried out as I clenched around him, a mix of pleasure and pain, and I moved without thinking, my senses dulled except for the feel of him in me and on me.

"Anora," he moaned, and I cried out again when he pumped into me rough and deep as he came inside me.

I collapsed onto him and he wrapped his arms around me. We stayed that way, sweaty and barely breathing, until the power of speech returned.

"One slight adjustment," he heaved quietly. "I want to live in the moment where you squeezed my cock as you came. That was the most intense thing I've ever felt. Watching your face and feeling you release. Fuck."

"Give me like 10 minutes and we can do it again." I spoke into the skin of his chest. I felt Owen laugh underneath me.

"I think we should take a day. You're going to be sore."

"I want to be sore. I want to feel this for weeks."

Owen laughed again. "We can make that happen, but not tonight."

I pushed myself up and we both groaned when I pulled off his cock.

I felt a rush of fluid and watched his come drip from me and onto him. I shivered, turned on by the sight of it.

"Go clean up, before I do fuck you again," Owen nearly growled, looking at the mess we made. As much as I wanted that too, I also saw the traces of red on his cock, and a hint of pink in his come. I had bled, and I needed to be nice to my body if I wanted us to keep having sex.

I nearly stumbled to Owen's bathroom. I took care of business and cleaned myself up, being as gentle as I could. After, I stood at his bathroom door.

"Do you want to take a shower together?" I asked, hesitant. That was intimate, and even though we'd just been as connected as two people could be, and even though I knew Owen's darkest moments, this was an unknown. A different layer to our relationship.

To my delight, Owen smiled. "Yeah."

He got up and walked past me, completely unconcerned about his nudity, and turned on the shower. I smiled when he pulled me inside and plunged me under the water. We kissed until it was nearly cold, and I didn't care at all.

19

Anora

I knew it was a myth that everything changed when you lost your virginity, so I had to assume that my life changed because I gave in to my feelings for Owen. It was like I'd always been standing on the edge of a cliff and I needed to jump. I was drowning now and I loved every second of it.

Instead of parting in the hall every night like we used to, I stepped into his room before anyone saw. We explored each other and what we liked, never rushed or hurried for the end, because our connection was already so deep we wanted to enjoy being together.

The first time I gave him a blow job, I asked him to use my mouth. I told him that I'd seen it in porn and thinking about it turned me on. He obliged, and it lived up to my fantasies. The feeling of his cock sliding along my lips and tongue, the press of the head into the back of my throat, feeling his thighs flex underneath my hands, the drip of saliva onto my thighs and down my chest was incredibly hot. I wasn't entirely ready for what him coming in my mouth would be like, but I did my best.

I swallowed some and then pulled away instinctively, the rest of his warm come hitting my face and chest. We both liked that.

Afterward, and after a shower, we laid down together before I had to go back to my room.

"So," Owen started, running his hand along my naked back. "What kind of porn do you watch?"

Instead of telling him, I grabbed my phone and I showed him.

While most porn is a terrible guide to sex in a relationship, it gave us ideas of things we wanted to try, or kinks to look into. We were both inexperienced in our mid-twenties, there hadn't been time to learn or experiment, and we'd been saving ourselves for each other. Now it was safe to explore and all I wanted to do was give him pleasure, and tell him things that pleasured me.

It's how I learned I really, really liked being bitten. I loved it even when the marks throbbed, the fissure of pain getting me aroused later when I'd remember seeing or feeling Owen sink his teeth into me. My favorite places were my inner thighs and butt, but I also loved when he bit my nipples. He liked to do that when I was close to coming and it would send me screaming over the edge. Neither of us was quite ready for him to truly bite my clit but I had a feeling I'd like that too.

Before this, I'd been pretty comfortable with self-exploration, and I trusted Owen so much it was easy to tell him what I did to myself, and teach him how to do it to me. He liked detailed instructions and had a flawless memory when it came to me.

Sex aside, he made my life better.

One night a week, we did something with Rafe and Sophie. It meant that I finally had a life outside of my charity obligations. Sometimes we'd go to their apartment and play board games or watch movies. I hustled them at their pool table, and we cooked together. Sophie and I took on baking experiments, swapping recipes over our texts during the week. Other nights we went to Montaigne clubs and partied discreetly.

Tonight the men were on cooking duty while Sophie and I worked on a homemade Black Forest Cake. The guys were grilling the main courses out on the deck, and we had taken over the kitchen.

"I never thought my life would be like this," Sophie laughed.

"Like what?"

"So domestic. So calm." She started layering the cooled cakes with the filling I made. "Has Owen told you much about me? We've talked about life now but I avoid the past."

"Don't we all?" I wondered how much she knew about Owen. I had a feeling Rafe knew everything, but I'd never asked Owen for specifics. Rafe had definitely known about me, and known that Owen was a virgin since he confessed he'd asked Rafe for advice about oral before anything happened between us. That was somehow both cute and embarrassing.

"I'll take that as a no. Rafe and I are technically an arranged marriage. My hand was sold to his family." I flinched but she didn't notice, lost in the work and her own recollections. "Except then we fell in love, and my family realized they had something to hold over the Montaignes and took me away. I was held captive for five years. I thought that was going to be my life until I died. Moving from hiding place to hiding place, used as leverage, having to bend to the will of my captors to survive."

I didn't know what to say, so I turned and put my hand on her shoulder. She stopped and turned into my offered hug. We held each other for a long time. Sophie felt like the first friend I ever made. Owen had been my friend but we'd always known it was more. The purity of the friendship and care I felt for and from Sophie was entirely new to me. I knew she was very guarded, and that Rafe always thanked me for being there for her. I don't think I understood until she told me this story what that really meant.

"How did you survive?"

Now Sophie smirked. "I told a very good lie, and cried a lot. While they did hurt me, often, I put the fear of Rafe into their souls so there were lines they never crossed. I knew he'd come for me, the second he had the means to find me. I was right. Owen was there, too."

Now I'm flabbergasted. "What?" I dropped the piping bag I was holding.

"You know Owen, but I don't think you know Owen when he goes dark. I think other than you, Rafe is the only person he'd be willing to tap into that side of himself for, and that's what he did. The Montaignes and Owen saved me. It's why he's my brother, because he united me with my love, and risked a part of himself to do it."

I think about what she said, about Owen being unwilling to go dark. He might be ruthless in business and cold to most people, but part of it is because there's a fire at the core of him that he keeps protected because he's afraid of burning too hot. If it becomes an inferno, he might never be able to quell the rage. It's the part of him he fears he inherited from his parents, an ability to do harm and damn the consequences.

Owen could never be like them, though. That inferno would rage for love and loyalty, not greed and selfishness. His fire only brings warmth, and I wish he'd let more people in to feel it.

"He's amazing." I looked toward the deck where Rafe and Owen were drinking beer and talking. Their friendship was so cute to me. Owen had been so good at keeping everyone at arm's length and I'd been afraid of him being alone when he pushed me away, even though he'd been right to do it. Sometimes I felt jealous of the years he spent with Rafe by his side when it could've been me, but I would never begrudge them their friendship.

"They both are. Rafe didn't really make friends outside his brothers. I'm glad he's got someone else to give him perspective."

We fell back into a comfortable silence and finished the cake.

"Our lovely ladies!" Rafe boomed as he came back into the house with a platter full of grilled chicken. Owen followed behind with asparagus and baked potatoes. Rafe set the plate down on the table then slid over to kiss my cheek before dipping Sophie and taking her mouth. As always, he kissed her for way too long and with far too much tongue.

I turned into Owen and ignored them. I looked up at him, absorbing the relaxed look he always had when we were here. When we could be Anora and Owen without the other pressures and obligations on our heads. Without fearing who would see.

I pushed up on my toes and he bent down to meet me. Our mouths pressed together and I opened for him, unafraid to show my unabashed need for him. I wished it didn't matter that we were together. I wished I could claim him forever, in front of everyone, and let them know that he was mine. That he picked me, too.

For a second, the fantasy I never let myself have moved across my mind's eye. A white dress, an aisle, Owen in a tux at the end of it. Unsmiling, but with a look in his eye that only I knew.

I kissed him harder, sending that wish out into the world. Begging life to make it happen. Begging myself to change, to find the will to fight expectations, to say fuck it to my panic and anxiety, and claim what I wanted.

Except the only person I can't disappoint in this world is dad, and this is what he thinks is best.

A wolf whistle sounds and we break apart. Rafe clapped and Sophie laughed.

"Listen, we're all hot, so if you're ever up for fucking in front of each other, I'm down." Rafe raised an eyebrow. Sophie slapped his chest and walked away to start setting the table.

I contemplated it for a second because they were both beautiful. It would be like watching super artistic porn as their gorgeous bodies fucked each other. I shivered a bit, but also realized that with my innocence in that arena outside of what I did with Owen, I'd be very uncomfortable to know what Rafe's dick looked like.

"Don't even think about it," Owen growled in my ear.

I laughed up at him. "Too late, but never happening."

Owen pulled the neck of my dress aside and bit me, and I had to muffle my moan by burying my face in his neck.

"I'll fuck you for that later," he promised.

I just grinned at him and went over to eat with our friends. I was in so much trouble because while I had always loved Owen, I'd learned what it was like to be truly in love with him, and I knew that I'd never get my heart back. It was his, no matter what happened.

20

Owen

For five fucking years, I let Anora lead me on.

We spent almost every night together, I went with her to every event, and we spent what free time we had with our best friends. I thought we'd told each other everything, were there for each other, and had both fallen deeply in love with the other. She was the center of my universe and everything I did was for her. I'd thought we were building our life together.

I'd let myself believe that we were going to get somewhere, that when the time was right, when she realized how strong and steady we were together, she'd tell Don. I had no doubt he'd give his blessing. A hundred times I'd thought about talking to him, telling him about us, telling him that Anora felt burdened by agreeing to the possibility of an arranged marriage. I'd thought about intervening, even if it exposed me.

What I couldn't stand was anything that exposed her. Any moment that would make her vulnerable, or send her spiraling. I did everything I possibly could to protect her. It went against every instinct I had. It hurt our relationship, but if she felt safe that was what mattered. If she felt sheltered from it all with me then I would have dealt with anything.

There had been a few offers of marriage in the last five years, and every time she'd said no. Then she would come and tell me about it, and we'd hash out why she wasn't ready to tell her father. She'd have a hard time for a few weeks, she'd fall back into that familiar pattern of feeling like she wasn't adding to her family.

It got worse when Aster graduated early and started working at Designation, because they'd always had trouble connecting, and now her youngest sibling was adding to the family legacy in such a large, meaningful way.

Anora had to go away on an actual retreat for a few days after that, one that focused on increasing feelings of self-worth as well as intensive sessions with a counselor. I'd never met anyone so wonderful who so easily believed the worst voices in their head. I could never really understand, and I knew that, but sometimes when she told me how she felt it made me want to rip into my own mind and find something to give her to fix it. Something to silence the voice that told her she didn't deserve to live, that she was meaningless, that we didn't need her.

Christ, I needed her.

I needed to talk to her about shit that pissed me off at work. I needed to tell her things that went well. I needed to celebrate her when she raised money for a cause that mattered, when she organized a flawless fucking fundraiser and helped people who needed it.

I needed to laugh with her and Rafe and Sophie at the absurdity of our lives.

I needed her to calm me down when the nightmares still hit from time to time, of reliving the last interaction I had with Roman. The nightmares I had where I was trapped in a room with Elaine, and I knew that pain was coming.

I needed her to tell me stories about the good things in the world, to keep me grounded and centered, and hear about all the people she was meeting and helping.

I needed her that way, and clearly she didn't need me or she wouldn't have betrayed me like this. It's worse than the first time. The first time we didn't know what it was like to be together, all we had was a dream and our imaginations. Now I'd had reality, and apparently I was the only one who wanted to keep it.

I didn't want to need her anymore. I wanted to rip her out of me.

Except I couldn't do that, because when I'd learned exactly what she'd done, we were having a family dinner in the Sorrelle house.

Don had implemented them in the last year or so because once Aster was home from college he wanted her to interact with them more. She'd always been more distant, and I knew exactly how fucking scary she was. In a weird way, I was proud of her. Once I'd officially joined Designation, and our criminal assistance enterprise, there were no secrets from me.

I'd watched Aster torture men twice her size for information. I knew what she was like when she turned off her humanity to protect her family. Even Alina couldn't stay in the same room as Aster when she played.

The sisters would probably be horrified by the things I knew about them.

Like I knew everyone Alina slept with on vacation, because while Don forced the trips on her, she didn't actually go alone. There was always a tail, and they would note who she went home with. I always had them checked out after she left them, just in case. Alina could probably beat me in a fight when properly motivated, so I made sure that was a secret she never found out.

I knew Aster was made a killer as much as she was born one, and I had a sneaking suspicion that she had more blood on her hands than we knew. Don didn't want to look into it unless it became a safety issue, and I had a plan for that. Not that she would care, but I liked Aster. We were more similar than she'd believe - nothing on the surface, everything buried underneath - and I trusted her.

Aro, on the other hand, had no secrets. She was open and dreamy, she wanted to be loved. It amused me that despite my relationship with Anora, Aro was the only Sorrelle sister that openly loved me. The amount of times she caught me off guard by hugging me was frustrating, but I let her. Aro was the innocent core that needed to be protected. Even if her joy annoyed me, I never wanted to see her lose it, and I tolerated her desire to give affection.

I'd thought that Anora had no secrets from me.

Until Don casually presented to the family that Anora had agreed to a marriage contract. Agreed to it so thoroughly in fact, that she'd already signed the preliminary agreement.

"Anora's agreed to ally us with Derick Clayton. It will be advantageous for Designation." Don seemed bemused, like he wasn't quite sure it was happening. All his daughters were in their twenties with nary a commitment in sight. Anora suddenly on the verge of being married probably felt like it came out of nowhere.

"Of Venture?" I asked. Anora heard my question and flinched, my voice deeper than normal because I was trying to maintain control of myself.

"Yes."

"That will be advantageous," I agreed. "What a useful connection to have."

Anora still wouldn't look at me, and I almost felt bad for throwing her reasoning in her face. Don, however, wouldn't look away from me.

"Do you have any concerns?"

"None that we need to speak about now." I wiped my mouth and stood up, excusing myself from dinner. I really wanted to talk to

Don about why he didn't bring this to me sooner, because I could've interfered. The matches proposed in the past didn't have to do with Designation, they were all social or political. If he was making a match that would fuck with the company he should've told me.

It was easier to be irritated with him than to be mad at Anora right now.

I wondered if she'd even have the guts to come to me and talk, or if she'd burrow away. I hoped that Anora had grown and strengthened enough now to be better than that. I paced in my room, holding everything in as best I could so that I didn't destroy everything in sight. I needed to call Rafe.

I'd give Anora an hour to come talk to me. If she didn't, I was out of here. I was moving out of the house, legitimate safety issues be damned. I'd live in Rafe's building and be protected by the Montaignes instead.

It took her 42 minutes to come to me. She walked in without knocking, closed the door, and leaned against it. I waited for her to meet my eyes.

"We always knew we were stealing time." Her gaze finally connected with mine, and I ignored the pain I saw. The explanation she gave me was shit, and it confirmed that she'd been lying to me. For. Five. Fucking. Years. Anora always knew this was how we'd end. Anora had always known there would be an end, period, while I'd been planning out forever.

"No," I snapped at her, and didn't care that she jumped. "You knew. You lied to me."

"I hoped this wouldn't happen. It's not the same as lying."

"You hoped, while also knowing that you'd still do this if it was asked of you. That you'd never tell Don, and you'd never truly committed yourself to me. It was a fucking lie, Anora."

"I didn't want it to be."

"You can enjoy going to hell with those intentions. I'm done. I love you, I will always love you, and I'm done. Get out."

"Owen," she started and took a step toward me.

"No. Get out. Get the fuck away from me. I need to leave."

"Where are you going?" Anora had the audacity to cry right now.

"Where do you think? To the people I can actually trust." I moved around her and left my room, not looking back to see if she left it too. I'd never look for her again. I didn't know what to do with myself.

I had thought I knew what it was like to be hurt. The destruction of my body, my mind, the way it had taken me a decade to regain the ability to trust others; I had survived and rebuilt from all of those things. Anora was inside my body, my mind, my heart, and this level of betrayal from her was nuclear. I hurt so bad that it was a physical ache in my body. The air had been stolen from me, my pulse was violent, and for the first time in my life I wanted to detonate. I wanted the monster.

I could not comprehend how Anora could do this to me.

I showed up at Rafe and Sophie's and got stupidly fucking drunk.

"Family pressure is so hard," Sophie tried to soothe me. "I don't think she'll go through with it. We know how much she loves you. We've seen it."

Rafe was nearly as pissed as me, and was busy pacing in the living room and cursing in a mix of French and Russian. He'd gotten attached, and it frustrated him to get attached. At least he still had me, pitiful monster that I was.

"Even if she doesn't, how can I trust her? Unless she tells Don everything, I won't get pulled in again. I won't set myself up like this."

"You're right. Of course you're right." Sophie hugged me, and with a curse, Rafe sat on the other side of me and joined the hug. I hated it and I loved it. I didn't really like affection, but I'd learned to accept it from them just as I was gradually accepting it from Aro. I loved that they cared about me, would do anything for me, and wanted to comfort me. I hated that I was going to pass out on this couch while they got to go to bed together.

I'd only slept with Anora a handful of times because she was scared of getting caught.

Looking back, all the red flags leapt at me. All the times I should have seen she was never going to tell Don the truth. She was never going to pick me. No one ever did.

I thought I'd worked through some of this abandonment shit in my own therapy sessions about my struggles with feeling worthy and safe, but one massive hit from the love of my life and it all crumbled.

Sophie's phone buzzed on the coffee table and we all looked as Anora's name appeared on the screen. We stayed still and watched it until the call went to voicemail and the screen went black. It buzzed again, Anora called again.

"Do you want me to answer?"

I sighed and took another pull from the bottle in my hands as Rafe still hugged me and Sophie moved away to pick up the phone. "I won't hold it against you if you're still friends with her."

Sophie and Rafe exchanged a look, then she stood up and accepted the call. I could only hear the murmur of Anora's voice, not what was being said.

"He's here. We have him." Sophie looked down at the ground, a flash of pain on her face, and Rafe growled. Aside from his own hurt, this was hurting Sophie, and that would be a hard thing for him to forgive.

"You made your decision, Anora. He deserves to heal." I winced as Sophie's voice got hard. "I don't know," she replied lowly to whatever Anora responded. "Maybe in the future, but not right now. He needs us more than you do."

Not waiting for a response, Sophie ended the call.

Rafe and Sophie sat with me for hours, letting me drink, letting me rant, and eventually they left me to my own devices until I passed out on their couch.

As I walked into the house the next day, not as hungover as I deserved, Don called me into the library.

"Wild night?" He joked, looking pleasant but concerned.

"It was fine."

"You said you had some concerns last night. Do you want to share with me?" Don sat back in his chair and folded his hands on his stomach. He waited, and I tried to sort out my thoughts.

"Clearly, this will affect Designation, and open up opportunities for us with Venture. I'd hoped that if that kind of agreement was part of a marriage, you would've talked to me about it first."

Don nodded. "No other...concerns?"

I frowned, trying to figure out what he was getting at. "No."

He sighed. "You know, the idea of any of the girls in a contract marriage was your mother's."

I froze. "What?"

"Roman and Elaine, really." I hated hearing their names, but I felt like I needed to hear this. "They shared with me first that in the world of the super wealthy, which we had entered, strategic marriages were often made. They first dropped the idea after Anora was born." Don's gaze bored into me, like he was trying to tell me something. "They talked about promising the two of you to each other, an engaged since birth kind of thing."

"That's..." My best fucking dream. That I'd had a legitimate claim to her my entire life. I would have loved that. "Intense," I finally said.

"That was my feeling as well. I wanted all of you to have a chance to be your own people and find your own way. I wonder if it would've worked out though, don't you?"

I forced a laugh. It would've worked perfectly. "I guess we'll never know."

Don's expression fell. "I guess not. Well, I'll keep you involved in anything regarding the crossing of Designation and Venture, and what that will look like. They'll be sending a significant amount of information in the next few weeks, and we'll be expected to share as well."

"Of course. We'll be family, right?"

I wanted to throw up. I didn't wait for Don to say anything else. The floor felt like it was moving beneath me, and I wondered if I might still be drunk.

Roman and Elaine somehow fucked this up for me. They planted the seed in Don's head, and rather than present the idea of Anora and I getting married, he presented it generally, and she accepted. The most strategic move would still be for Anora to marry me, but if Don didn't think I wanted that he wasn't going to force it. If he thought for even a second Anora would be interested, I think he would've pursued it.

Life conspired to fuck me over. All the right things were there in the wrong order.

I was destined to be alone now because even when I hated her, I loved her. Even full of fury and betrayal, my heart beat for her. There would never be anyone I trusted with my secrets, my past, my pain, or my weaknesses because I'd never be able to open up enough for them to earn it. I was built for one woman, and if I couldn't have her, I wouldn't have anyone.

The only satisfaction I felt was that she'd be miserable too.

21

Anora

Before, there was a mask.

Behind the mask was a wall.

Now the wall was a fortress.

It was where I let myself be crushed under the weight of my betrayal, and at the same time where any piece of myself still lived. Where sometimes I'd retreat to live inside the memories of things I would never experience again.

Everything outside the fortress was fake. A scripted act of a person in my position who lived a life like mine. People thought they saw me when what they saw was a fiction of me. A performance.

I felt so little after he shut me down and left that it almost took me out when the pain finally hit for what I'd done. I drowned so deeply in hurt that even the worst of the voices in my head had gone away.

There was no need for me to die because I was already dead.

Owen was so deeply entwined in me that when I killed our love, I killed the most vital piece of myself. The apathy I felt toward my own existence should have worried me. I couldn't dredge up enough energy to worry.

I'd do what needed to be done because my family mattered more than what I wanted. If that meant I wasted away until I was a parody of a person then I would.

Even though they didn't talk about it with me, I knew that something was going on with Designation. I knew that there had been aggressive hacks and I knew that our safety had been compromised in some way. Dad and Owen were doing a lot of work at home, and that was never a good sign.

I didn't care about my safety. I went and did the things I was supposed to do to make us look like social benefactors and I smiled and spoke and then came home with no memory of the evening that transpired.

Dad started making me take two guards when I left the house instead of one, and even Alina was expected to be part of a two man team.

We needed allies. We needed a show of strength. Marrying Derick Clayton accomplished both. I had to follow through because we were in even more danger than when I'd agreed to it in the first place. The weight of that dropped me even further from myself.

The silence echoed in my mind when I was alone.

If I wasn't doing something for one of my charities or meeting an obligation, there was nothing inside me. I'd find myself losing time if I was by myself. I would sit down on my bed and hours would pass without me being aware. I'd come back to the present and instead of concerned I'd feel grateful. Grateful that I didn't have to be aware of my own existence.

That I didn't have to think or feel, or pretend to think or to feel.

The voices had stopped, so I must have made the right choice.

He still messaged me every night. The words were there, but I could feel the hatred behind them. It was a punishment, and I accepted it. He loved me, and wanted me to be punished with the truth of it.

My therapist knew something was wrong but for the first time in my life, she couldn't crack me. I said all the right things that demonstrated

I was maintaining my well-being. I was taking my medication, and I was talking about the intrusive thoughts I no longer had because I was overwhelmed by the nothingness. I mined my own past to tell convincing lies, and there was nothing she could do about it.

This was always the price I was going to pay.

IV

Fractured

22

Owen

That was the closest I'd ever come to working myself to death. Between the desire to get away from Anora and the Sorrelle house and the threats to Designation, my life was nothing but my job. Even Rafe and Sophie were worried.

Every day followed the same pattern, and the pattern gave me sanity. I'd wake up, get ready for the day, eat breakfast, and then drive Aster and Alonzo, sometimes Gio, to the office. Alonzo had been my guard for years. While I never confided anything to him, I knew he knew about Anora and I. He never said a word, and for that I was grateful.

At work, it was non-stop. Meetings, research, planning, coordinating. I worked to make sure our people and property were protected. That in every way I could possibly control, nothing could harm that building. The innocent people inside. The ones that knew nothing of our connections to darker things, or the way that wealth puts a target on your back.

I could see Anora retreat inside her mind and had to fight with myself that it was not my responsibility to fix it. If she asked for help or recognized what was happening, I would help, but I couldn't be that person for her anymore. I had to move away and so did she. We'd be separated by the country as well as matrimony soon and if I held on, I'd destroy any dignity that remained inside me.

The time passed faster than I wanted. I'd had preliminary conversations with Venture programmers, had talked to their security staff about the server farms, had tentatively started making plans for collaborations between the two companies. Aster and I worked to keep our vulnerabilities quiet, and so far there had been no successful attack. Her team worked well together.

Derick Clayton was coming to meet Anora and the rest of the family tomorrow. There would be little to no business discussed, and even though Don requested my presence as part of the family, I couldn't do it. I couldn't watch Anora sell herself to the most useful connection. Not yet. Not until there was nothing I could do to stop it, or I trusted that I wouldn't try and kill the unlucky, unaware man.

It wasn't his fault that I hated him. Hated her for being etched into every fiber of my being.

"Come to our place. Please," Rafe begged. "We'll distract you."

"No offense, but seeing the two of you might make it worse." I dressed casually, and watched the clock. I needed to go when Alina was distracted. I'd never seen her so paranoid about sticking to the schedule and looking good. For her, this was a demonstration of her capability as head of security. She worked hard but struggled to accept that some things were beyond planning, and couldn't be fixed with a fight. Sometimes surrendering to the inevitable was the only way to survive.

"At least see me," Rafe answered. "Tell me where. Sophie won't care."

I already knew where I was going. Alonzo was smuggling me out and dropping me off, hours before my presence was supposedly required.

"Fine. I'm going to the Orchid. In about twenty minutes."

"It's a little early, isn't it?"

"I have to be out of the house before he gets here. I can't watch this."

"Fair. I'll be there as soon as I can. Stick to the good stuff. No tequila."

"Fuck off," I snarled. He knew how I felt about tequila.

Rafe laughed but it was forced, and we hung up without saying anything else. Someone knocked on the door and dread pooled in my stomach.

"What."

The door opened and I was relieved that it was Alina.

"Do you have any questions about the itinerary for this weekend?"

I placed my hands in my pockets so she couldn't see me tense or fidget. "No. It's been well-planned. Nice work."

She gave me a tight smile. "I have a weird feeling."

I'm surprised she told me. "I'm listening."

Alina hesitated at the door and then stepped in and closed it behind her. "I don't want Anora to do this."

It took everything I had not to react. "Why are you telling me?" I didn't ask it harshly, but genuinely. Alina took it as I meant it.

"Can't you tell dad this isn't necessary? He'll listen to you. If this is a business thing, then it needs to come from the business side of things, and that's you."

I sighed. "If I thought he'd listen, I would, but it's not an exaggeration that being connected to them is good for us. Really good. Don also isn't going to contradict Anora. If she says she wants to do this, she will."

"I know," Alina groaned and I almost smiled. "It's archaic. Why can't we marry you off instead?" Her hand snapped to her mouth. "I'm sorry, that was a dick thing to say."

"Yeah. And it's not out of the question in the future." It had already crossed my mind that instead of being alone, a strategic but empty marriage might be the way to go. It would keep women I didn't want from pursuing me and give some woman the assurance that she'd done what was expected of her. As dorky as it sounded, maybe I'd even gain a friend in the process. Someone who wouldn't hate me for never falling in love with them, and see me for the broken idiot I am.

"As long as it's not me. No offense." Alina waved her hand. I nodded, because, same. "I tried. Thanks, Owen." The door snapped smartly closed behind her as my phone buzzed with a message from Alonzo that he was ready to go.

When I left my room I stared at Anora's closed door, knowing that she was behind it and getting ready to meet her soon-to-be fiance. I wanted to know how she was feeling. I wanted to know if she was crying for me and I wanted to revel in her tears, but I wasn't capable of it. If I saw her cry, I'd be on my knees trying to fix it.

I hoped she cried for me every day for the rest of her life.

I hoped she took a second every day to recognize her misery and know that she'd never be happy without me. I hope she wallowed in guilt knowing that of all the things I'd been through in my life, she was the thing that had truly broken me.

If I met Derick Clayton today, my feelings for his future wife were still too strong, and I'd want to kill him. I'd destroy all possibility of a professional relationship by either being a total, monstrous asshole, or a murderer. Neither was acceptable to me. This was what Anora wanted, this was what she'd get.

I pulled out my phone as I walked straight out the front door and to the waiting car.

O: *I hope you can live with this, my love.*

Anora didn't reply.

The bartender at the Orchid looked skeptical when I said I was opening a tab, and I'd cover anyone who came into the bar for as long as I was there. Then I slid my card across the glossy wood and when he saw the black plastic, he nodded.

"Are we celebrating or..." he trailed off.

"Or," I answered. "What's your name?"

"Kyle."

"Welcome to the second worst day of my life so far. I'm going to start with bourbon. Rocks."

Kyle nodded and made my drink.

I was halfway through it when Rafe joined me. I introduced the two and Rafe ordered a vodka tonic because he was going to pace himself in order to make sure I didn't do anything so stupid I couldn't come back from it. Rafe could drink vodka like water so it would take a lot to impact him.

My watch taunted me as it ticked closer to the meeting. My phone rang incessantly because Alina realized I'd left. Alonzo was going to cover for me, and he wouldn't break, even for Alina. I felt a little bad for ruining the perfect orchestration she'd attempted, but I was only one piece out of the machine, the rest would be fine.

Rafe watched me drink, and we didn't talk much.

He tried to pull me in to reminiscing about college and some of the weird things him and his brothers did to train me, but all I could think about was how I threw myself into those things because I had missed her.

I was a miserable idiot. I'd believed that she was committed to making us work, and our future. I'd thought she was looking at forever instead of for now.

Despite my earlier thoughts, I didn't want her to be as miserable as me. Not really. Not ever. I wanted her to find some sort of happiness in her decision. If it comforted her to know that she was providing safety and stability to the family and Designation, then I couldn't hold it against her. Eventually, I would mean it when I said that. Right now, I was past my anger and into a combination of denial and depression.

"I used to think love was stupid," Rafe started, but I shook my head at him. "No, I mean, that love made us stupid. Not that loving was stupid. I was wrong, and you're not stupid for having hope or thinking that things were something they weren't. You weren't stupid for trusting her, and you're not for still loving her."

"And I'm sure someday I'll feel that way."

"Not to sound like a hippie, but love puts good shit out into the world. You love her, her family, Don, my family, and it means you'll work hard to keep those things safe. To do things that benefit them. We never know the ramifications of our actions, but I know you. After everything you've survived…you're the only person that "hurt people, hurt people" doesn't apply to because you've lived that. The only person I'm worried about you hurting is yourself."

"But that would hurt her." I finished my drink and signaled to Kyle for another.

Rafe shook his head. "There are an infinite amount of ways to hurt yourself."

I thought about how Anora is hurting herself now, by forcing down all of her own wants and needs that don't align with the wants and needs of her family.

I downed the drink Kyle placed in front of me in three large gulps, barely feeling the burn.

"Switch to whiskey," Rafe directed him. "Top shelf, so he has to sip it or die."

Kyle looked at me for confirmation and I knew I was going to double the kid's tip for that. I nodded in agreement because Rafe was right. If I was going to be drunk all day I needed to start spreading it out. The bar was still empty, and it would be for a while since it was the middle of the day.

I forced Rafe to let me kick his ass at pool, even though that also made me think of Anora.

We talked shit about his brothers until I sent them a barely readable text demanding their presence. If anyone would agree with me that love was a waste of time, it was those three single jackasses. They'd side with me. I was sure.

Alina called again and again, and I didn't answer. I promised myself I'd apologize in a few days when I was sober and sorry. She didn't deserve this from me, but I couldn't exactly tell her what was happening either.

The Montaigne brothers showed up, took one look at me, and rearranged any plans they had for the next day. They were going to be with me and that meant they were getting fucked up too.

Michel agreed to stay sober and Thierry, Lothaire, Rafe, and I did shots of something with cinnamon in it that made my tongue numb. I hustled them at pool while Rafe laughed, noting that even drowning in alcohol I could still kick their asses. I wished I'd had a chance to see Anora do it. We'd never had a chance to play pool with Rafe's brothers, although she'd always hustled Rafe.

I'd never let her hang out with them outside the occasional times in clubs. I'd kept her distant from them because I knew what they were and I knew what they did, and I didn't want that touching her. Maybe I'd been wrong. Maybe if I'd let her see the realities of the world, the blurred lines I lived in, maybe she'd feel less like this was the only way she was useful. Anora wanted to hide the criminal connections of Designation behind a sheen of perfection. The shine of her philanthropy. She wanted the world to be black and white.

I didn't tell her enough how powerful she was, how much the work she did helped her family. Helped me and Designation. I didn't remind her enough that what she did had value, even if the others didn't see it. Even if Don didn't tell her enough, and even if he didn't take the time to be part of it like he should have. It was me that didn't work hard enough. She was our shield, and we didn't need her to marry anyone to protect us. Anora was already doing that.

If I'd said it more, would I have been able to change anything?

Thierry made me do more shots, then I poured myself onto my barstool and Kyle handed me water. Good man.

"Have you ever been in love?" I asked him.

"Yeah," he nodded, but he frowned.

"Didn't work out?"

"She moved."

I nodded. "You still talk?"

"Yeah."

"Would you go after her, if you could?"

"Yeah. There's not a lot for me here, but I don't have the means to go to her."

I waved my hand at him. "I'll take care of that. Promise me though - that I'll get you where you need to go, and you're going to fucking chase her."

"Sure." He smiled but I know he thought I was full of shit.

"Give me your email. Right now."

"What?"

"Kyle. Do what I tell you."

Kyle rattled off his email and I had to close one eye to see what I was doing, but I navigated my banking app just fine. I had him check it before I did anything and he confirmed it was correct. Then I sent him $15,000 because that seemed like an amount that could get him anywhere, and put down roots to stay there.

I watched him take his phone out of his pocket and his face when he checked his notifications.

"Is this real?"

"Yeah. Someone should be with the person they love."

Kyle was too stunned to say much more, but went back to serving. I hoped he'd get on the next plane to wherever the person he loved was and never look back.

I was face down on the bar and Alina had stopped calling, so when I checked my phone I was relieved to see the worst time was past. They'd met. The thing happened. Without thinking, I called Anora.

"Where the fuck are you?" That didn't sound right, but I was pretty drunk. That sounded like someone who was ready to rip my head off. That could only be one person. They were right next to each other in my contacts, it's reasonable that I did not press the right name.

"Alina? I must be more fucked up than I thought, I meant to call Anora."

"You did call Anora, but I saw and took her phone. You're drunk?" Alina sounded even more pissed now. Too bad for her.

"Yes ma'am." I laughed because I could almost see her fuming on the other end of the phone. I had abandoned the plan, I was a fucking mess, and I was messing with her. It was a combination of all her least favorite things.

"Why are you drunk?"

"None of your business. Let me talk to Anora. Is she okay after meeting the hubby?"

"He's not her hubby, he's mine, butt wipe."

What.

WHAT.

Also I'd never heard Alina say "butt wipe" because she had no problem calling me a myriad of creative insults and swear words, so I focused on that longer than I should. Sometimes I couldn't tell if Alina actually disliked me or just enjoyed saying weird shit to me because it didn't bother me. My unflappability unsettled her.

Then I focused on what really mattered - he's not Anora's. As in Anora was not going to marry him, and the agreement had been broken. It was so absurd and I had so many questions that I didn't know where to begin. I didn't know what to ask first, and I didn't know if I would even be able to understand given how much I'd had to drink.

141

Was this a dream or a hallucination? Was there something in my drink?

I looked down at my glass but it was empty so if there had been anything in it, it was too late now.

Was I actually unconscious on the floor, drooling like an idiot, instead of sitting on this stool and having this conversation? Had I died? Was this a weird punishment that was between heaven and hell?

"Am I dead, Lina?" She'd be honest with me, so I had to ask. Alina would definitely tell me if I was dead.

"If you don't tell me where you are so I can get you home, I'll make sure you are."

If things had really shaken out this way, then I needed to get home. I needed to know what had happened, and I needed to know if I could claim my woman and make sure this shit never happened again. I had to understand.

If I had another chance, I was taking it. Despite my anger with Anora, I wanted her back. I'd take her back.

I told Alina where I was, slammed my phone on the bar, then climbed on top of it.

"She didn't get engaged!" I shouted to the entire bar. All 20 or so of us. It didn't matter though, I'd been paying for their drinks, so they all cheered riotously.

I was quickly surrounded by a sea of Montaignes, those redheaded fucks.

"Hey!" Michel protested. I must have said that out loud.

"Redheaded fucks I love," I amended and they cheered too.

"You should get out of here. They're coming to pick me up." I tried to get down from the bar and ended up flopped over onto Lothaire, who set me on my feet.

"What happened?" Rafe asked as his brothers gathered their things.

Rafe would wait with me until I was picked up, even though he was pretty drunk too. Alina knew Rafe Montaigne had been my roommate but we'd been pretty cagey about my overall relationship with the family, or the friendship I maintained with him.

"Alina said that he was hers. Anora didn't get engaged. I don't know anything else." I burped spectacularly in his face. "I didn't think I'd understand if I asked questions."

"No, probably not," Rafe patted my back. We walked to the door of the bar and watched for a car to come for me.

Some guy pulled up to the bar in a truck and gave us a disgusted look.

"Sweet Avalanche, bro."

He glared at us as Rafe and I busted into drunken laughter. I felt light and heavy at the same time, and I also kind of wanted to vomit.

When a car pulled up I was grateful to see Alonzo, and not Alina herself. It occurred to me that if Alina was now the one getting married, she was probably freaking out. She had never planned on getting married at all, and had already dropped hints about being my head of security when the time came. I would've given her the job, no question.

Rafe and I hobbled to the car, both unsteady on our feet, and he flopped me into the backseat, shut the door, and pounded the hood to let Alonzo know he could go.

"What happened?" I grumbled, and moved to smash my face more comfortably against the leather.

"Remember how we had trouble finding Alina's one night stand from Seattle?"

"Yeah." I was confused about that turn in the conversation but whatever.

"It was Derick Clayton."

Not what I expected. I giggled, and Alonzo laughed too. "He said he'd keep the deal, but he wanted to marry Alina instead."

"Oh shit," I sat up quickly and overbalanced, and ended up smashing my face into the window. "Was Anora okay?"

"She was going to agree to the marriage anyway," Alonzo said quietly, and silence collapsed over us. "I think she's relieved."

Alonzo checked on me in the mirror repeatedly the rest of the drive, worried that I was going to lose it. I wasn't. I was plotting, as much as my inebriated brain would allow.

"Are you going to get her back?"

"I don't know," I answered honestly.

"I hope you do."

I'd thought hope had died inside me the second I found out she'd agreed to this contract, but one infinitesimal spark remained, and I had zero ability to stop it from igniting back into a flame. My love for her could never burn out.

23

Anora

I spent the day reassuring Alina that I was fine, and checking to make sure that she was. My little sister never intended to get married, and now her wedding was happening tomorrow. She was shaken, I could tell. I couldn't figure out how to convince her that I was fine.

I was better than fine and I felt terrible for it. I had wanted to run from the house, run from the agreement, but I stayed because I'm a dutiful daughter and would do what was asked of me. It almost amused me that the Brody my sister had spoken of so minimally, so protectively, was the man that walked into our house.

I had seen the obsessive glint in his eye when he realized who she was, and the fear in hers when she realized the same. Alina was afraid because she didn't want to be hurt. She didn't want anyone to have power over her. Derick Clayton already did, and she wanted to deny it.

If he hadn't, she wouldn't have said yes.

Alina wanted him.

And it worked out that she had the excuse that it served our family's purposes. I understood that feeling and motivation well. I had lived it all my life.

The burden lifted from my shoulders was immense, and the desperate hope that ravaged my heart was dangerous. Perhaps it was time to fix my mistakes, and take responsibility for what I wanted.

I called Dr. Landry. It was after hours and it wasn't an emergency, not really, but I had to speak with her before tomorrow. I had to speak with her before this contract was officially concluded when my sister married Derick Clayton.

"Alina? Are you alright?" her soft, worried voice reassured me immediately. She'd started her career as a specialist in pediatric mental health. There were some of us who stayed with her as a client even as adults because consistency of treatment was more important. I was endlessly grateful to have her.

"I'm not getting engaged."

"You called it off?" She sounded surprised and relieved.

"No, he did. He uh, knew Alina, and wants to marry her."

Dr. Landry's silence was astonished, I could tell even over the phone. "How do you feel?"

"Relieved. Like I've been given a second chance."

"You sound like yourself again. How bad did things get?" I liked that she cut right to the chase.

"A new bad. I didn't feel anything. I collapsed."

"I don't like to hear that, and we'll work through that in our regular appointments, but I need to know why you called."

"I'm done with arrangements. The way I felt isn't worth it."

"I'm happy you feel that way. What about Owen?"

"I have a lot of work to do where he's concerned, but if he'll have me, I don't want to walk away anymore."

"And if he won't?"

"I think I'll need to leave for a while."

"Okay. What do you need from me?" Dr. Landry asked, and we spent the next several minutes talking about my feelings and fears.

Sometimes I needed her to tell me I wasn't being irrational, because I couldn't always tell the difference. Sometimes what felt rational to me was dangerous, and I needed a reality check.

"I need to accept that I'm an adult, not a child. I think I made the decision from a child's perspective on what the adult in my life wanted. Or what I thought he wanted."

"That's possible. Are you going to talk to your father?"

"Eventually. I think I need to get my family through this first." Dr. Landry laughed at my response, and we ended the call.

There were other ways I could step up for my family. I opened a fresh spreadsheet on my computer and started making a list of everything I needed to do tomorrow for a wedding to happen in our backyard. I texted some of my favorite and most trusted vendors or their staff members that I knew that could get work done for me.

Dad would handle the judge, one that he'd supported in the past to look past some of Designation's ties to arrested criminals and keep law enforcement out of their business. It didn't make me feel good, but whatever got the job done.

I checked off the last thing on the list as the chef and I confirmed that last details of dinner, and she showed me the lovely cake she'd made Alina. It was her favorite.

The reality that Alina would be leaving hit me this morning. I had planned for my own travel to Seattle but I thought I'd have months to adjust and to say goodbye. Instead, my closest sister was going to be gone in a matter of days. I would make today as perfect for her as a I could, as low key as possible, and then I'd be by her side. Do anything she needed.

Owen wasn't at dinner last night, and I heard one of the security staff say that he was sobering up. Instead of being with us, Owen had gotten drunk. That felt like my fault.

"Anora."

I felt his voice inside my skin and down my spine. It haunted me. Sometimes I heard it in my dreams and I'd wake up in tears. Wake up with regret eating me alive.

I turned to face him and bumped into his chest. He was closer than I expected. I looked up into his icy blue eyes, and found them to be unreadable. Owen had never been so closed off to me, but I deserved it. I deserved it if he never spoke to me again.

"Are you alright?"

I was caught off guard by the question. "Yes?"

"This was what you wanted."

"No," I shook my head at him, and maintained his gaze. "It's what I thought I needed to do, and I don't think that anymore." My shoulders dropped, and I let him in. "I was so relieved, Owen. I know now..." I shook my head. "I know better."

Owen stared at me as if he could will his way into my thoughts and see everything. Everything that I wasn't saying to him. I would say it all, he only had to ask me.

"What do you know?" There was a threat in his voice. "Do you think I'll come crawling back to you, now that you're free again? That I'll wait for the next time you hurt me?" Owen towered over me and it aroused me. The danger in the way he moved and spoke. The power he had over me was intoxicating. I would give him anything he wanted.

"No. *I'm* going to crawl to *you*. I'm going to beg you." My voice was barely a whisper, but I couldn't keep the lust out of it.

Owen's nostrils flared and his eyes dilated, the imagery seeping through his brain. "We'll see, Button." He leaned in, almost as if he was going to kiss me, and then pulled away and left before I could say another word. I shivered and pulled myself together.

After checking that Alina was dressed, I joined everyone else in the gazebo in the backyard.

Owen stood next to me, and even though I tried to pay attention, all I could feel was his nearness. I was wearing a purple dress with an open back. It was a warm day and I wanted to be comfortable.

When Owen palmed my back, the tips of his fingers dipped beneath the edge of my dress, and it took all of my control not to react. I leaned into him as we moved to our place and waited. He didn't drop his hand. It slid further beneath the material and wrapped around my waist.

His fingertips dug into my vulnerable skin, hard enough to leave marks. Hard enough to turn me on, and he knew it. When Alina walked out of the house, grumpy and barefoot, he let it drop back to his side. I could feel the burn of where he touched and marked me.

I watched my sister as she said her vows. I watched a man that was now my brother preen like a predator who captured his prey. There was no denying that he wanted her, badly, and I hoped that would turn into love. I was afraid that Alina had already started to fall, and a determined man would be lucky to have her. I hoped Derick was that man.

When the ceremony was over, everyone walked to the house for the dinner I had arranged.

I stayed in the gazebo and handled the last details. I said goodbye to the judge and paid her. I instructed the few staff about cleaning up and what I needed them to do.

Owen was still there when I turned around. I was used to his intensity, but he was putting me on edge. An edge I liked, but I wasn't sure what would happen when we went over it. I'd always been so careful, loving him with a backup plan, and now I had to be vulnerable to the possibility that he would hurt me. Scar me irrevocably.

I wanted that.

I wanted to be marked by him, forever, even if it was a reminder of what I'd lost instead of what I had.

"When dinner is over, come to my room."

He waited until I nodded, then walked away, leaving me standing alone.

My stomach was a riot when I knocked on Owen's door an hour after dinner ended. We'd all been shocked when Derick dragged Alina away but it had also been quite amusing. Everyone had finished their dinner and then we'd gone off to do our own things, as if this was any other night.

Aro had seemed upset but she retreated to the library like usual.

I didn't even bother to change out of my dress.

"Come in."

I opened the door and closed it behind me, then turned the lock. I took a deep breath and faced him.

Owen was sitting in a chair by the window, still in his suit but distinctly ruffled now. His tie was gone, his shirt unbuttoned, and he'd been running his hands through his hair.

"On your knees." He commanded and I obeyed before I could think about it. I lifted my dress out of my way and dropped to the carpeted floor.

"Beg."

My eyes welled with tears. I couldn't stop them. It wasn't because I wanted him to feel sorry for me, it was because I owed him my tears. I owed letting him see the pain I was in over him. I'd never let him see when I cried because of us. The tears I cried because of loving him and the lie I was telling that meant I would lose him. The lie was done now. He would know. He would know what these tears were for.

I didn't mind that his expression remained unmoved because I could see his body stiffen.

"Please forgive me. Forgive me for letting you down, for leaving you, for lying and being selfish. I love you. I love you so much that without

150

you I was dead. There was nothing," I sobbed, my hands clasped to my chest. "Everything I am was gone without you. I will spend the rest of our lives showing you, but please. Please."

I got onto my hands and knees and crawled to him, and pressed my head to his knee like an animal trying to apologize to its master. I rested my cheek on his thigh and looked up at him.

"So pretty on your knees, Button," his voice still held that low threat from earlier. He stroked my hair. "How can I trust you?"

"I don't know, my love," I whispered. "I already told dad that I won't enter into anymore contracts. That I didn't want it."

Owen stiffened under me, and his fingers dug into my tresses, gripped hard enough to hurt.

"Why would you do that?"

"It's you or no one. Only you."

Owen moved and threw me to the ground. At first I thought he was throwing me away, but then he gripped my dress and tugged, ripping it from the hem of the skirt to just above the hem of my panties. He tugged those down, baring me to him, and I watched eagerly as he undid the belt and fly of his pants, freeing his large, hard cock.

I pulled him down to me as he lined himself up with my aching pussy, and shoved inside me. I cried out, bowing to bury my face in his jacket and fight against the power of the intrusion to find my breath.

"You or no one," he repeated my words as he started slamming inside me. "There's no leaving now. No escape," he groaned as he hit deeper and I flexed around him. "Even in death, it's us."

"It's us," I moaned in response, grinding my hips into him and chasing my orgasm. I wanted him so badly. Owen slammed our mouths together and savaged my lips and tongue. We panted against each other's mouths, as if we were trying to break our bodies. I wanted us to be one. I wanted him so badly that nothing he did would be enough.

"Hurt me."

"What?" Owen growled.

"Mark me. Do it," I encouraged, turning my head and baring my neck to him.

Owen rumbled against me and then he did what I asked. He bit into the top of my shoulder before it curved up to my neck. The pain was perfection and I cried out in pleasure. Owen clenched his teeth harder and I felt him break the skin.

I orgasmed around his hard, battering cock. Owen loomed over me, red on his lips, and kissed me as he pressed deep and came inside me.

We stayed together, hands gripped so tight to him that my joints hurt, the places he held already bruising beneath his desperate touch.

"That's going to scar," he grumbled, out of breath.

"I know." I bumped his nose with mine.

"Mine," he pressed against me and into me.

"Yours," I agreed.

Eventually, Owen got up and pulled me into his bathroom and the shower. That was when we made up in a softer way, and took care of each other. After, he put antibacterial gel on the bite mark and covered it with a band-aid. I was curious what it would look like when it healed, and I loved knowing that it would hurt while it did.

I wanted to hurt for him.

Owen pulled me into his bed, and I felt like I was back where I was supposed to be. We both stayed quiet, watching it get dark out the window. There was a lot to talk about, and I didn't know where to start.

"When are we telling Don?"

"When you trust me again," I answered after a moment. "He'll see through us otherwise, and he'll doubt. The only person I want to fight to be with you, is you."

Owen was quiet and it made me nervous. I twisted my head to look up at him and found him looking back.

"Okay," he agreed. "Let's fight, Button."

24

Owen

I spent the next few days showing Derick and Jack Clayton around Designation, coordinating relationships between our teams, and serving as a witness for a fuck ton of paperwork. The timeline on our companies working together was vastly sped up. Even though it would take months to decide how we wanted this to work, there were some things we could start now for our mutual protection.

Anora was with Alina, and I didn't pursue her until the air was cleared and Alina was gone.

I'd said goodbye to Alina the night before, and wished her luck. Anora was under the impression that this would work out for her sister, and that Alina had feelings for Derick. I liked him, now that I could give him a fair shot, and I hoped that was true. I would miss her, even when she annoyed me with her need to control every situation. I would miss someone who didn't feel the need to make small talk, and was efficient in communicating what needed to happen.

I'd miss her because Anora would miss her, and made her feel safer.

Don pulled me into the library after dinner, and I gave Anora a look that said I'd find her when I was done.

"What do you think?" He settled in, smiling and content.

"I like Derick. We could do worse than working with Venture. The girls like him, too."

"I noticed. How is Anora?"

I hesitated to answer because we'd always been protective of how close we were. "She seems to be okay. I want to take her at her word as an adult that she's fine." My voice came out harsh, but Don only smiled bigger.

"She told me she didn't want to find another arrangement. I think she thought I'd be angry, but I was relieved." Don chuckled to himself and leaned forward to rest his arms on the desk. Something loosened in my chest to hear him say it. It wasn't that I didn't believe Anora when she told me, but our trust was broken enough that hearing it confirmed by Don made it feel final. It was real now. Anora was truly moving forward with me. She'd taken a concrete step to remove one of the barriers that had kept us apart.

"I'd never be able to choose someone worthy of her," Don continued. "She's so protective of her own emotions, so protective of her heart, that I'd never be able to find the right person."

I wondered what he'd think then if he knew it was me. Would he see me as worthy? Or would the taint of Roman and Elaine make him doubt me? If I were in his position I'd fear that they would infect my relationship. The doubting fear would always be in the back of my mind that I could turn into them and hurt Anora, or hurt this family. I wanted to believe that I was never capable of that, but I also knew that once upon a time my father and Don had been best friends.

That couldn't have happened if Roman was the person he was when he died when they met. Don wouldn't become friends with a monster, and Roman hadn't been very good at hiding it. Don never said that he blamed Elaine, but I think he holds Elaine responsible. Even though Roman made his own choices, she twisted something inside him. Made something more powerful than his self-control come out. The worst impulses inside him were strengthened by her viciousness. Roman had been good at one time, I believed that, but Elaine had always been a snake. That could live inside me too.

I could only hope that the darkness inside me would only ever be used in defense. Of Anora. Of the Sorrelles. Of Designation.

"Do you think she will?"

"I think Anora holds back when she shouldn't. Time will tell." Don gave me a look I couldn't quite interpret, and it was on the tip of my tongue to ask him if he knew about us. Then I realized it wouldn't matter if he did know because he's waiting for Anora to tell him. I can't be the one that does it. When she's ready, he will be too. Even though I wanted to ask and I wanted his approval, at the end of the day I wasn't his son. It needed to come from her.

"Things are going to be okay," I reassured him. "We'll get through what's ahead. We always do."

Don agreed, and we talked shop for a little longer until I couldn't wait anymore. I needed to get my hands on my woman. I excused myself and went to find her.

Anora was in her room and I entered without knocking. I rarely ever went in her room before. It was the place I'd let her go to hide from me. To hide from us. This was her space and I never violated it. Things were going to be different now. Everything was ours. Every space, every inch, every breath she took was shared between us now.

Something in the intensity of my gaze scared her, but in the way that she liked. Anora adjusted her shoulders and I knew that she was feeling the echo of my bite. My cock was immediately hard.

"Crawl to me," I demanded of her. Anora slid from the bed and did as I said, moving on her hands and knees until she knelt before me. "Suck my cock."

Anora went to work undoing my belt and fly and removing me from my pants. She opened her mouth and I slapped the head against her tongue. She wrapped her soft lips around me and started to move, going deeper with each stroke. I let her get comfortable before I grabbed her hair and thrust deep. Anora gagged around me, then pushed herself harder, giving me permission to fuck her face.

She liked it rough, but not all the time. This wasn't going to be a gentle make up or a gentle rebuild. This was going to be the destruction of everything we had been, and building it back up from the foundations. Burn away the mistrust, the betrayal, the reasons that we had kept things a secret. I was going to remind Anora that I've owned her all her life just as she always owned me.

Anora's mouth was so hot and she sucked me so tight. I loved hearing her groan after she gagged on me. Her spit was dripping down my balls and soaking my pants. I looked down and watched the ecstasy on her face as I ruined her. Mascara and tears ran down her pink, blushing cheeks. She was wearing dress pants and a demure white blouse and the contrast of her actions with her modest clothes made me so fucking hot.

I pulled her off my cock and tilted her head up as I jerked myself to the finish line.

"Mouth open, Button." I felt my orgasm build, and then burst through me, sending waves of pleasure through my body. I watched my come paint her face and shirt. It wasn't enough. I was still painfully hard. I let go of her and stepped around her. She turned, not moving to wipe me from her face or clothes. I liked her submission in this moment.

"Clothes off. Then bend over the bed."

Anora moved to do what I said, arousal burned in her gaze. When she removed her bra, her nipples were hard and tight. She stripped and walked toward me. Before she could bend over I grabbed her to me and forced her back to arch so I could take one of her tight buds between my teeth. Anora moaned and pressed me to her, grinding shamelessly against my body for relief. I sucked each nipple back and forth until she was whimpering and on the edge.

I moved her body and bent her over the bed. I knelt behind her and spread open her ass cheeks to see her pretty, wet pussy. It was pink and glistening, and as much as I wanted to taste her, that wasn't what she needed or deserved right now. I stood up and ran my cock through her wetness, teasing her until she was whimpering again.

I lined up and pressed inside her. It was so tight it took my breath away. Every single time felt like the best time. Every time I entered her it was heaven, and my cock was where it should be at all times. All I ever wanted to do was fuck her and pleasure her, take everything from her that I could.

"Owen," she cried out, and pressed her face into her boring beige comforter. I looked around the room as I fucked her, as the real Anora was unleashed. The feral animal that lived in her heart that was as fierce as me. That loved and fought, that wanted and craved, that had color and fury. The one that would've killed Roman and Elaine for me. Not the tied up, tied down person she thought she was supposed to be.

Anora wasn't beige, she was shades of violet, indigo, and purple, a riot of deep dark color. Color that concealed and hid. Anora was the color of shadows, a shape that could appear as one thing but in reality it was something else entirely. I never understood why she hid herself so thoroughly, but I wouldn't let her hide who she was from me.

I dug my nails into her hips as I slammed into her, giving her the bite of pain she wanted. "Anora," I groaned, "let go. Show me what a desperate slut you are, that you'll do anything for me."

"I will," she moaned as she pushed her hips into me, fucking me back.

"I have to punish you for what you did."

"Yes," she nodded vehemently. When she looked over her shoulder at me, fresh tears trailed down her cheeks.

"You almost married someone else." I slapped her ass as I continued to destroy her. "You denied me. You denied us." I slapped her again in quick succession.

"I'm sorry."

I pushed Anora down so her chest was on the mattress, her face half buried in the blanket as I leaned over her prone body. I pressed myself against her and whispered in her ear.

"You have to earn back my gentleness, Button. I want you to feel how I've fucked you with every step you take. Every time you sit down. Every time you move I want you to remember me inside you, and remember that you're mine."

"Yours." She nodded.

"Good girl." I slid a hand under her body and palmed her pussy before my finger started toying with her clit. I moved away from her and watched as my cock disappeared inside her, watched it get shiny with her arousal.

"You take me so well, Anora. You were made for me. Never question it again."

"Never. Please, please, I promise, never," she started to mumble into the blankets as her orgasm approached. Her pussy worked me, sucking me in deeper, and when I pressed hard on her, she turned and buried her face in the blanket as she screamed.

I fucked her through it before grabbing her ass in a punishing grip as I came again, filling her pussy with my come. It lasted forever, the muscles in my legs and ass flexing and twitching, the pleasure of owning her so powerful that I almost fell over.

I pulled out of her but kept a hand on her back as I knelt to look at her well-pounded cunt.

"Push it out. I want to see you dripping."

I watched her flex and push, and groaned in satisfaction as pearly beads of come started to drip out of her pussy and down her thighs.

"Someday, I'm going to push that come back inside you. Hold your hips up and make you keep it."

"Yes," she moaned in response.

I bit her ass cheek and she giggled before I stood up and moved us so we were laying on her bed. I held her to me as I looked around her room.

The only color was the large painting on her wall. Aro had gone through a phase. My own canvas hung on a wall in my room. I hadn't hung it up myself; I'd walked in one day and there it was. Aro gave me gifts and when she did it outside of a holiday, she did it in secret or behind my back. The painting was one of those times. There was a small note attached that said the painting represented me, to her.

It was shades of red. At first I thought it meant she saw me as angry or bloody, and it made sense given how I came into her home, but the more I sat and stared at it, the less I felt that way. There were bursts of yellow and orange, too. It looked like a fierce sunset, and for some reason I liked that. I liked being that last fiery burst of color before the sky turned dark.

Anora's painting was interesting, and I wondered what she saw when she looked at it. It was shades of white, tan, and pink, that gradually darkened to a deep purple-blue. As if moving from bland to color. It reminded me of the way I thought of her. It was especially interesting because the more bland colors had chaotic strokes, thick globs of paint, they looked messy and textured. As it moved to the darker parts it was smooth and even. Still waters running deep. Aro saw her, too. She saw the mask Anora wore was the trouble, and the part she hid was the part that was calm.

I knew Anora's struggles. She'd told me, she'd called me when she needed help, and I'd always give it to her. The darkness she had inside her wanted to pull her away from the world, and I hoped that wouldn't always be the case. That darkness and doubt didn't make her weak, it made her whole. It made earning her so much more powerful because she had to overcome it to let you in.

"I love you." I'd said it a thousand times, but looking at that painting, and thinking about the person that I knew and held in my arms, I'd never meant it more.

"I love you, too."

We didn't know then the way our love would be tested, but I never doubted that we could make it through anything.

25

Anora

In one aspect of my life, things were better than ever. Owen and I were together and working on trusting each other. We'd opened up to one another again, and while I wasn't screaming from the rooftops we were together, I wasn't trying hard to hide it anymore either. We slept in each other's beds. We would sneak off to make out, or leave dinner early together to rip each other's clothes off before doing whatever else needed to be done.

This time, Owen was the one that asked to wait to tell my dad.

It hurt at first, but I accepted that it had nothing to do with us, and everything to do with what was happening around us.

He finally confessed to me that someone had been sending threats and wanted to kill Aster. As much as I'd felt a similar need to strangle my youngest sibling, I wouldn't let anything happen to her. It also coincided with an attack on Designation. Everything was in chaos and dad was stressed. I'd started adding afternoon tea delivery to his meal schedule to try and keep him calm.

They tried to keep me out of it but that's hard to do when you run the house. It's hard to do when I'm the social face of the family and rich people prefer to trade gossip and secrets. Things made their way back to me, and I was worried, too.

The summer was one of the hardest of my life. Alina was hurt, Aster was threatened, and I was an island all alone while everyone else tried to fix it. They were fighting battles I couldn't help, so I worked hard to make home feel safe and comfortable. I made sure our security staff had everything that they needed, that they felt valued, and like members of our extended family.

I made sure they knew they mattered and that we'd honor them when we lost Gio. I was the only one at his graveside when we buried him because I was the only one who didn't have a death threat hanging over my head. I put flowers on his casket and thanked him for saving my sister, and for being a member of our family.

Dr. Landry and I had some complicated conversations. I couldn't tell her what had happened or what was happening. She had obligations to report crimes, especially ones where someone might be harmed. It was easier to talk about feelings of stress and inadequacy.

I threw Aster a birthday party that blew up in my face when it ended up she'd been sleeping with her bodyguard who was also her co-worker Isaac, and that she also went around murdering people who hurt people. I was proud of her for the second part, a little confused about the first. Then again, Aster was even more private than me about her romantic life, so if she wanted to have sex in parking garages with masked men, so be it. I wouldn't worry about her. She was deadly, and I'd never mess with her.

Aro found the whole thing hilarious, and I was glad to see her out of the library. Since graduating college she'd been lost. I tried to get her involved with my work but she wasn't interested. It hurt a little, but I had to keep telling myself that we all found our own way eventually, and that each of us had our own thing.

She read so much she'd come across something in some book eventually that she wanted to pursue with her life.

Life was tense and scary, but I had my family. We were working hard to protect and comfort each other, even when some of us were across the country. I had to believe that it was going to be okay.

I'd been working on a run to raise funds for cystic fibrosis research for what felt like forever. It was a group and a marathon I'd built from the ground up, and I was thrilled when Owen agreed to run the half-marathon with me. He could run, but he didn't like it. Finally, Alonzo had talked enough crap about how he could run it without training that they both agreed to do it with me.

Alonzo needed to be with us for security reasons anyway, and the staff sometimes assigned to me would be around as well.

Things seemed to be looking up. Owen told me the hit on Aster had been dropped and it had given us some freedom after being trapped in our house for weeks for security reasons. Aro hadn't even noticed. This race was the first time I'd really been out in a while, and I was enjoying the cool air of summer turning into true fall.

Dad was still being paranoid, and I worried about how this was going to affect his health. I'd made him a doctor appointment and made Gailen promise to make him go. The thing I liked most about Gailen being in charge of security was that he tried hard to do what was best instead of what he was told. Alina always bent to dad's authority when she should've stood up to him. Gailen charged ahead a lot of the time, and it made me feel safe.

"Think you can keep up?" I taunted Owen as we took our places at the start.

"I'll keep pace with you," he sassed back, "wouldn't want you to fall behind."

I leaned close and brushed my nose against his, unafraid of who would see us here. They could think what they wanted. The rumor mill could go crazy about the eldest Sorrelle and the Carver heir, or our Disgraced Ward as I was sometimes heard him called in impolite company. It didn't matter what they called him, he was mine.

Owen pressed a quick kiss to my lips and then the race was called. We started running. I loved this. I loved feeling the power of my body and feeling confident in myself. I loved running side by side with him. We didn't say anything, and I loved the sound of our feet falling into a matching rhythm. This was why I loved runs, and I loved this one especially. It was well-organized and I handed it off to the charity on the day of the race so I could enjoy this piece of it.

I'd help them later, and if they didn't need me, I'd see them when we debriefed on how it went.

Alonzo trailed behind us by a few paces, and I could tell he was almost bored. I noted that his eyes were on a constant scan, still in guard mode, still protecting us even as his body worked.

It took me a few minutes to realize that Alonzo had stopped on the course. The participants had spread out so it was easy to grab Owen and turn around to head back to where he stood. My stomach dropped to the ground when I saw his face. He was pale and horrified, sweat broke out on his skin that hadn't been there from running, and it took him too long to meet my eyes.

He handed his phone to Owen.

I watched the man I loved and trusted, the man I knew better than anyone in this world, react to that phone conversation. I watched as something came over him that I couldn't explain or articulate, and I saw something in his eyes when he looked at me that I might never recover from. It was pain and a horror so deep that I knew it was about to pull me under. He hung up the phone.

"We have to go."

"What happened? Tell me what happened."

Owen didn't say anything. He physically picked me up, stepped off the trail, and started moving back toward the park. Alonzo was making another call, and when we made it to the street our town car was waiting. He practically threw me inside before he and Alonzo got in too.

He took my hands in his and I felt like I couldn't breathe.

"We're going to the hospital."

"Okay…" That could mean anything, but panic was starting to crawl up my throat.

"Aro and Aster have been hurt." Owen's voice was so measured and still, I knew there was a storm inside him. I knew he was putting off telling me something.

"There was an attack at the house and…" Owen's eyes closed.

"And what?"

"Your dad is gone."

I took a breath in, and then couldn't let it out. The car swirled around me as I processed what he said and I knew that I was passing out but I couldn't stop it.

Nothing I did could protect my family. Nothing could keep us safe.

It didn't matter who I married, what I did to strengthen our home, how much I cared, there was no way to keep anyone safe. My presence, my work, it made no difference.

I was alone in the world in a new way now.

Mom had died a dragging, agonizing death that I never entirely recovered from, and now someone had killed my father. I prayed it had been quick. I prayed he didn't feel a thing. Agony ripped through me and that breath finally escaped, carrying a sob with it.

My vision narrowed to a pin, and then faded into nothing.

So did I.

26

Anora

I lost two days. Two days that I remembered nothing and had to be cared for in the hospital. When I emerged, things were better and worse.

Aster and Aro were going to be okay. Owen sat with me and told me everything that had happened and that had been done. I was discharged shortly after, and thanked Isaac for saving my sisters. They would both be in the hospital for a few days longer.

"You're one of us now," I warned him as the three of us ate dinner at the house. We'd been home for a few hours and I'd already hired someone to come clean the library. It was loud, but it was like they were chasing out a ghost. I couldn't bring myself to even stand at the door. Like I'd needed another reason to hate that room.

Another breakdown was imminent, but I could hold it back behind the need to take care of this. Owen and Derick were working on the cover up, which pained me beyond words, but I knew was the best way to protect them all. If we wanted to be the ones to handle this and find out who hurt us, we had to keep it a secret. We had to tell one story while hunting down the truth ourselves. I hated it.

"I'd warn you that if you hurt Aster we'll kill you but..." Owen trailed off and smirked slightly. I could tell he liked Isaac. They'd worked well together these last months while he watched Aster, and I knew he was also a good programmer. He fit our family in a way I didn't expect, but I was glad to have him.

"I'll warn you that if you hurt her, there won't be anything left when she's done with you." I pointed at him with my butter knife. Isaac laughed. "How is she?"

"Honestly, pretty freaked out. The physical stuff, she's healing fine, but I think the reality that she was facing an opponent she couldn't beat hit her hard. I'll be here, but don't press her." Isaac glanced at me and then away, as if he was afraid I'd be the problem. I never pressed Aster for anything. Most days I did what she wanted and left her alone. For reasons I didn't understand, I frustrated her. I was her least favorite sister unless we were running together.

"Should I get a therapist?" I offered.

"Not yet. I was going to talk to her about it." Isaac sighed and gave up on his dinner. "She's mostly worried about Aro."

"She still hasn't spoken," I whispered.

Owen and I shared a look. Losing dad, and the way it happened, had shattered our family in ways we'd be dealing with for the rest of our lives. Pieces of us might never be recovered, and I think we'd be blaming ourselves in circles until the situation was finally put to rest. Until we knew who was coming after us, and the assassin they hired was dead in our basement.

"We'll make them all pay," Isaac vowed.

"We will."

After dinner, I climbed into Owen's bed and cried like I did every night. In his arms, I emptied myself of all the fear and blame so that I could make it through the next day. I had a feeling it was going to get worse before it got better.

27

Anora

The thing people don't talk about when you're wealthy and well-known is that when the patriarch of a family like that dies, planning the funeral requires an event planner.

I hired someone that I trusted to be sensitive and private, and not play up the spectacle. It helped that she was from a mob family and was working hard to be legitimate. There were details and decisions I didn't need to think about. I could focus on myself and my family and that was what I needed.

Aro wasn't okay. It was like watching a natural disaster happen in slow motion, and there was no power to stop it. Even Aster couldn't get through to her. She shut down and shut everyone out. Occasionally, she would talk to Owen, but even he couldn't get her to talk to a therapist.

Alina and Derick were their own little bubble and as much as I wanted to be with her, I also loved seeing her lean on someone else. I loved seeing my sister find the only man in the world she was willing to be weak around.

Almost two weeks after he was murdered, we celebrated my dad's life and laid him to rest beside my mother. Aster had to attend in a wheelchair because her injuries were still too fragile for that much movement, and it helped play into the narrative that there had been a tragic car accident.

Owen stood by my side every second. I spoke to Dr. Landry every day, and for the first time in a long time it felt easy to back away from the edge. I didn't collapse. I pulled myself together, and I got over the idea that any of this was my fault. That I could have done anything to change what happened. That any of us could have. I was hurting and missing him, but I wasn't descending into darkness again.

It wasn't satisfying to be mad at the universe, but it was a lot more productive. It was easy to take action and move forward out of anger.

We would find this bastard. I would keep everything running, everyone fed, rested, and resourced, and they would get our vengeance. I vowed that to myself and to them.

After the burial, we had a reception at a hotel downtown. There were too many people and I didn't want them anywhere near the house. Aro went home, and Gailen agreed to go with her. I wished I could blame him, but I couldn't. He blamed himself enough for all of us.

Owen was making his rounds of the crowd, when a hot hand landed on my shoulder.

I turned and saw thick fingers that led up to the arm of a suit jacket that didn't fit quite right, and then to Elton Forrester's bland face. His mouth was turned down but it didn't feel like the expression was real.

"Elton, hello," I said as I stood up. I gave him a brief hug and his hand landed far too low on my back for comfort or familiarity. I knew Elton but had only seen him a handful of times since high school, and we hadn't been that close. I thought that was possibly the first time I'd ever hugged him.

I pulled back and he gestured for me to sit back down before he took the chair opposite me.

"How are you?" he asked, and reached out to take my hand. He rubbed it in a way that irritated my skin. After a moment I pulled it back to fidget and comfort myself, as well as an excuse to end the contact.

"Still in shock," I gave my rote response.

"Your father was a very interesting and decisive man."

"Yes," I agreed, confused by his direction.

"He was so protective of you and your sisters," Elton sighed. "It's tragic they were hurt in the same accident."

I held my face in a neutral position. That was an oddly rude thing to say, so I said nothing in response. Elton had always been like this, always pushed boundaries while wearing a mask of kindness. He'd always been nice to me, so there was never anything specific to call out. He was harmless and awkward, so I was always kind in return. Probably kinder than he deserved.

"Sorry," he continued after another beat of silence. "I know how hard it is to lose a parent, and you've lost both." Elton took my hand again. "We're their legacy, don't ever forget that, and I think they'd be proud."

It was a genuinely kind thing to say, and it had tears springing to my eyes. "Thank you." I sniffled and he moved to pull me toward him, but a throat clearing interrupted us. I looked up at Alina and Derick. She gave me a head nod and I used it as an excuse to step away.

"Thank you so much for coming, Elton, it was nice to see you." There was a flash of fury on his face and then he nodded, putting back on that patronizing smile he had to have practiced in a mirror. He tried, and I appreciated it.

Alina linked her arm through mine and I leaned on her, perpetually amused that she was so much taller than me. We walked around the edge of the room and didn't say anything, just watched people use this as another excuse to be seen. There would be a separate celebration at Designation, and that was the one that mattered. Dad's employees had adored him, and they deserved to remember him and be appreciated for how happy they made him.

"How much longer do we have to be here?" Alina grumbled.

"You can leave any time. I'll stay."

"No," she sighed. "I can't let you carry this alone. I'm better at this social thing now."

"Your last big social thing ended with a bullet in your shoulder."

Alina shrugged. "I'll take a bullet over a knife, speaking from experience."

I laughed, and something further inside me relaxed. I was going to be okay. I wasn't going to fall apart. We still had each other. We were still the Sorrelles, and we were going to survive. Life without dad would always hurt, and the moments in the future that he should be there for would be devastating, but I would make a life that would make him proud.

I would stop holding back. It killed me already that I never got the chance to tell him about Owen and me. I think he would've been okay with it, and I wish we had his blessing. I would live without it, but I hate that he left this world not knowing how truly happy I was after a lifetime of worrying about my depression.

"Our lives are so weird. I can tell you ten different shades of purple and you can tell me the difference between wounds."

"Aro is still the weirdest. There's way more bizarre things that she knows than any of us."

"All those books," I nodded in agreement.

I looked around the room. We'd already been here for hours. Spoken to most people. I was exhausted, and despite what decorum demanded and our social standing expected, I was done.

"You know what? Screw this. Let's get the fuck out of here. These people don't deserve any more of our time or energy. We deserve a chance to mourn dad together."

Alina looked stunned, but nodded. "I'll round up the crew."

I stepped away from her to find Owen, and wove my hand in his. He looked down at it and a hint of pink came across his cheeks. One day when we were finally, truly public, I was going to enjoy making Owen blush from public displays of affection. He was so untouchable that it caught him off guard when I crawled beneath his walls and touched him.

"We're leaving. I'm done."

"Are you sure?" he looked at me hard, afraid that more was going on.

"I want to be with my family."

"I can stay, handle things."

I shook my head hard. "You're family. You lost him too, Owen. Don't think I haven't seen you hiding your grief. Don't do that, not even with me. Come be with your family."

Owen blinked hard and I pulled him out of the room and around a corner, out of sight. I pulled his forehead down to mine and watched as two fat tears dropped down his cheeks. I brushed them away and held him close.

"I love you. He loved you."

"I know," Owen's voice wobbled.

"You're my family, Owen. You know that, right? You know that my sisters love you, and that you belong with us. If you try to say otherwise, Aster will cut you."

He laughed then. "I'll work on believing that."

I shook him until he opened his eyes and looked at me. "You deserve us, even when you tell yourself otherwise."

"Sometimes I hate it that you know me so well," he drawled. We laughed, and then he stole a quick kiss. "Let's go home."

28

Owen

Life moved on, but our minds were trapped in the past. Who had done this? Why were they doing it? Once Don was gone, the direct attacks on Designation stopped. It felt like the calm at the eye of the storm. We were waiting for the next wave, the next clue that would lead us to the enemy, and trying to lick our wounds while we did it.

Aster was fighting and running because that's what she did. Isaac moved into the house with us and it was like he'd always been there. Outside of the Montaignes, I counted him as a friend. Someone I trusted to keep not only Aster, but the family safe.

I believed it because he would get up at all hours of the night and drive into the city to rescue Aro.

The one and only time I offered to help and pick up Aro was the first time I thought Aster might hurt me. The expression on her face had been a war of fury and pain. I knew she had a knife in one hand out of habit and was fighting not to use it. I was the target for her anger in that moment. I'd have taken a cut if that's what she needed.

"I have to do it," she hissed at me.

"You don't. I would. Anora would."

Aster scoffed. "Anora wouldn't know what to do with her." I couldn't exactly tell Aster that Anora had taken care of many a drunk person, and would be even more tender and careful with Aro. I don't think it would've made a difference anyway. This was Aro's penance and we couldn't get in the way of that.

"Whatever you think is best," I finally answered and left it alone.

There was only one way for me to move forward and take a step that felt like it was making anything better.

Sophie took Anora out for the day, and the Montaigne family had them under protection so I knew that Anora was safe. She was going to drop Anora off at Designation when they were done, and then I'd be ready.

When she walked into the atrium, the sun was going down and cast her body in shadow. I couldn't see her expression until she was closer, and when her eyes met mine she smiled. It hit me hard that it was a smile I only saw when she looked at me, and I knew that all her smiles came more freely when she was with me. I was so proud of her for doing the work to stay well through all of this. Don would be proud.

"I have a surprise for you." The building was empty and I took her hand and walked her toward the far end of the building. I pressed the button for the elevator and we stepped inside. When I pushed the button for the basement, Anora smiled.

"I can still kick your butt."

"We'll see."

She swung our clasped hands between us and laughed. "Rafe keeps me in practice. I've never met such a sore loser."

"I think it's because he's the youngest. He can't let anyone get one up on him after being on the bottom for so long."

"I'll keep teaching him a lesson then." Anora made the turn into the game room and stopped when she saw everything inside.

The pool table and games were still there, but now it was filled with twinkling lights, and a table set for dinner for the two of us. She turned to look back at me, and heat crept into her cheeks. She knew.

"This is beautiful."

"Play first, or eat first?"

"Play. Sophie kept feeding me."

Of course she did. She knew my plans and wanted me to get to the good part first. We racked the balls and I held my breath that this would work and she would like it.

"Can you check the pockets for the cue ball?"

I pretended to be busy with the cue rack as she walked around and checked the pockets.

"Here -oh." I turned and Anora was holding a white ball, but it wasn't a cue ball. It had a line down the center and a small hinge. At first I'd thought it was a dumb idea but when I told Sophie she was so excited she got it made before I'd settled on anything.

Anora was frozen, and I stepped toward her softly. She looked up at me then with tears in her eyes, and they fell as she followed my move onto one knee.

"No one in the universe has ever hurt or broken me the way you have. No one could ever hurt me like you. You destroyed me. I looked into my future and saw it empty and loveless because without you I didn't even want to try. I hated you almost as much as I loved you."

"Owen," she sobbed, pain pulling her lips down.

"I would go through it all again to get us here. I would let you hurt me endlessly just to be with you. I would give my life up to love you."

"Please," she whimpered.

"I wanted to ask you this a long time ago. I've wanted to ask you this question all my life." I took the ball from her and opened it. The ring was a white diamond with a purple amethyst on each side. It had belonged to her mother, and I knew she knew as soon as she saw it. It was one of the reasons purple was her favorite color, because she had played with it often as a child. I remember her telling me about this exact ring.

It was one of the assets that had been left to me by Don, and I wondered yet again if he'd known about us. I wanted to believe that he did.

"I have loved you since the first day of your life, and I'll love you until our last no matter what happens in between. I decided that this isn't going to be a question, because me and you, that's beyond anyone's control, even our own. We're going to get married, Anora. You will be my wife."

Anora laughed and more tears spilled over her eyes. "Yes, I will." She held out her hand to me and I slid the ring home on her left hand. It hadn't even needed to be resized. Anora took my hands and tugged me to stand up. We wrapped our arms around each other and lost track of time and the world as our lips met.

29

Owen

Everything changed with a letter.

It was delivered by courier. All it said was: *I can find your assassin.* It had a username on a messaging app. I was suspicious, of course, but I wanted to chase down every lead. We had so few of them.

Once again, Anora and I had kept things a secret. We wanted to wait until a better or more necessary moment to talk about what was moving forward with us. I wanted them to believe in us. She did too. It was going to catch them off guard and we wanted to ease everyone into the idea of us, and that it wasn't a strategic move. Given Anora's agreement for an arranged marriage in the past, we knew we had perception to fight.

Time didn't let us figure it out though. With the contact from Sphinx, we needed to lay out the plan in front of the family and we needed everyone on board.

The first conversation with Sphinx was stilted, but when he said Clive Branson would vouch for him I knew that he was legitimate. That didn't mean I ignored my due diligence. I called Clive and Clive stood for him. He seemed to know more than he let on, and I wondered if they'd had a suspicion about our assassin before. I wondered why they waited this long to say anything.

After Sphinx had confirmed everything regarding the details of the attack and the similar cases, I asked what he wanted. There were only two demands: that we hunted and killed Shadow together, and he wanted to take Aro away to help her.

O: *How do I know we can trust you with her?*

S: *I've been in her place. Scarred and drowning. I can help.*

O: *Help how?*

S: *Refocus her on the fight, and fight through the blame she feels.*

O: *Can you guarantee her safety?*

S: *Yes. No one could find us unless I wanted them to, and I can give her the chance to get revenge, and closure. Your family deserves this. She deserves this.*

I don't know why that was what convinced me, but it did. I gave Aro the option - if she'd said no, I would have respected it. But she didn't. I demanded that Sphinx come meet us before he took her. I wanted to see the man for myself. If there was even a hint of him that felt off to me, the deal would've been done. I told him so.

We sat together in the front room of the Sorrelle house and I watched him watch Aro. There wasn't anything predatory in his gaze even though everything about Sphinx screamed danger. He couldn't or wouldn't speak, but he communicated nonetheless. He didn't look at Aro with pity either. He understood her and what she was going through in a way that we didn't, and I felt oddly relieved.

Our dreamy romantic was broken and I wanted her back. She might not be the same on the other side, but we needed her as much as we needed everyone else. This family functioned because we were all so different, and having Aro so far from herself made us vulnerable.

Of course meeting the assassin who was taking Aro away would be the easy part.

"When Aro returns, and after we kill the assassin, Anora and I will be getting married."

I didn't expect the chaos the room descended into, and all of it was focused on Anora. I thought they'd be angry with me and think that I was taking advantage of the family's moment of weakness. Instead, they all believed that it was her idea to keep everyone safe. They thought that *she* was taking advantage of *me*, which was shocking and slightly amusing. I'd tease her about it later.

Then I yelled for everyone to shut up and broke up the meeting. Nothing productive was happening and I needed it to stop. I watched Sphinx stare at Aro one more time, waiting for her to meet his eyes. I needed to protect her, but I think Sphinx wanted to protect her from himself just as much. The end of this situation would be fucked up, but I'd weather that storm.

Everyone left the room or the house except us, Aro, Aster, and Isaac. Alina had hissed that she'd call Anora later.

Aster stared at the two of us, then turned to look at Isaac. "I owe you."

Isaac smirked. "Told you so."

"You're sure about this?" Aster asked us both. I'd question Isaac later about that interaction.

"We are," Anora answered before I could, and took my hand. "I want this."

"Cool," Aster nodded, then focused on me. "Fuck this up and you'll wish for death."

"If I fuck this up, I won't stop you." I held her gaze, and after a moment, she nodded and left the room. Aster was suitably convinced that she didn't need to intervene.

Aro was curled in on herself, and I wanted to feel sorry for her but it was hard. It was hard to watch someone you loved repeatedly reject help, and even hurt the people around her while she was hurting. After everything Anora had done to take care of her own mental health, she struggled the most with what Aro was dealing with. Anora didn't know what it felt like to have someone's death on her head, and I tried to get her to see it differently. Instead, she was short on sympathy with Aro sometimes.

"Are you okay?" Anora asked her.

"Yeah," Aro nodded. "Just scared."

Anora moved to sit by her sister and I moved away, out of their sight. I wasn't going to leave because they were both so fragile right now, but I'd give them as much privacy as I could.

"We're all scared. I want you to get better."

"Me too. I think I mean it this time."

They hugged. Aro got up and walked toward the door, but stumbled when she saw me. Our eyes met and I felt the anguish in them as if it was my own. Aro didn't deserve this. She'd always been the innocent one, and I hated that life had taken that away from her.

"I can do this," she said to me as much as to herself.

"I know you can," I agreed.

As soon as she was out of sight, Anora plowed into my arms. "It can only go up from here."

"It will. I promise, Button, it will."

Anora lifted her head and pressed her lips to mine. It was time for us to make it official because I wouldn't let anything keep her from me anymore.

Finally, it was our wedding day. I could declare to the world that Anora Sorrelle was mine.

I watched the most beautiful woman I'd ever known walk down the aisle toward me. People stood on either side of the aisle, watching her come toward me, witnessing this event. My best friend was escorting her to me, cementing our bonds to each other in another way.

I wanted to smile. I wanted to cry.

All I could do was stare at and tell her everything with my eyes. Telling her the things that only she could read in them.

I never thought I'd get this moment. I never truly believed that she'd be mine in this way. I thought my past and her fear would keep us apart forever. The taint of Roman and Elaine lingered, but I was freed of them when Don Sorrelle accepted me as part of his family. When Anora said yes, and we started dreaming of a family of our own.

No one knew it yet accept Anora, but I was taking her last name. I was leaving behind the Carvers forever, letting them fully die like they deserved. I wanted to be a Sorrelle. I wanted her name to be the one that lived. I wanted to declare to the world that they were my true allegiance, and always would be.

Anora and Rafe took a step toward me.

The world around me rattled, went black, and everything I'd ever dreamed of turned into a nightmare beyond my imagining.

Rafe was dying. Anora was gone.

V

Determined

30

Anora

PRESENT

When I wake up, I'm still in my wedding dress, laying on a bed in a room with no windows. I shake my head and take a deep breath, trying to clear it. Between the bomb and the drugs, I'm a mess.

As I sit up, there's a clanking sound. My brain can't comprehend the manacle around my ankle, and I follow the chain with my eyes to where it's bolted to the floor. I hear footsteps shuffle closer.

"Hello, cupcake."

The voice is familiar, and my body freezes. I blink a few times to clear my eyes before seeking out the source of the sound.

"Elton?"

Knowing that he was the one doing all of this to us and having it proven to me is an odd experience. I look at his bland face and notice for the first time that his eyes are dead. There's nothing there. Everything about him is flat.

"It's me, love. I've saved you."

"What?" I shake my head as if I could clear it like an etch-a-sketch but the drugged haze lingers.

"I know you felt obligated to marry Owen, I know that your family has been through so much, I couldn't let you make a mistake like that." He comes to kneel down next to me and I am too dulled to move away when he tucks a stray piece of hair behind my ear. "We're together now. I can take care of you."

My chest is tight and I'm struggling to pull in a breath. I can hear my heart racing and thumping in my ears, my skull pulsing with the rhythm of it. I try to breathe but nothing happens. I fight against myself as my body locks and my vision narrows. Elton is speaking to me, but I can't hear anything.

I've been taken. I was kidnapped and drugged, and I am now a prisoner of the man who has destroyed my entire family. Who paid people to hurt them and bring them down, and I still don't understand why.

I want to live. I want to live.

It's all I can think before the world goes black.

Days pass and my eyes are open, but I'm not in my body. Elton tries to talk to me, and I see him, but I can't comprehend anything that's happening. I sit in my wedding dress and I'm seeping in my own bodily functions, barely alive. There's a girl who comes to look at me sometimes, and I think I'm hallucinating a version of myself. I see her but don't see her. Sometimes when she speaks I can hear her, like I'm hearing my own voice in my head.

"You have to get it together or he's going to hurt you. Please. Please snap out of it."

I shiver on the bed, all of my muscles tense, my teeth chattering. I am frozen. I am in a constant state of panic that I can't escape. There has to be a way for me to regain control of myself, but the drugs make it hard to think. It's hard to use the thought processes I've learned to cope when I'm incapable of clear thought.

"I know you're delicate, cupcake, but you can't go on like this." Elton touches me and it only makes things worse. I spiral again, and dry heave until I think I've rubbed my throat raw and hurt my diaphragm. Everything hurts.

"He's not going to hurt you if you behave," the girl tells me. "If you talk to him he'll calm down. You need to be good. You need to come back."

She holds my hand and it's so warm I almost believe she's real.

On what I think is the third day, Elton comes in with a needle. I don't feel the prick in my arm but I feel the relaxing of my body. I pass out, and get what might be real sleep for the first time in days. It's something different than he gave me before.

I start to wake up but don't open my eyes. I let myself believe for a moment that this was a terrible nightmare. That when I open my eyes it will be my wedding day and that I'm going to marry Owen.

Even thinking his name hurts.

I take a deep breath and open my eyes. There's no one in the room this time. I breathe again, then again, feeling my limbs come awake after being so stiff and so useless for days on end. I sit up and take stock of how disgusting everything is right now. My dress is ruined, I'm covered in days' worth of body oils and waste, my stomach is hollow with the need to eat, and I'm parched from a lack of water.

"Hello?!" I yell, and hope that someone is around to hear me.

The door opens a few moments later and Elton comes in. He stands by the door and his face wrinkles in disgust.

"Have you rejoined us?" I can hear the barely restrained anger. Fear causes my stomach to cramp but I cling to the mask I've always worn and hid behind. It might save me now.

"Yes, I'm so sorry, Elton," I decide kissing up is the way to go. I think about what little me said when I was out of it. "Please let me clean up so we can talk."

"Of course," he agrees. He walks into the room and unlocks the chain from the bolt on the floor. He holds onto it and looks at me expectantly. It takes me a moment to understand that he's going to lead me around by that chain to wherever I'm going. With another fortifying breath, I follow him out of the room.

We're definitely in a basement somewhere, but it's a warren of brightly lit concrete and turning hallways and doors. He leads me a few doors away to a bathroom. I step inside and wait, hoping that he'll leave. Elton steps inside and locks the chain to a bolt on the wall. I can get into the shower, as well as reach the toilet and the sink.

"Clean up. Yell when you're done."

"Thank you so much," I reach out and grab his arm even though I'm recoiling at the feel of him. Elton looks down at where my hand rests but says nothing before he leaves the room. I look around for cameras and don't see any, but I'm sure they're there. I need to bite the bullet and do this, even if I feel violated and vulnerable.

I step into the shower and strip off my ruined dress. It's got mud and grass stains, not to mention what I did the last few days. When I get it off me, I throw it out of the shower. I'm standing in my wedding lingerie and now is when I break, crying over something as stupid as the sexy bra and thong I picked especially to wear for Owen.

I strip down to my skin, ripping the underwear from my body, and turn on the shower. At first, feeling cleansed by the ice cold and then the increasingly hot water. I let it run so hot it hurts and my skin turns red. I use the soap on the shelf to wash my body. The shampoo and conditioner on the shelf are my preferred brand, and my skin crawls again. I finish washing quickly before reaching for a towel and stepping out.

There are clothes on a shelf - yoga pants, a tank top, and a hoodie.

All new. The hoodie still has the tags. I put on the tank top and the hoodie and I'm grateful when it goes down almost to my knees. I realize that if I want to get the pants on, I need Elton to unlock my chain.

I pound on the door and hear him coming. I pull the sweatshirt down around me and try to protect my modesty. Other than my doctor, Owen is the only person who has ever seen me naked and I'd like to do my best to keep it that way.

When he opens the door, his eyes drop down my body, heating when he sees my bare legs. I swallow thickly. I know I'm in danger at the possessive look in his eyes. Elton thinks he owns me.

"I need the chain removed to put on my pants."

"Of course," he says after too long a pause. Elton kneels next to me and undoes the manacle. His eyes never leave my barely covered crotch, and I look away. My body is turning red with embarrassment, and he smirks when he sees it on my face. Elton doesn't leave as I tug on the pants and do my best not to show him anything.

"There you are," he says as he locks the cuff around my ankle again. "Much better, right?" I nod. He looks at the pile of white dress and lingerie on the floor. "I'll burn that. You never have to think about it again."

"Okay," I answer, and follow him back to my prison. The bedding has been changed and it smells like cleaning supplies. I don't think he did it himself, which means there's somebody else here.

Elton chains me to the floor again and I sit on the bed, trying to get comfortable. He leans against the wall and we stare at each other. I don't want to look away. I can't show weakness.

"I'm going to bring you food, and you're going to eat it. You're going to sleep. Tomorrow, we'll talk about everything, when you're rested."

"Okay." That gives me more time to figure out what I can say or do to get out of this. Owen will come for me. My family will come for me. I think about Sophie, trapped for years, and have tonight to remember everything she told me about surviving. She's the blueprint for making it to when Owen rescues me. I'm not half as strong as her, but channeling even a little bit of Sophie will get me far. I know it.

"If you behave, I'll allow you to come upstairs."

"I will," I promise. If I can get upstairs I can figure out where I am.

Elton comes over and cups my head, then kisses the crown. I hold myself still, holding my breath, so I don't flinch or move away. When he closes the door, the lights go out, and I'm trapped in pitch dark.

31

Owen

We search every property that had ever been touched by a Forrester, a Lassiter, or any company connected to either of those names. We burst into occupied places, not giving a fuck, searching for Anora. I'm not a man, I'm a machine, and the longer we go without finding her, the further I get from my humanity.

The Montaignes stepped up, as did Dinah and the Rileys, using every resource all of us had to find out where she went. Every favor I ever owed was called in. It got us nowhere.

It wasn't a leap to know that she was taken by Elton Forrester, but I never thought he'd be smart enough to get so far off the grid that I can't find him. His desperation to have her made him careful, and that's making him hard to find. Given the fact that his whole family disappeared almost a year ago means that he's had a lot more time to learn a way around us than we've had to learn anything about him.

He had the luxury of time to plan this. We have no time to find her.

I will kill him with my bare hands. I fantasize about it when I want to fall into a pit of missing Anora. When I feel the tether between us pull tight, it eats me. I center myself by imagining him dead at my feet, ripped into pieces after screaming for mercy that will never come.

Rafe is alive, but still in intensive care. Sophie sits by his side and I give her regular updates. She's the only one with any optimism in this situation.

"I told her everything I'd been through, O. Everything I did, every thought I had, every way I kept myself safe. She's prepared for this. She'll keep it together until we find her."

Sophie knows Anora struggles, but I don't think she knows the extent of it. I'm not afraid I'll find Anora with a broken body, I'm afraid I'll find her with an irretrievable mind. I am terrified that she will be so inside herself in order to survive that I will never be able to coax her back out.

But I also know she's been stronger than ever lately, and I know that if she was doing it for her family, it would be what she needed to stay present. I can only hope all the work of the last few years has been enough. She is strong, I know it, but I need her to know it. I need her to believe that I will find her. I need her to believe that she's strong enough to save herself however she can.

All of Aster and Isaac's digging has been investigated; there's nowhere else to look. We're sitting around the dining room table, thinking and wallowing, depending on the person. There has to be somewhere else to look.

Alina leans forward around her belly. "What about Roger Forrester?"

"What about him?" Derick sneers at the thought.

"That's his uncle, right? We know he's fucked around in family business before. I think we should find out what he knows."

"If he knows anything," I add. I'm one of the wallowers at the moment. My anger is temporarily exhausted from lack of sleep.

"It's something, isn't it?" Alina responds, a plea in her gaze. We're both people of action, and this is an action. It's better than sitting around thinking about what else can be done. She's not wrong. At this point, every Forrester is suspect.

"Then let's go. We'll escort you home." It's better than nothing.

Derick nods in agreement and steps away to make a call and ready their plane. The rest of us decide who's going to Seattle. Michel and Thierry Montaigne are coming, as well as Alonzo. We've got plenty of men left here to keep an eye on everything. Even Gailen, although he's recovering from a broken arm after his car was hit chasing the van that took Anora.

I might be angry with him for not being there when Don was attacked, but he was the one who held it together and chased my woman. In my book, he's forgiven.

Aro and Harp are going to New York to check out the other Forrester branch. As far as we can tell they don't even speak to anyone else in their family, but we'd rather check everything than miss something. It's a relief to be able to rely on her now. I wish I was in a place where I could tell Harp I was grateful, or even express any of my emotions to Aro.

Derick gets Roger Forrester to come to us with one phone call. He acted as if he was interested in selling one of his clubs, and wanted to talk to Roger about it directly, rather than working through their companies.

The man was arrogant enough to be amused and agree to meet.

I'm waiting with Thierry and Alonzo as Derick shows him around. The plan is that they'll walk him to the office, but it's really this room. It's empty, windowless, soundproof, and has a drain in the floor. I knew the Claytons were criminal but I'm entertained by the ingenuity of interrogation rooms inside clubs. It's easy to cover the screams with thumping bass and any good club has questionable garbage and sewage even without crime.

I still prefer our room in the basement of the Sorrelle house, but that's because I like having control. Not just over who is there but also over Aster. It's too easy for her to lose herself when she's somewhere else, when no one is around to pull her back into herself.

I almost wish she was here, but I need her computer skills more than her interrogation techniques today.

Their voices reach us before they do, and after Michel opens the door, Derick shoves Roger inside. The man goes down on his knees, already turning around to grumble at Derick rather than notice his surroundings. It makes it easy for me to string a rope around his neck and pull it tight, strangling him as I pull him deeper into the room. I hold him at my feet and look down at his purpling face.

I release the rope and he takes a deep breath.

"What the hell is this?" he rasps.

"My name is Owen Carver, Mr. Forrester. I was supposed to marry Anora Sorrelle last Saturday, but there was an incident. Would you know anything about that?" My voice is cold and level, hiding the rage inside.

"No," he has the audacity to lie. I tighten the rope again, pulling it taut as he struggles underneath my grip. His feet scramble ineffectually against the smooth concrete, and I push down with enough strength that he can't get them underneath him. Thierry laughs, and then we all do. It's mirthless. It's the laughter of the ruthless as they penalize the weak.

"Let's try again." I release Roger and he heaves in deep, ragged breaths. "Did you know Elton Forrester was attacking my family?"

"Yes," Roger answers, looking down and massaging his throat. "I helped him."

"Helped him how?"

I'm surprised it took so little to crack him, but then again, he might be involved in criminal things but he's no criminal. Roger Forrester has never been the man behind the gun, the one who took responsibility and took action. He's directed others from afar and never got his hands dirty.

"Put him in touch with a broker, helped him set up some shells under different names, how to use their legitimate businesses to hide money."

For good measure, I strangle him again. I hold the rope until I have myself back under control. Until I know I won't kill him.

"Where is he?"

"I don't know! I swear I don't know. He took off with his mom and his sister and I haven't heard from him in months. I swear, I swear," Roger is sputtering now, making a mess and fearing for his life. Good.

"His sister?" Alonzo steps forward and kicks Roger's leg. "He doesn't have a sister."

"He does, he does," Roger gets excited now, as if this piece of information will set him free. "Gloria had her late, kept her home because she was sick a lot. Maybe you can find him through her. Aspen."

While it's an interesting piece of information, I'm not sure it's useful. It could mean that Anora is victim to two captors instead of one. It could be a loose thread to pull, or it could be nothing. It gives us another name to look for, but that's about it.

Derick kneels down in front of Roger. What happens today is up to him. Roger Forrester is his enemy for funding his now dead brother's attempt to steal his life. Derick never had a clear way to get revenge before, and I have no problem helping him exact it.

"You're going to forget this happened." Derick holds Roger's head by his hair and forces the man to meet his eyes. "You're going to stay the fuck away from my family, my extended family, anyone I've ever looked at for longer than a second. Right?"

"I swear," Roger agrees.

"You're going to call us if you hear anything, even a rumor, about your nephew."

"I will." He starts to move as if we're going to let him go.

I tighten the rope enough to hurt, and he can barely breathe. I get down so I'm speaking right in his face and finish the threat. "If I find out you know anything and haven't told us, your death will be beyond your worst nightmares. If I find out you hear from Elton and don't call us immediately..."

Roger holds up his hands. "I got it," he gurgles, and I let him go. I drop the rope and kick him over, and the room fills with that mirthless laughter again. Roger is a minnow in a room full of killers. He has no idea the true danger he's been in this whole time. We are men who kill for love and loyalty, and even if he was involved indirectly, he was part of hurting someone we all care about.

We wait as Roger crawls out of the room. Alonzo follows to make sure he gets to the door and leaves the building.

"Kade will keep an eye on him," Derick assures us.

"Aster is tracking his every move now as well." I feel unclean. We learned nothing overly important other than how Elton managed to go off grid and get in touch with someone who could hire an assassin. At least that's been handled - both the broker and the assassin are dead.

The answer is somewhere.

I have to trust that Anora is fighting with everything she has, and that I will find her.

32

Anora

The door slamming into the wall wakes me up the next morning. The light from the hall burns my eyes and I squeeze them shut. Elton grabs me by the wrists and pulls me up, and I'm caught off guard by his strength.

"Do you want to go back to them?" He screams it in my face.

"What?" I'm still coming awake and trying to get myself into as neutral a mindset as possible. He's volatile, and I need to calm him down.

"Your stupid family that's ripping everything apart to find you, do you want to go back to them?"

"Yes," I answer but it sounds like a question.

"Then you'll fucking behave, won't you?"

"Yes, Elton, of course." I shift my wrists in his harsh grip and he lets me pull away to put my hands in his. "What's the matter?"

"I don't like people messing with things that belong to me." His voice is hollow and creepy. Whatever they're doing to find me, it's setting him off.

"I'm sorry. They're just worried."

"Of course," he nods, the mask of calm falling over him so quickly it's unnerving. "Come on. Upstairs." Elton steps away from me and undoes the chain. I follow him out the door, down a long hallway, and through another door that opens on a set of stairs. It's hard to maneuver the stairs with the chain being held, and I fall twice.

Elton huffs. "Hurry the fuck up."

I try and rush but I'm afraid I'll trip again. We emerge into bright daylight in a large kitchen. Elton leads me through it and into a sitting room. Wherever this is, it's a very nice, enormous house. Outside there is a thick swath of trees and nothing else. The furnishings are dated but nice.

In the sitting room, there's a fire going. He directs me to a chair, and connects the chain to another bolt in the floor. It's clear he prepared this whole house with the idea of keeping a captive inside it. I can go anywhere because there's a way to chain me. Giving me the illusion of free movement probably makes him feel better about all of this.

I stare into the fire, feeling clear for the first time since he took me. No more drugs in my system, no more shock, but the harsh, cold reality of what's happening.

Elton is the most dangerous situation I have ever been in.

This man is responsible for my father's murder.

For the harm to my sisters.

For anything that happened at my wedding. For anyone that might have been hurt there. This was all him and I don't understand why.

Tears stream down my cheeks before I can stop them as these truths strike like a hammer.

"Don't cry, cupcake." Elton comes over and kneels in front of me, and I can't even stop him when he roughly wipes away my tears and holds my head just a little too tight. He thinks he's being romantic and caring but I don't think he knows how to touch someone gently. He's only got brutality in him. I see it now.

"I did all of this for you," he whispers to me and kisses my forehead.

Nausea overwhelms me and I close my eyes.

"I know I had to hurt you to get us here, but all of it was for you. I needed to free you from your family. They were holding you back. They didn't appreciate you at all. I see you, Anora. How special you are." He kisses my forehead again and then lets me go, moving to sit on the chair next to mine.

"You'll forgive me for it all in time. I'll love you the way you deserve and you'll see." Elton nods talking more to himself than to me. "I had to do it this way. I had to show you that I'm strong enough to take care of you, and take care of anything that could ever get in our way."

Silence falls again, and I don't break it. I'm afraid of what I'll say.

"You belong to me now." Elton's voice sounds sinister, something dark creeping in it that I haven't heard before. "You're mine."

He moves swiftly, yanking me down to the floor and crawling on top of me. I thrash against him as he paws at my clothes, his hands diving under the hoodie and tank to squeeze my bare breasts. I'm sobbing again, saying no over and over. I have to think of something. I have to say something.

"Elton, please, I'm a virgin!" It screams out of me, and I don't know why I said it, but it makes him freeze. His hands are still cupping my breasts but they aren't hurting me anymore.

Carefully, he slides his hands out from under my shirt but he's still pinning me to the floor with his body.

"What?" He's incredulous.

I look at him and then away, feigning embarrassment. My cheeks blush with the lie.

"I knew I had more value in a marriage if I stayed untouched." My voice wobbles and I lean into it. "I kept myself pure." I break on the last word and squeeze my eyes shut. For some reason I want to laugh, and I know that would be terrible.

"My precious princess, you were waiting for me, weren't you?"

I nod.

"You'll love it, baby. I'll make you feel good."

"Elton," I whine and wiggle underneath him. "I want to be married before I do that. It's important to me."

"Anora," he huffs.

"Please?" I beg. "I want to build our connection first. I want to be with you and know you, so I can give all of myself to you when we get married."

He stares down at me before his face softens. "Okay. If it will make you feel better, we can do that."

I nod and he leans down and presses his lips to mine. I don't kiss him back but I don't fight him either. I'm finding a way to survive.

Elton pulls me up from the floor and over to the couch, where he sits beside me and wraps his arms around me. He turns on the television and I turn off my brain, sitting beside him, trapped in more ways than one, as he watches the show and laughs like this is normal. Laughs like he isn't doing anything insane or wrong.

"Where are we?" I ask softly. "Is this one of your family homes?" The Forresters are an old family and have a lot of money. It wouldn't surprise me if the ownership of this house is buried in their history and hard to find.

"No," Elton snorts. "We'd never own somewhere like this." I'm not sure what he means by that. The house is nice, and clearly isolated. To some people that would be an asset. "I acquired it through a company. It served my purpose until you're ready."

"Ready for what?" I blink up at him like I'm confused. If I remember anything about Elton from school it's that he got insecure about anyone being obviously smarter than him. He was very book smart, it was his social skills that lacked. If I play dumb, he might over explain things to me and give me more information.

"To leave. When I can trust you, we can leave this place behind."

200

"Of course," I nod in agreement. "After we get married."

"Yes, cupcake, after we get married." He squeezes his arms around me and goes back to watching the show. At least I know for sure he's got the internet here, which is something else Aster and Isaac might be able to track. I'm trying to find anything I can use to get some sort of signal to them. I doubt he'd let me get in touch with them, that's too much of a risk and he knows what my family is capable of, but maybe I can do it without him knowing.

I sort of wish I'd paid more attention to all the technology my family is involved in, but it's never been my skill set. They made things, I kept things in order. That's how our lives worked. I'm not sure it would do me any good anyway.

I have to make Elton vulnerable. That's how I get out of here. I run, or I'm rescued.

Eventually, he drags me into the kitchen and chains me where I can sit at the island on a stool. I watch with surprise as he cooks.

"You once said men who can cook are men worth marrying, so I learned." He says that like I should know exactly what and when he's talking about. I went to school with Elton for so long it could have been any time. It's not something I remember myself saying, but I can't disagree with my past self. Owen can cook and it was part of the reason I thought that.

Quickly, I push the thought of him away, afraid of what might show on my face, and focus on what Elton's doing.

I imagine grabbing the cast iron skillet he's using and smashing him over the head.

Pushing his face down on the burner, charring his skin until it's unrecoverable.

Stabbing him with the knife he's using to cut up ingredients until my arms give out.

All the ways in which I would hurt him in order to escape him.

I'm fantasizing about it while Elton makes me an omelet, and when he slides the plate across the counter to me I almost can't eat it. He sits beside me and I force myself to take bite after bite. I have to stay aware. I have to stay strong.

Elton leads me down to my cell, as I've come to think of it. After securing my chain, he steps into the hall and comes back with some books. He sets them on the bed, grabs my head, forces my lips to his, then leaves me without another word.

I wonder if he's watching, so I take one of the books and open it.

I don't notice the title or even read the words. I stare and turn the pages when I think I've been staring for long enough.

When the doorknob turns, I flinch, caught out of my daze.

A girl appears in the gap. I'm afraid I might be hallucinating, and then she steps inside and closes it behind her. I watch as she moves with her back against the wall into the corner next to the door.

"This the blind spot," she tells me. I must look confused because she points up. "The camera. He can't see this spot."

"Can he hear us?"

"No. I don't think he's watching right now anyway."

"Who are you?"

She's small and even now that I'm awake, I see the similarities in us that made me think I'd been hallucinating a younger version of myself. Although her hair is dirty and stringy, it's the same shade as mine, and our eyes are a similar deep brown color. There are other features in her that look familiar, but I'm not sure why.

"I know you lied to him," she says quietly.

I freeze. "About what?"

"You're not a virgin. I mean, I can see why he believes you, but I know."

"How do you know?"

"I know all about all of you. He made me learn. He made me dig."

"I'm sorry." I mean it, but it just makes her frown.

"I won't tell him, but you have to keep up whatever game you're playing. He's dangerous."

"Are you safe?"

"Not a day in my life," she answers, smiling but defeated. "It'll be okay here if you do what he says." The girl stares at me for a little longer. "Don't let him get angry. Don't fight him, okay? He'll hurt you."

"Has he hurt you?" I already know the answer, and when she meets my eyes, it breaks my heart. "Who are you?"

The girl shrugs, and then slides back to the door and leaves the room. I'm not sure if this is another way Elton is messing with me, or trying to get information from me, but I feel like whoever comes to save me, they need to save her too. If I find a way out, I'm taking her with me. I can't leave anyone at his mercy.

33

Owen

I finally get good news shortly after we land back in Chicago: Rafe is awake.

I leave everyone except Alonzo behind and we race toward the hospital straight from the airfield. I've been to see him as often as I can, and make sure that someone is always keeping an eye on Sophie. The Montaignes have it covered, but I need to know that they're both taken care of at all times. It's keeping me sane to know that I'm protecting them. The Montaignes have offered us extra protection around the house, but I don't think it's necessary.

Elton has what he wants, he doesn't care about us anymore. Elton has Anora, and I believe she was his endgame all along. Yes, he wanted to defeat the Sorrelles, but more than anything he wanted her. I'd always noticed the way Elton watched Anora, the way he spoke to her, or watched her at events but never approached to talk to her. Elton wanted her, and she was entirely oblivious. I liked it that way. She would have niced herself into to trouble if she'd known.

Now he had her, and I couldn't let myself think about what he could be doing to her. My girl would fight and survive, of that I had no doubt.

Sophie is stepping out of Rafe's room when I turn the corner. She runs to me and I embrace her. Rafe is a possessive asshole so I'm one of the few men allowed to hug her. Even his brothers get the eye if they do it.

"Any news?" she asks, pulling me back toward the room.

"No." I drop my head. Sophie closes the door behind us and I look up to see my friend, paler than usual, but with his trademark smirk on his face.

"Hell of a wedding."

"Fuck off," I retort. "I'm sorry."

Rafe scoffs. "Fuck that. I'd do it again." I walk over to the bed and we embrace the best we can. They both fill me in on where he's at medically. Despite the blood loss, he's doing well. Healing fast, and he should be out within a week.

"Always so fucking lucky," I shake my head. We stare at each other, and then his face drops. "Don't," I warn him.

"We'll help. Not just me and Soph, but the Montaignes. You're family, Anora is family. Whatever you need."

"I know. Your brothers are already on it." The tightness builds in my throat and I try and keep it down. Sophie's warm hand lands on my back and I shake my head, trying to fight the panic and overwhelming emotions.

"I owe you," Rafe continues. "You saved my girl, I'm going to help you save yours."

"She's going to be okay, Owen," Sophie says as she rubs my back gently. "I know you're worried, but she's got fight in her, and she's smart. We will find her."

"Fuck," I croak, and I break. I break with them like I can't in front of anyone else. In front of the family I have to stay strong and confident. They need to believe that I'm certain we're going to save her and that I have a plan to figure out where she is, that I'm not throwing random things into the air and hoping we get a result. I need their faith. With Rafe and Sophie, I can be myself.

I press my face into the blanket on Rafe's bed and I let everything out. Rafe grips my hand and Sophie rubs my back. Because of this monster I almost lost everyone that matters to me - Anora is gone, Rafe almost died, and Sophie would have fallen apart. They already spent enough time forcibly separated and I am so lucky she doesn't hate me for almost taking him away from her.

When I feel like I can't cry anymore, I sit up. Sophie leans on my shoulder and we both hold Rafe's hand, the three of us connected like we always have been. They might be married to each other, but she is my sister and he is my brother, and they are my family. Family I never thought I would find or deserve, who I know, even if I ask them not to, will put everything they have on the line to find Anora.

Because they love me, and know that I would do it for them because I love them too.

"So what's the plan?" Rafe asks, shifting uncomfortably in his bed.

"There isn't one. We're turning over every leaf, tracking down every tiny bit of the existence of the Forresters to try and find where he would take her. Aster and Isaac are sleeping in shifts to keep looking around the clock." I put my head in my hands, pulling back from them and retreating into myself.

"Something will turn up. I believe that." Sophie nods, and I know she's telling herself as much as she's telling me.

"Whoever we have to bribe or hurt, we'll find her. Then we'll destroy him." Rafe pounds a fist on the railing of the bed. It sets off a series of beeps and he panics, checking that everything that's supposed to be attached to him still is.

A nurse rushes in and presses a button. "Whatever you're talking about, it's done. You need to rest more, then you can go out and cause trouble."

"How do you know I'm trouble?" he grins at her.

The older woman circles her finger around his face. "That right there. That face."

I laugh at him and let the tension snap for a moment. Rafe is going to be okay. I have my friends and my family by my side, and we are going to save Anora. The nurse leaves, and Rafe and Sophie share a look.

"I'm sorry," Rafe starts.

"For what?"

"I didn't protect her. You literally had me in a role that was meant to do that and I fucked it up."

"You say that shit to her and she's going to punch you in the face."

Rafe snorts. "It won't hurt that bad, and I deserve it."

"You don't. None of us were ready for this. There's nothing to be sorry for."

"I'll believe it when you believe it."

We stare each other down, and neither of us cracks. Sophie waves her hand in between us.

"Enough of that."

"Fine," we say in unison, and she laughs.

34

Anora

The days blur as it's a cycle of Elton feeding me, sitting with me, and touching me. I try and get him to talk more about himself and his plans, but he always redirects. Most of the time he reminisces about interactions we had in high school that meant everything to him and nothing to me.

He has a journal. Correction, he has journals.

He's kept them since 7th grade and they are all about me. Every interaction, when I wore clothes that he liked or didn't, when I did something he did or didn't like. There were ranting entries about being angry with me, or glowing, obsessive ones for days after we spoke to one another. It went on for years.

There are programs from almost every charity event I hosted or helped organize.

A napkin where I blotted my lipstick.

The discarded lid of a coffee cup with my lip print on it.

There's even a tissue from a time I got a bloody nose at an early morning running event. I hadn't even known he was there. That's probably how he wanted it.

There are pictures of me that I wasn't aware were being taken. Even when I was out East at school. Walking around campus, through my dorm room window, at parties with my acquaintances. I don't know if he was there or if he had someone following me.

There are pictures of me going in and out of Sophie and Rafe's apartment, which is the more shocking thing. Their security is so aware I would think they'd notice someone taking a picture of their place, but maybe he was covert enough.

I'm surprised he's never gotten a photo of me and Owen out, but I also realize he'd never be allowed inside a Montaigne club. There's photos of me going there, but never of the inside or what we got up to in there. He has no idea that Owen and I are more than friends or have more than a sibling-like relationship.

I know, because he talks about it. Sometimes he thinks about the wedding and gets angry.

"You had to know I was coming for you, cupcake." He grips my jaw hard and makes me look at him. "Owen was never for you. He's like your brother. He's lived in your house for years. It's like incest. It's disgusting."

I can barely nod, but I do, agreeing with anything he tells me.

"The Carvers are dirty. You were almost tainted," he sighs, and pulls me into his body like he's shielding me from something. "I got there just in time. I would have had to kill him otherwise."

"Of course. Right in time," I murmur, breathing in until the tears dissipate. I can't cry because it's harder to lie when I'm crying. It's harder not to scream Owen's name and pray that he hears me. That he finds me wherever the hell I am and that he takes Elton apart.

His touches are getting more brazen. He kisses me for longer and grabs my body. There are bruises on my hips, waist, and neck from how hard he holds me in place as he grinds against me. I go somewhere else in my head, I'm good at it, and let him touch me until he talks himself out of taking it further.

I've been here at least a week.

I never see the girl when we're up in the house. I don't know if he tells her to stay away or if she's kept prisoner somewhere else. I hope that she's eating, I hope that she's safe. I'm afraid to ask him about her. I don't want to get her in trouble since she was clearly hiding her presence from him when she came to see me.

We're eating dinner in the kitchen when I try and broach a sensitive subject.

"Elton, where's Gloria?"

The last information we had was that both he and his mom had disappeared. I would assume she went off with her son, but it's possible he sent her away somewhere, or hid her somewhere like this. We couldn't find any sign of her. I'd seen her over a year ago at an event with Elton, but that's the last time I clearly remembering noticing and interacting with her. She always made a point of talking to me and I liked her even when Elton annoyed me. I saw him at a few more events, but she was never with him.

"Why?" Elton's voice is deadly, and I already regret asking.

"I thought she'd be with you. I haven't seen her in a long time."

He stares at me and then stands up, the stool he was sitting on clattering to the floor as he stalks over to me. I gasp when he grabs me by the throat and pulls me up from the chair, then slams me into the wall. Pain radiates down my head and back at the force and I automatically reach up to scratch at his arm. Elton doesn't react. Like he doesn't even feel my nails digging into his skin.

"Are you going to betray me, like her?" His face is ruddy with fury. He pulls me away from the wall and then slams me back into it again. "Another woman who thinks she knows better than I do? Are you like my mother, Anora?"

"No," I rasp out, and instead of scratching at him, I wrap my hands around his forearm and squeeze, as if I'm trying to soothe him. "I'm sorry."

"You'll be sorry." Elton drops me and I fall to the ground. I take a breath but when I turn to him, I hear the slap before I feel it. My head snaps to the left and then the pain radiates out across my face. I barely turn back when he slaps the same cheek again.

"You don't question me," Elton growls, and I whimper in response. I grunt when he kicks me in the side, just below my rib cage. I breathe in through my nose, trying to fight the desire to vomit. "Ever." He kicks me again and again, and I lose count of how many times. It hurts, but I know he could kick me harder if he wanted. I can almost feel him holding back.

"No!" A voice screams. Bare feet pound on the tile floor and I see a tiny tangle jump at Elton. I can't move but I watch as he flips her over and slams her onto the ground. It's the girl.

"Elton stop stop stop," she wails out, trying to claw at his face. I cry out when he hits her with a closed fist in the face. The girl never stops fighting, and I watch in horror as he lifts her up and slams her into the side of the island, smashing her tiny body against the solid wood.

I scramble up and run over to them both, but my chain yanks me back. I keep fighting it, trying to grab at him as he keeps smashing her into the floor and the wall. It's going to hurt later as the metal scrapes my skin and the tendons and ligaments are stretched beyond their limits as I try to reach her.

"Elton!" I'm screaming it, and finally he turns to look at me. The expression on his face is inhuman. "Please," I beg him. His eyes drop to where one arm is wrapped protectively around my torso and the other is reaching out. The frightening expression melts from his face and leaves behind a neutral nothingness that's almost scarier.

He gets up and walks out of the room.

"Hey," I call to the girl. I can't reach her, but I keep my arm out as if I could anyway. She lifts her head and stares at me. There's already a bruise forming on her cheek. "Come here."

She slides closer, hesitant but responding. When she's close enough I pull her to me and wrap my arms around her. The girl is stiff at first, and I start rocking the two of us back and forth, running my hand along her snarled hair. She's got to be a teenager but she's so small.

"What can I do for you?" I ask as I keep rocking her and rubbing her gently wherever I think it might not hurt.

"What did you ask him?"

"About Gloria," I answer her. The girl stiffens again and then sags deeper into my embrace. I feel wetness on my arm and realize she's crying. I try to look at her but she presses her face into my skin and hides from me.

"He killed her," she whispers. So quiet I almost don't hear it, and I don't want to believe it. *Elton would never kill his mother.* It's my first thought, but I also never thought he would kidnap or beat me. Elton has always seemed so harmless to me it's hard to rearrange my view in spite of everything. Owen always saw through him. I thought he was just awkward.

"Why?"

"She tried to stop him. He locked us in our house first, and then when things started happening he trapped us up here. The bolts were for her, first." She sniffles and her breath shudders. "Mom got free and ran into the woods and he went after her and only he came back."

"Mom?" I ask. Apparently Elton isn't the only one who keeps secrets. If Gloria was her mother then Elton is her brother, and he's still treating her this way.

"He's my brother," she confirms. The girl still looks away from me as she wipes off her face on the grubby sleeves of her shirt, and slides out of my lap to lean against the counter.

I try to figure out the most delicate way to ask my question. She intuits it based on my confused expression.

"It was a late pregnancy, mom was sick, then I was sick, so she kept everything quiet. I'm also scary smart," there's a slight lift of her cheek when she says it, "and after a while it was normal to be a secret. Mom didn't like it but Elton convinced her. Said people would ask questions we didn't want to answer."

The world of the wealthy is so freaking weird. "Why is he doing this? Why does he hate my family?"

She shakes her head. "Knowing won't make this any better."

I don't press her. "We should get some ice on your eye." I stand up and wince at the pain radiating all over my torso. It makes it hard to breathe but I manage to hobble to the fridge, right at the extent of my chain's reach. There's a bag of frozen vegetables so I grab that instead. I've seen our guys use that over ice or an ice pack. I kneel down in front of her and gently place it over her eye.

She takes over holding it there, and stares at me with her good eye.

"You have sisters?" I know she knows that I do, but I nod. "Tell me about them?"

I adjust so I'm more comfortable sitting on the floor and keep my arms wrapped around my middle. For some reason that makes it hurt less. Talking would also be a good distraction as long as I breathe careful and shallow.

"I'm the oldest, then Alina, Aro, and Aster." It hurts to talk about them, but I do. I tell her that Alina is married and having a baby - a baby I realize I might never get to meet. I share with her that Aro struggled after our dad died but she's doing so much better. I talk about my computer genius baby sister and how proud I am of her for working at Designation. I tell stupid stories about us as little kids, about fights, birthdays, pranks, and parties.

"What about Owen?" her voice is quiet.

"I don't want to talk about Owen," I whisper back, afraid that Elton will hear.

"It hurts too much," she answers. Then her eyes meet mine. "You love him."

I nod, feeling a lump in my throat and a burning in my eyes and nose that I'm about to cry. It's been days since I lost it and I don't want to do it again. The reality is, my sisters' lives will go on without me. If I don't make it back to them they'll have their husbands, children, jobs, a purpose, and even though I know they'll miss me, they'll keep living. They'll make a life for themselves and find happiness again.

That won't be the case for Owen. I know because if the situation was reversed and I didn't find him, I'd never recover. I destroyed him for so many years thinking I was doing the right thing, but the times when I was with him were the best of my life. Those were the times I was a whole person, living and breathing, creating and loving, finding my own purpose. I can't imagine how it could have been even better if it hadn't been a secret. He is my life and I am his, and if I die, so will he.

Maybe not literally, but he'll never move on. Owen will never find someone else and make a life for himself. I hate that truth. I hate how deeply he's hurting and I can't do anything about it except fight to survive.

"He'll find out eventually that it's real. He's convinced it was strategic."

"I'm a good liar."

"I hope so, or we're both damned." The girl crawls to her feet. "I'm going to get you something for the pain, but you'll have to stay here until he comes back. He has the only key."

"Thank you." My head thumps against the cabinet and I close my eyes, waiting for a reprieve that might never come.

35

Anora

I must have passed out, because I wake up back in my cell. My body aches everywhere and when I lift my shirt there are bruises everywhere from below my ribs to around my hips, and I can feel them on my back as well. The skin of my cheek is still tender from where he slapped me.

The lights are on, which means Elton is coming soon.

I crawl back into the corner of the bed when he enters, and the condescension on his face makes me want to scratch his eyes out.

"Did you learn your lesson, cupcake? Are you going to be good?"

I nod. He comes over and yanks me out of the corner and tilts my face to his. The feel of his lips on mine is repulsive, and he forces his tongue inside my mouth. It's wet and slimy and I try to keep my face relaxed so I don't bite him and earn myself another beating. I need to lull him into feeling in control of me again so that I can find out more about what's happening. What's happened.

"Let's go upstairs." Elton steps away to unlock the chain and wraps it around his wrist a few times. He yanks me to him and keeps me pressed up against his body as we walk through the kitchen and to the living room again. He makes me stand as he locks the chain in place, and after sitting down he forces me onto his lap.

I sit stiffly until he presses against the side of my head until I'm resting on his chest. I tense as his hand slides up my inner thigh until it's pressed against the seam of my pants. He didn't give me underwear so there's only thin, stretchy cotton between his digging, disgusting fingers and my core.

He presses against it, trying to tease or arouse me. I feel nothing.

"Aren't you curious, cupcake? Don't you want pleasure? We don't have to have sex for me to make you feel good. I'll keep your virtue intact until my ring is on your finger."

"Elton," I force myself to whine, and squirm as if I'm feeling something from his touch. "It's more than that."

"What?" He kisses my neck and presses harder into me. It only hurts.

"I want to be your partner. I want us to last, and take our place in the world like we deserve. I need to trust you. I need my family to trust you."

He jerks away from me. "Your family." The glare on his face almost deters me.

"I'm the heir, Elton. We have to take over."

Elton's face relaxes and he smiles at me. "We will. You're right."

Taking a chance, I lean forward and kiss him. My mouth is closed but I know I'm earning points for initiating it, even if I know I'm going to pay for it. His hand slides up, under the hoodie, until he's playing with my breast. My nipples react from my fear, and I almost breathe a sigh of relief. He can play with them all he wants. It doesn't scare me the way the idea of him trying to invade my vagina does.

"Please, Elton," I beg and arch my back. "I can't give myself to you until I understand. I need to know you, baby." My lip curls at the pet name but I'm hoping it worked.

Elton grunts and removes his hand, then tips me off his lap and onto the floor. I land with a thud and almost smash my head on the coffee table. I scramble away from him and curl up, preparing for another attack.

He yanks my arm hard, and throws me into a chair. "Stop it, I'm not going to hurt you." His voice has taken on that weird dull tone again. "Some of this is going to upset you, cupcake, but I need you to know I did it for us."

I look up at him and think of Owen, letting my face show love and trust. "I believe you."

Elton smiles at me with affection and runs his thumb down my cheek.

"Your sister killed my father."

I drop my head so he can't see even the hint of a smirk. "I know, I'm so sorry."

He scoffs. "He might have deserved it, now that I look back on it, but it's what your father did that cemented his fate."

I look up at him and wait.

"Our families negotiated a settlement for the loss, and to keep it quiet. My uncle Roger helped my mother. Roger offered that the best way to fix it was to create an ironclad agreement - a marriage. He wanted a marriage contract for you and I. He told me all about it, and that's when I started paying attention to you. Noticing how perfect and beautiful you were, and I knew even at 12 that you were meant to be mine."

At 12, I already belonged to Owen. He'd gotten into my soul on day one. Elton never stood a chance.

"Your father rejected it. He didn't want our family connected to his after what my father did, and my mother agreed. She agreed!" Elton is building up a head of steam now, and I can see the red spreading across his skin indicating his fury.

"You were mine! They kept me from having you!"

"I'm sorry, Elton."

"It's okay, cupcake." He takes a few deep breaths. "They kept us apart, but apparently, that didn't stop our parents from fucking each other."

My head snaps up. "What?"

"Oh yeah," he laughs without humor. "They were "grieving," according to my whore mother, and found solace in each other. Our parents fucked and then my mom got pregnant and kept it a secret. I made her keep it a secret, even after Aspen was born. That little mutt turned out to be useful, but fuck I hate her."

"Aspen, the girl, that's Aspen?" I feel frozen, my body still as my brain processes everything.

"The bastard Sorrelle sister. She connects us forever," he growls as he turns to me and stares me down. I nod, accepting this.

Of course she looked like little me, she's one of us. Bastard or not, she's one of us. She's one of my sisters, and I have to fight for her. I might not be able to save myself, but I have to find a way to save her.

"Did my dad know?"

Elton snorts. "Fuck, no. When I say secret, I mean top fucking secret. I made mom keep her at home, and Aspen joined her little hacker collective, and I made sure she hated everyone and everything except that fucking computer."

More pieces fall into place. Aspen was the hacker that was messing with Designation, or at least, she was one of them. It makes me feel even more connected to her because I see pieces of my sisters in her now. She looks like me but she thinks like Aster, could even out-maneuver her on a computer. I feel a weird sense of pride.

I want to talk to her so badly, but I need Elton to keep going.

"Why do this, then? Why not come to me?"

"You don't get it," he rages and wipes everything from the fireplace mantle. "I tried again. I approached your father and he said no. He rejected me without even bringing the option to you, and I know you would have said yes. I had to have you."

"Wait...this is about me?" No. That can't be true. I'm...nothing. Sure, he's been obsessed with me but there would be no reason to go to these lengths only for me. My mind rejects it.

Elton rushes over to kneel in front of me and takes my hands in his, then kisses them fiercely. "Of course it is. I love you. We are meant to be together. I needed everyone to be out of the way. There could only be me. I needed them to understand what I would do to have you, to fear getting in my way. Anyone who stood between us needed to be dealt with."

"You killed my dad. You tried to kill my sister."

I was trying so hard to hold on to my control and the facade, but knowing this all happened because of me shatters the mask. I can't fake anything anymore. I would rather hurt than lie. He is beyond deranged. Not only because of his delusion of us, but because of what he had done to Aspen. To Aster. Even though he hadn't held the knife, my father's blood was on his hands. The marks on Aro's soul that she tried to drown were on him. He had tried to ruin my family. Elton didn't know or understand me at all if he thought I could let that go.

I'd always feared that somehow I was to blame for what had happened. That it was all my fault because I wasn't doing enough.

It was my fault. I had done this to us by existing.

This psychopath had decided on me, and he had put my entire family through hell to have me.

Later I'll remind myself that his choices did this to us. That I didn't consciously do anything to cause this, but right now, all I can feel is blame. A swirling whirlpool of guilt that wants to drag me under.

My breathing is getting thin.

"Not this again," Elton grumbles as he stands up. He slaps me. "Snap out of it." I gasp but it's not good enough for him so he does it twice more, until I can look up into his face.

"This is my fault."

"Of course it is," he sneers at me. "I gave you so many chances and you were oblivious, and then your family got in the way. I had to do this because you didn't see me, Anora." He roughly grabs my face. "Now you only see me. Forever."

He forces a kiss on my stiff mouth and leaves me there.

I don't know how much time passes. I can hear him humming to himself and moving things around in the kitchen as he cooks something. A movement in my periphery wakes me up, and I see Aspen tiptoe into the room.

Tears well as soon as we lock eyes and I reach out for her. "You're my sister."

She stills, then comes closer, more tentative than before.

"I thought you'd be mad."

"No," the tears fall and my voice cracks. "You're ours. If we'd known..."

"Your dad knew. He rejected me." There's fury in her voice, and I vehemently shake my head.

"No. Elton said he didn't know."

Her head whips to the kitchen and her teeth pull back in a snarl. "That motherfucker." Aspen curls her hands into fists and I watch as she forces herself to let it go. "He spent my whole life telling me that I was unwanted. That I was your dad's dirty little secret. Not good enough to be with his real daughters."

"He wasn't like that. We aren't like that. We would have loved you so much."

"I hate him." There's venom in her voice that resonates with me.

I smile at the strength of her hatred and when she looks back at me she's confused.

"You might have grown up a Forrester, but you're a Sorrelle, Aspen. That fire in you, that's us. I have to get you out of here."

220

"There's no escape. If we run, he'll kill us."

"We don't run, we stand." I reach out for her again and she takes my hand. "Can you get to a computer?"

"Yeah."

"Drop a crumb. Aster will find it. They'll find us."

"I don't even know where we are."

"It doesn't matter. Make it something she can follow, and she'll find us."

"If he catches me, I'm dead."

I hate that I know it's true. I know that if she openly crosses him, he'll kill her.

"It's our only chance to get home."

Aspen stares at me, a war in her gaze.

"It's your home, too. Let me take you home, Aspen. Where you belong."

She shakes her head. "I don't belong anywhere."

"You're wrong. Everything he's ever told you is wrong," I whisper and squeeze her hand.

Aspen shrugs. "If the chance comes, I'll take it."

That's all I can ask of her.

36

Owen

Days pass with nothing. I'm in Aster's room reading through financial records, Isaac is snoring softly on her bed, and she's writing code that I can barely follow. I'm good, and I'm smart, but I am nothing compared to Aster.

We're tracking every relative, every account, everything that Elton might have touched to do all the things that he's done. It's not impossible to go off grid, but I know Elton likes things a certain way and some of those things will require payment that can't be done in cash.

Aster's phone buzzes and she ignores it. It rings again, and I look over to see "Dominic Kanso" on the screen. I know Dom, he works in her team at Designation. He's a good guy, and he knows something is going on with our family. Everyone knows that there was an "accident" at the wedding and it's why both Aster and I have taken a leave of absence. I'm glad I have people I trust keeping it safe until we can come back.

I take Aster's phone as she continues to ignore it.

"Carver," I answer. There's a long pause because I'm sure he's confused.

"Uh, I thought Aster would want to know we got a weird ping in the system."

"I'm listening," I prompt him.

"One of the systems we built for the hacker awhile back, it was triggered, but it left a trace."

"Is it the same hacker?"

Aster has tuned into the conversation and whirls her chair around to face me.

"The signature is there."

"Find the location–" I start but Aster rips the phone away from me and starts talking rapidly, and then turns back to her computer. I watch her remote in and mirror Dom's screen so she can see everything he sees.

She moves over to another setup on her desk and starts running a program. Aster pulls the phone away from her ear and taps the screen to put it on speaker.

"What's going on Aster?" Dom asks and I can hear him typing and clicking in the background. "What are we getting into?"

Aster looks at me and nods. She trusts Dom.

"Someone took Anora. We think this might be her location," I answer him.

"Fuck. Okay. Whatever you need."

"I'll call you," Aster says and then ends the call. "I'm tracing the source right now. It might be where they are, it might be another stop in the path."

"It's a lead."

Aster nods and wheels over to shake Isaac. "Get up babe, we got something."

Isaac springs up and looks around, then shakes his head. "Let's work."

I leave them to it, and go pace in my office until Aster runs in almost an hour later.

"We got something."

Derick flew to Chicago as soon as I called him and Alina; she made me promise that we'd wait until he could be there. It worked out, as that's as much time as we needed to the Montaignes to pull everything together. An unmarked van, weaponry and tactical gear, and Michel had gone ahead to scout out the location.

Gailen was staying at the house, since he was still recovering from his broken arm. I tried to convince Aster and Aro to stay, but they both gave me a look so furious I was very sure they were sisters, and unsure which one was scarier in that moment.

The van ride was quiet. The tension was thick, and it made my skin crawl. We were all on alert, ready for anything when we got to this house in the middle of the woods. Michel hadn't seen anyone go in or out, and he hadn't even seen anyone moving in the windows. It looked empty, except the electricity was running, there was a fire in the hearth, and smoke from the chimney. Someone was using it and even inside they were keeping a low profile.

The house was bought with an all cash offer from a friend of Gloria Forrester's father. He had died and the house had been sitting doing nothing for years. Elton purchased it directly from the man's heir. I don't know how he knew about it, but it was a connection far enough removed that we hadn't looked into yet. I want to believe we would have found it eventually.

As it was, Anora had been with him for almost two weeks. Anything could have happened.

I don't let myself think about exactly what that might entail. I can't now.

"We've already lost enough family to this asshole," I tell everyone. "We will not lose her. If we have to take him out, I don't care who takes the shot. I want him gone more than I want him punished."

"Dibs," Aster raises her hand.

I give her the finger, and she gives it back. "No dibs. We get Anora, we take Elton down."

"Okay," she relents.

The van stops at a seemingly random spot in the road, and we pile out. Michel emerges from the trees.

"Follow me. There's no sensors or security of any kind." He meets my eyes. "She might not be here."

"I know."

He nods, and we follow him through the woods. I fall back, keeping an eye out behind us just in case. I watch Aro reach over and take Harp's hand. He looks at her with such stunning care, and I'm jealous for a moment of how open they are. I've held back around everyone for so long, and I vow to myself I'll never waste another second not letting the entire world see how much I love Anora.

No one will be able to look at us and not know how devoted I am to her. That she's my entire world. I have wasted time trying to do the right thing instead of what I wanted, and that's done. Even with us finally getting married I was letting the idea that it was a strategic marriage live instead of declaring that it was love. That I loved her, owned her, was owned by her. That I was lucky she'd agreed to marry me, that I didn't deserve her love, I didn't deserve her being willing to tie her fate to mine forever.

Maybe we never had a choice. No one else has ever drawn my attention, it was only ever her. Anora never even looked at anyone else. Even when she was supposed to marry Derick, who was handsome as hell, she didn't care. Maybe it's because we loved each other so young, or maybe it's because we're fated. One soul, one heart, one purpose in two bodies. It would never make sense with anyone else. I could never feel with anyone else the way I do with her.

We reach the edge of the woods and the house is in sight.

Michel is in charge, as he had been when we rescued Sophie, and directs each of us to an entrance, and an assigned role once we were inside. Rafe is at my back, even though he's barely healed. Sophie is waiting at the Sorrelle house with Gailen, furious that Rafe would go but also understanding why he needed to. I think I'd apologized to them too much in the last few weeks and I hoped I wouldn't have to do it again when this was done.

On Michel's signal, we open both doors. They're unlocked. If anyone is here, they aren't expecting to be found.

Michel's plan is to draw out any security, so after looking inside and seeing no one, I throw a flash bang into the hall in front of me and close the door. The bang rattles the door, and it's shortly followed by a second bang from the back of the house.

After minutes of waiting, no one comes. There's not a sound.

I open the door, gun ready, Rafe covering me. There's still no one. We move through the house, checking each room. Thierry and Lothaire go upstairs, and come back down shaking their heads. The house is lived in but there's no one that we can find. We aren't exactly quiet in our search, opening doors and moving furniture.

Derick calls to me and when I approach, I see he's found a door to the basement.

I head down, hoping like hell she's here.

37

Anora

I wake up in semi-darkness to hands on my body. The door to my prison is open and the light from the hall spills inside. Elton's shape looms over me, running over me over my clothes. I took the hoodie off to go to sleep, and now I regret it as he palms my breasts over the thin tank top and pinches my nipples.

"I need more from you. I need to touch you," he murmurs in the dark before putting his mouth on me. I don't move. I can't. He'll do what he wants and then he'll go. I have to believe that. I have to believe he won't take things too far or I'll disconnect from myself so thoroughly I'll never find a way back.

He rips the tank top down the middle and starts sucking and biting my skin. It hurts but I barely feel it. I hiss when his teeth sink into the flesh of my breast, and strangle a whimper when he bites my nipple.

I was scared that I'd like it. I was scared that my body would react to his rough touches the way I did to Owen's. There's nothing I love more than Owen biting and marking me. There's a scar near my shoulder from the time I made him break the skin and truly, permanently, mark me. I get off on pain and I was afraid that I would feel the same arousal.

I don't respond to Elton's roughness because I don't want him. My body is repulsed.

Elton shoves his hand under my pants and forces a finger inside me. It burns, and my body tries to buck away from him, but he groans as if I'm into it. He starts shoving his finger in and out of my dry vagina, pressing his face into my skin as he grinds his hips against me and then shoves in a second finger.

"So untouched. So pure." He bites and sucks the side of my breast. "I'm going to ruin you."

I take a deep breath and hold it, trying to force the muscles in my lower body to relax and not fight his invasion. It hurts so badly and I am trying to control my reactions.

A loud bang echoes through the hallway. We both freeze, wondering if it was something intentional. Another bang.

Elton rips his hand out of me and I cry out at the pain.

"I'll be back to finish you, cupcake." He kisses me and wipes his hand on my pants. I'm relieved when he doesn't close the door and I can still see. I discard the torn tank top and put the hoodie back on without looking down at my chest. I don't think I could handle seeing marks made by someone else on me. Not yet. I close my legs and curl up in a ball. The burn is still there, and I feel raw. I try and tell myself it could've been worse.

There's rumbling and banging upstairs, like furniture is falling over, and I hear the thump of feet. I'm afraid to yell for help. I want to, but this could be a trick. Elton could get to me before they do and hurt me for betraying him. I have no idea who's up there.

"Anora!"

I know that voice. Tears immediately fall. "Owen!" I start screaming it over and over, hoping that I haven't lost my mind. There's another loud thump above me, something more is happening up there, but all I can focus on is his voice getting closer.

A silhouette takes up the door and I can't see who it is. I cower back on the bed as the lights flash on. I nearly scream when I see Owen instead of Elton.

"Anora," he sighs and rushes to me. When he gathers me in his arms I cling to him, my nails aching with how deeply I'm digging them into his clothes. I have to hold onto him. I have to touch him to believe that this is real. He's here. I'm safe. I'm saved.

He kisses my forehead and presses himself against me like he can't believe it's real either.

"I've got you."

"Get me out of here," I sob. He has to let me go so he can take out a pair of pliers. It takes a few tries but the lock on the manacle snaps. My ankle is free for the first time in days. I scramble into Owen's lap as soon as his hands are free.

Owen rearranges his hold on me and then stands up, carrying me in his arms. I can't look away from him as we move through the house, afraid that if I look away he'll be gone.

"He's got her!"

Then we're both engulfed in familiar arms and there's ginger hair in my face. I start crying harder and I try to speak but I can't. Rafe is alive. Alive and well enough to come with them to save me. The three of us stay trapped in this hug, standing in place, and it reassures me that we're safe now.

"I'm sorry," I sob at Rafe when I can finally speak.

"It wasn't you, peanut. I'm fine."

Owen starts moving again and I feel free air for the first time since the wedding. I take a deep breath and shift for Owen to let me down. I turn to face my prison. It's an old, huge hunting lodge. In other circumstances it would be a beautiful place, a beautiful location.

My family converges on me - the only person who isn't here is Alina. It wouldn't be safe.

They surround me and I let the guilt drain out of me with each hug. Even Aster hugs me, and Isaac pats my back awkwardly. It makes me laugh and feel so much better. The euphoria of being safe is indescribable.

Aro holds me so tight I can't breathe, and I can't stop smiling.

The three remaining Montaigne brothers surround me, and I laugh as I disappear inside the cave of their bodies. I want to laugh and smile uncontrollably, I want to scream with joy because I'm free.

I turn around to look at them. "Did you kill him?"

Owen and Rafe exchange a look. "He got away."

I nod, because nothing on this earth will stop us from hunting him down. He's a dead man walking. "What about Aspen?"

"Who?" Owen asks.

Now my chest tightens in panic. "The girl in the house. Did you find her? Did you see her?"

"There was no one else." Aster sounds confused. "It was just you and him."

She must be hiding. Without thinking about it, I charge back into the house. It doesn't scare me to go back inside, it scares me to think that he took her.

"ASPEN!" I shout, running through the upper levels that I never saw before. I push open each bedroom door and look under the beds and in the closets. I find a room full of computer equipment and look around as best I can trying to find her.

Owen and Aster are standing in the hallway when I step out. "We have to find her. We have to save her."

"Elton's sister? Why?" Aster steps into the room. "She clearly helped him."

I take a steadying breath. "How did you find me?"

"We got a ping from..." Aster trails off, looking around. "Son of a bitch. Shes Sn0wWh1te."

I nod. "And she's our sister."

Aster flinches and steps back like I hit her.

"We have a lot to talk about."

"Let's get you home." Owen offers me his hand and I step past it and into his arms. I keep close to him as we leave once again. We pile into a van and I crawl into Owen's lap, burying my face in his neck. I'm never leaving him again.

"Where are we?"

"Michigan," Aster answers. "It's only a few hours to get home."

"Is Alina there?"

"No. She's back in Seattle."

I turn toward my brother in law. "Derick. You didn't have to do this."

He pats my arm. "Yes, I did." We smile at each other, and I'm so glad I didn't marry him.

"When we get home, I want to tell everyone, all at once. I need to get it out. Okay?"

They all nod in agreement. I lean on Owen and close my eyes. We won this battle, but the war isn't over.

VI

Whole

38

Anora

"Well, medically, you're fine. Dehydrated and bruised, but nothing that won't heal with rest. A lot of rest," Dr. Napoli looks at me over her glasses. She's been our family doctor for years and was willing to make a house call.

"Rest sounds good." I put back on the giant fuzzy sweatshirt I picked. I want to drown in my clothes. My body still hurts and I don't want to see myself.

"Honey," she says as she scoots closer to me on the bed. "Were you assaulted? Do I need to prescribe prophylaxis?"

"He touched me," I gulp, "but I'm okay. Dr. Landry and I can unpack it all."

She nods. "And mentally?"

"Not spiraling. I'm happy to be back on my medication, but I'm okay. Glad to be home."

"I don't know a lot about trauma, but I know it's going to come in waves. Don't hesitate to ask for help." She pats my hand and packs up her things. "Call if you need me."

"Thank you." I slide off the bed and follow her out of my room. We walk downstairs together and everyone is in the main sitting room.

They turn to look at us as one. I thank Dr. Napoli again and step into the room.

"I'm all good. Let's get this done."

"We can wait," Owen starts, moving toward me as if to guide me out of the room. I shake my head but step into him.

"No. You don't need to know what happened to me, but you need to know what I learned." I stare into the fireplace and watch as Derick pulls out his phone and in a few rings, Alina's voice comes through, a slight edge of panic.

"I'm okay!" I reassure her, another burst of euphoria giving me the energy to do this. "But I need to get this off my chest. As soon as possible. Please."

"Okay. We love you," Alina answers. I nod even though she can't see me.

Then I start talking. I can't look at them. I can't see Aster understand the part she played in this when I talk about what spurred Elton's obsession with me. To be honest, I can't deal with anyone else's emotions yet. I tell them about Roger's role in the negotiations over Benjamin Lassiter's death. I gloss over Elton stalking me for the last decade and a half, but I'm honest that all of this is because he wanted me.

That he killed dad to punish him for rejecting his offers of marriage, and thought dad was in the way of Elton having me. It breaks me, even though I have so much more to say. This was because of me.

"We don't blame you," Aro rushes as silence falls. "He made his choices and you didn't do anything. This is not your fault."

"Isn't it? If he'd never wanted me this never would have happened."

"If I hadn't killed his father," Aster trails off. "Even if I hadn't, what if he'd become fixated on you anyway? What if there's no reason any of it happened?" Her voice is harsh but it's a defense because she's emotional. Isaac puts his hand on the back of her neck and I watch as

236

she melts under his touch.

"The only person to blame is Elton Forrester," Alina says through the phone. "None of this is on you."

"Okay," I nod and take a deep breath. "After that was done, dad and Gloria…got close." I'm trying to be delicate. "Gloria got pregnant."

The silence is heavy. "What are you saying?" Aro asks.

"Dad got Gloria pregnant. He didn't know. She had the baby. That's Aspen."

Everyone looks as shocked as I felt, and I don't say anything. I have to let that bomb sink in. If dad had known, we could have saved Aspen from a life of Elton's abuse and control.

"Elton forced his mom to keep her a secret, but Aspen is our half-sister."

"Are you sure?" Aster asks. "He could have just told you that…"

"She looks like me. Like us. I know it." I look around at them all, willing them to believe me. "We have to find her. I'm afraid he'll kill her."

"She saved you, of course we'll save her," Owen answers. The others nod.

"It won't be so easy for him to hide again. I'll keep everything running." Aster stands and wipes her hands on her pants. "I have to start looking."

I stand and make her hug me. In that moment I'm so grateful for her support there's nothing else I can do except show her. She didn't question our responsibility to Aspen at all. Aster lets me embrace her, and even though her arms don't wrap around me, I feel her lean on me. That's all I needed.

"She's one of us," Aster says gruffly.

"She is." We step back from each other and she gives me a firm nod, before jerking her head at Isaac to go upstairs and get to work.

I turn back to everyone else. "Thank you. For coming for me."

"Of course we came for you," Aro answers. "We'd fall apart without you."

I laugh through my tears. Enough peopling. I'm burnt out and need that rest the doctor ordered. "Come on, Owen."

Without looking back, I leave the room and walk back upstairs. I don't go into my room, I go into his, and crawl beneath his covers. His pillow smells like him and I press my face into and inhale the safe, familiar scent of him. I want to wake up in this bed with him every day for the rest of my life.

Owen slides in on the other side but doesn't touch me. I scoot back until my body is lined up with his.

"Touch me, you idiot."

Owen rolls onto his side and wraps his arm around me, spooning me into his body. I sigh happily. This is where I belong. This is my home.

We lay there for a long moment, and then I notice my phone sitting on his bedside table. He must've gotten it from my things after the wedding was attacked. I turn it on and watch the buzz as a million notifications find their way to me. After it stops, I start with my messages. I pause when I see that I have multiple from Owen.

I open the thread. There's a message for every day I was gone. Sometimes it was his usual, simple, *"I love you,"* but other nights there was more.

O: *I'll find you. I love you.*

O: *I'm never living without you again, I won't survive it. I love you.*

O: *I can't wait to see your smile. I love you.*

Then the last message from yesterday.

O: *I'm coming for you, Button. I love you.*

"Owen," I stutter as tears form in my eyes. I roll over to face him and the reverence mingled with pain in his expression undoes me completely. "I love you."

He gives me a small smile. "I couldn't miss a night. It would have felt like giving up."

"I don't deserve you."

Owen glares. "Yes you do." Then he rolls me over and roughly pulls me back to him, lining up every inch of me to him. I am completely surrounded, and completely safe. We breathe together for a long time and enjoy the feeling.

"What happened to you?" he whispers against my neck.

"I don't want you to think I'm fragile. Or that you can't be with me."

"You are fragile, but nothing could take you away from me. Never again."

I nod and pull his hand up to my mouth, kissing his knuckles. It's a little bit like deja vu because we were in this same bed when he told me the truth about his parents and everything they had done to him. The first time that Owen truly opened up to me and showed me all of the hurt inside of him. I'll give him the same in return, because even when it hurts, it's better to know.

I tell him everything. Every bruise, every bite, every touch. I tell him every lie I told to keep Elton at bay. We laugh together, probably hysterically, when he hears that I told Elton I was a virgin. That Elton believed it.

"I got the idea from Sophie. You know that's why they didn't touch her, right?"

"No. I think I owe her a lot of gifts."

"We both do. I don't know if I would have made it through the same without knowing what she went through. I could lie because of Sophie."

"What are best friends for?" he replies, and I snort into his arm.

When I'm done telling him everything up until the moment their rescue began, I roll over to face him. His blue eyes are stormy and full of heartbreak.

"How can I help?" His voice is low and raspy. He's barely keeping it together.

I push him back and he goes, looking wary when I throw my leg over his hips and straddle him. Keeping my eyes on his, I remove my fluffy sweatshirt, then my tank top. Owen doesn't look away from me. I know it's not pretty - there are bruises from the beating and hickeys from the assault.

I take Owen's hand in mine, and press it to my hip.

"Touch me. Remind me that I can feel good. I can feel pleasure. Remind me that I can feel at all. Love me, Owen. Love me like you always have."

"The way I always will." His grip is firmer, and I let my hands drop so he can move. He trails his fingertips over the bruises, and the little flashes of pain have me clenching around nothing. He's taking the pain someone else caused and making it ours. I moan when he cups my breasts and my head falls back when he tweaks my nipples. It's not about how I'm being touched, it's who is touching me. I am a lock and he is the only key.

"Fuck," he growls before arching up to take my nipple in his mouth. Owen sucks deep and hard, and my hands dive into his hair. This is the last piece I needed to feel safe and whole again. I'm where I need to be, I'm the best version of myself.

I grind in his lap and smile as I feel him get hard under me.

"I need you," I beg. "Please."

With a snarl, Owen lets my nipple go and rolls us over so I'm underneath him. I start undoing his pants but he moves away from me as he yanks down mine. He's a desperate beast and I am happy to be his prey as he moves between my legs and dives into my core with his mouth. His tongue slides through me and he sucks my clit ferociously.

I hold him there and roll my hips, chasing the feeling of him.

Relishing the way he touches me and the way it makes me feel. Owen bites my clit and I cry out, the pleasure overwhelming.

"More," I beg, and he slides his fingers inside me. I tense for a second, afraid that it will hurt in the way I don't like, but I'm so wet they glide in easily. My body relaxes again, moving with and against him as he works me toward an orgasm. With his free hand, Owen reaches up and toys with my nipples, teasing the tips softly and then pinching hard, over and over. The contrast drives me crazy, and I'm milking Owen's fingers with my body.

"Come for me, my love, give me your pleasure."

Hearing his voice and the hard press of his fingers against the front wall of my pussy sends me over the edge. He pushes as my core muscles convulse around him and I cry out in bliss as my orgasm overwhelms me. Owen sucks on my clit through it all, driving me to the brink of my comprehension. I'm breathing hard when he lets me go, and flinch and then giggle when he slaps my clit as he sits up.

"More," I beg again, and sit up to finish removing his pants. "Fuck me like you lost me."

He leans over me and lines his furiously hard cock up with my entrance. "I've done that before." Owen slams into me and I scream at the pleasurable intrusion, all of my muscles spasming as I try to keep control. My thighs squeeze his hips and I writhe, pressing my hips up to take him deeper.

"No one will ever take you away from me," he grunts and thrusts, slow but unbelievably forceful. "You are mine, Anora Sorrelle. Your heart, your mind, your sweet pussy," he groans as he presses deep and stays that way, grinding his hips into my clit. "Your soul." Owen looks down into my eyes and I can only nod, incapable of speech because I'm mindless with how good this feels. "I own every inch of you, and no one is going to touch what's mine."

Owen presses against me and sinks his teeth into my neck, right over the scar he already left. My orgasm hits like lightning at the mix of pain with the ecstasy of the way he's fucking me. I bury my face in his shoulder and scream, clinging to him as my body is ravaged, every nerve alight and awake. It's so powerful I think I'm losing consciousness.

As it ebbs I crash back onto the bed and Owen groans as he comes, releasing himself now that he knows he got me.

"I love you," he says as he presses kisses over my cheeks and eyelids. "You are my soul. All the things about me that matter are tied up in you, and I cannot exist without you."

My eyes open slowly and I ache for the pain that's still swirling in his.

"I love you. I live for you. I will never give up as long as I have you."

Owen kisses my lips gently. Now that I'm whole again, I'm ready to keep fighting.

39

Anora

We get a few hours of sleep before we're awakened by a pounding on the door. Somehow I manage to get to it and open it, only to find a terrified and disheveled Derick.

"Alina's in labor."

"Fuck," I hiss. "Okay. Front door, 15 minutes, you get your plane ready."

"You're all coming?" He looks so scared, and knowing what I do now about his family's history, I understand. The fact that he's here, even at Alina's instruction, instead of with her, means he needs us more than ever.

"Of course we are."

"Are you sure?"

"I'm good. I wouldn't miss this for the world."

Derick swallows heavily and nods, and then backs off down the hall. When I turn around Owen is already dressed and heading toward the bathroom with a small travel bag.

"My stuff, too."

"Of course. Rally the troops. Again."

I go from room to room, banging on every door, waking everyone up. Rafe and Sophie were crashing here as well, and they decide to come along.

"I feel like it's bad luck if we leave," Sophie tells me, throwing on her clothes and throwing some essentials in her purse. "We have to be with you right now."

"There's room on the plane," I reassure them.

Everyone is waiting in the front hall, and Owen takes charge dividing up guards and cars to get us to the airfield. He drives with Alonzo, and I pile into the back with Derick, Rafe, and Sophie. I take Derick's hand and reassure him.

"Alina is the toughest person we know, the pregnancy has been really healthy, and labor has been normal so far. It's going to be fine."

"It's going to be fine," he repeats.

"First babies take a long time, her contractions are still far apart. Cara and Kade are with her, and she sounded excited when she called, right?"

"She did." He nods. We're speeding along the roads in the early hours of the morning, and definitely aren't obeying speed limits.

"Do you have a name picked out?"

"I'm not supposed to tell," Derick smiles a little.

"Okay. I can't believe you agreed on a name, actually."

He laughs with me. "She got a baby name book and would open a random page and put her finger on a name. The first time she did it, the name it landed on happens to be Welsh. She never got it out of her head, and I wasn't going to argue with that."

"I love that."

"We want the middle name to be Donald," Derick says quietly, like it's going to upset me.

"I love that even more."

After 22 hours of labor, Wyn Donald Clayton joins the family.

If they'd rescued me a day later, I would have missed this.

Derick or I were with Alina for the entire labor. I held her hand and her leg as she pushed my nephew into the world, encouraging her as she gazed into her husband's eyes and he told her she could do this. Derick told her she was the strongest, most beautiful woman in the world and with a little more pushing they would meet their son.

It was the most amazing thing I'd ever experienced.

I cried as Wyn was placed on Alina's chest, and after kissing her on the forehead, I left the three of them to bask in the moment until they were ready for us.

When I walked into the waiting room where our entire crew was assembled, I got to announce the arrival of our nephew. We were catastrophically loud, even for the labor and delivery floor, and a nurse came in to tell us to quiet down.

Everyone hugged, a bottle of sparkling grape juice was popped, and we passed it around taking sips and toasting baby Wyn.

I find myself in a corner of the room with Aro and Aster. As always, Aro starts the group hug but Aster doesn't resist. We stand together, arms around each other, acknowledging that this changes things. A new generation is in the world now. We're growing.

So much has changed for us in the last year. More than we ever could have anticipated, but this is the thing that remains: we love each other. We don't always like each other, but I love my sisters so fiercely that I would do anything for their safety and happiness. It makes my heart ache for Aspen. She doesn't know what this feels like, and I know without a doubt that we will make space for her.

After we step away from each other, I find Owen and bury myself in his arms.

"I want a baby." I tell him.

He smiles down at me and I go up on my toes to kiss him. "I'm ready when you are."

I grin up at him, feeling more content than I thought possible. In a way, my ability to retreat and hide inside myself saved me while I was taken. I know that what I went through is going to hit me, but right now I keep getting distracted and I can't be sorry. I'm beyond exhausted, but I wouldn't change a thing.

Alina needed me, and because the people in this room saved me, I was there for her.

The group settles back down into our seats and I curl up on Owen's lap. He throws his coat over me and my eyes close.

A few hours later, Derick wakes everyone up. Wyn is ready for pairs of two to meet him. I offer to go last since I saw him first. I doze against Owen until it's our turn.

In the room, Alina is holding the tiny bundle that is our nephew. She smiles, still tired, but happier than I've ever seen her. I lean into Owen as I look down at Wyn's little face. He's a scrunchy old man and I love it.

"You can hold him." She holds him out to me and I take him, almost surprised by how light he is. I haven't held a baby in a long time. Automatically, I sway him. Owen puts a hand on my shoulder and leans over me, looking down at Wyn.

"Congratulations. He's perfect," Owen says, then kisses my temple. "As soon as we get married, we'll get to it." I laugh with him and look up to see Alina and Derick exchange a look.

"Let's do that then," Alina says. "There's a chapel here. I won't be able to travel for a while. I don't think you should put it off another day."

I stare at my sister. "You were questioning this literally up until the moment you left me to walk down the aisle."

"I know." She looks ashamed. "And I'm sorry." Her gaze slides from me to Owen. "But I saw him when he realized you were gone, and I know that I was wrong. I don't want anything to keep the two of you apart. Please."

"Our license is still valid," Owen says. "As long as we have witnesses and an officiant."

"I think I can handle the officiant. Go home, get cleaned up, I'll call you." Derick nods at us, and finishes a text. "Now give me my baby."

I smile as I hand Wyn over to his daddy, and delight in seeing my sister's family grow. I vow to myself that it's only the beginning, and nothing will stop any of us from flourishing.

"You want to do this?" Owen asks as we walk back to the waiting room.

"I don't need the big wedding. I only need you." I tug his arm until he leans in and kisses me. "Marry me. Today."

"Anything you want, Button."

In 6 hours, we put together a wedding. That's a new record for me.

Derick found an officiant, Aro found me a white dress, and Aster and Isaac got me flowers. Everyone is inside the small chapel, and Rafe and I wait outside the doors.

"At least this time if someone stabs me, I'll get prompt medical attention," Rafe jokes.

"Too soon." I lean on him and he kisses the top of my head. "Thank you for taking care of him when I couldn't. When I wasn't ready."

"I knew you'd come around," he winks at me. "What's meant to be always finds a way, right?" He steps forward and opens the door to the chapel, and we step inside.

It's a cozy space with a few rows of pews and a small altar at the front. Owen stands next to a man in a dark suit, who I assume is the judge that owed Derick a favor. A lot of people in this town owe Derick a favor.

I can't stop smiling when my eyes meet his, and this time, as Rafe starts escorting me toward my future husband, nothing happens. We walk past my assembled family and Rafe hugs Owen before he joins our hands together.

"We don't have our rings." It hits me then that we're missing this one detail.

"Yes we do," Owen replies, and pulls a box out of his pocket. "I've had them with me since the first time."

I start to cry as I open the box and see my diamond and amethyst ring with the matching band already soldered together, ready to be placed on my finger. His thicker, plain platinum band glints in the light. Owen hands them to the officiant, and turns back to me, taking both of my hands in his.

In this moment, there is nothing more important than for me to pledge my life to him. We repeat after the judge, we vow to be all things at all times, and then Owen is sliding my ring on my finger. It feels new and foreign, but it's a weight I want to get used to. I slide Owen's ring home. We made it. Finally.

"You may kiss the bride."

I don't wait. I jump into Owen's arms and kiss him. My husband.

40

Owen

We stay in Seattle until Alina, Derick, and Wyn go home from the hospital. It's a teary goodbye between the sisters, and I love seeing that the damage the last year has done is being healed. The tension that was between them all before our first wedding is gone. The Sorrelles are back, and they are not to be fucked with.

Aster and Isaac have been having a much easier time tracking Elton. He's gotten sloppy because things didn't go according to plan. Even though we don't have a location, we know he's spending money. On the flight back to Chicago, she lays everything out for us.

"He's out of support, even though he's got financial resources. He's just not smart enough to do what he did before, and he doesn't have the time. He knows he's a dead man and he's panicking." She pulls up his financial records. "He bought tickets to a bunch of different destinations thinking he could fool us with that, but he never got on any of the flights. I think he's got a car. I think he's mobile, but it's figuring out how to narrow down the search for which direction he went."

"Do you think he crossed into Canada? A day's drive across Michigan would get him there." It's what I would do.

"No," Aster shakes her head. "There's too many ways for us to find out if he did."

"I think he's going to New York," Aro chimes in. "David didn't seem to be involved at all, he didn't speak to Gloria or Roger based on his records, but I think Elton is desperate enough to try."

"Check their property holdings. They might not help directly, but they might be willing to give him some place to lay low," I muse. "What was your impression of David Forrester?"

Harp types on his tablet and I wait. Aro whispers something over his shoulder and he nods. The computerized voice starts speaking: *He's a rich bastard but not up to anything criminal. Faithful to his wife. Good with his kids. Nothing that seemed out of the ordinary and no contact with anyone else in the family. He seems to have distanced himself from their reputation but he's also loyal.*

"If I reached out, how do you think he'd respond?"

"Family first," Aro answers. "He's not going to stop you, but he's not going to help you."

I nod. "See what you can find, track their communication and see if Elton gets in touch."

"Anything from Aspen?" Anora asks.

Aster shakes her head. "I've got Dom on it. I'm sure she's helping cover their tracks but she's not being as careful. I don't know that there would be time to do anything to alert us. Especially not if he's over her shoulder and watching every move."

"I hope she's okay," Anora sighs and leans on me.

"I can't wait to meet her." Aster shakes her head and closes the laptop. "The little shit nearly beat me."

"Only nearly," Isaac reassures her.

"I don't know what his next move is." A frustration headache is starting to build behind my eyes. "He's too arrogant to go on the run, but he's out of moves. He has to know there will never be another chance to get Anora."

"I think that makes him more dangerous," Anora says quietly, and we all turn to her. "This has been his purpose for so long, and to lose it means he's unmoored. Elton was already out of touch with reality, but now...there's no telling what he'll be willing to do to get his sense of control back."

I don't like the feeling that wells in me because I know she's right. Elton is more dangerous than he's ever been because it's an all or nothing situation for him now. It means wherever he is, whatever he's planning next, we might never be prepared enough. There's no way he's giving up or running. Not with the way he wants to take us down, and not with the delusional belief that Anora belongs to him.

The fear I feel for her resonates down to my bones. It's my job as her husband, as the person who loves her most in this world, to keep her safe. I feel like a failure already. I've worked my whole life to hold her up when her demons overwhelm her. I can get inside Anora's mind, I can fight beside her when she's fighting herself, but this outside threat is such an unknown. To most people it would be the other way around, but Anora and I are so entwined in one another's psyche that I think she could step inside my head just as easily.

We've grown up with so many of our experiences laid across one another that sometimes it feels like her memories are mine. In those years and years we spent together and talked every night, there were almost no secrets between us. We were still so innocent we didn't even know that maybe there should be. The only thing I kept from her was what happened at home, and even that came out eventually. Boundaries didn't exist for her and I, and they never really have. If we're together, we're one.

It's why losing her for so many years nearly killed me, but it was an experience I had to have in order to truly appreciate her. Even if I disagreed with her choices, it was important for us to be apart and try and find some semblance of what it meant to be our own people. After being on our own, it made coming together so much sweeter.

For the hundredth time, the pang of sadness that Don will never know runs through me. I think he did know about me and Anora, but I wish he could see it. I wish he could see the way she flourishes being open and in love. He never really saw her happy. He saw her content at best, even fulfilled when it came to her charity and non-profit work, but he never got to see his daughter when she wasn't keeping secrets. Don never got to see her beam with happiness because every part of her was finally free, and I hate that.

It's the closure we'll never get.

41

Anora

A new kind of anxiety is eating at me. It's not as overwhelming as what I've dealt with my entire life, but a constant thrum in the back of my head. We have to save Aspen. I'm more concerned with saving her than I am with finding Elton, which is saying a lot. If I had to choose between punishing him or getting her home, I'd pick her.

Owen can feel it churning inside me. I think they all can, but he's the only one that knows what I've dealt with my entire life and watches for it to turn into something more dangerous. Right now it keeps me going. It gives me energy to work and prepare, to make sure that everything in the house is running smoothly, and in a position where we can leave at a moment's notice.

I don't feel useless. I'm not drowning in a feeling of worthlessness, sure that I've let everyone down. I wish I'd never been taken, but I can't regret that it feels like we're racing toward a conclusion now. We will find Elton, we will remove the threat, and we will make our family complete. The threat has been nameless and faceless for so long that the more answers we have, the more confident I feel that we're on the edge of it being done.

It's like I've been living under a pendulum the last few years, watching it swing back and forth, getting closer and closer, bracing for the first cut. The first cut came and it was painful, but I survived.

The time is going to come soon when I get to figure out what comes next for me, and I have to figure out how to be more honest with my family. They think Owen is the only secret I've kept and they couldn't be more wrong. Given Alina's reaction and doubt regarding Owen, I highly doubt she's going to take the knowledge that I've tried to take my own life on more than one occasion in stride.

I'm going to be spending the next decade apologizing.

Part of me feels like I shouldn't have to, and part of me feels like it'll never be enough.

Owen wraps his arms around me from behind, stopping me from wearing a path in the carpet. After a very tense discussion with the assembled family, it was agreed that Owen and I should move into the master suite. It has enough closet space for both of us and at the end of the day, this is our house. With dad gone, the house passed to me.

It's time we start chasing out some of the ghosts.

"I love you," he whispers against my neck. "My wife."

I close my eyes, delighting that those words are true. "My husband."

"We found them."

I spin in his arms. "Where?"

"Upstate New York. A cabin belonging to a family member of David Forrester's wife. Aspen got a message through."

Relief floods me. "Of course she did."

"She gave us a name, Aster followed the thread. Then she hacked into a camera on the smart TV on the wifi network for the cabin and there they were." Owen's brow furrows.

"What?"

"Aspen doesn't look good. He's definitely been hurting her."

My blood boils and my hands clench into fists. "When do we leave?"

He steps away from me and I don't let him, closing the space between us. I know what he's going to say before he even opens his mouth, and it's not going to get him anywhere. This time, I'm the predator, and I track every step he takes back. Owen lifts his hands, trying to calm me down before he even sets me off.

"You're staying here."

"The fuck I am. I'll stay back until you have him, but I'm the one Aspen knows. She won't trust any of you. I need to be there." Owen pauses like that thought hadn't occurred to him. "She's an abused, traumatized teenage girl. I need to be there."

After watching his thoughts flash across his face, the resignation I see him settle on relaxes me.

"Okay. I understand." Then he dives into my space and wraps his hand around my neck, pulling me to him until we are forehead to forehead, and he is in complete control of me. "But you do everything we say. If I tell you to stay back, you stay back. I tell you to move, you move. I don't want you anywhere near him ever again. Got it?"

"Got it," I whisper in response. Owen smashes our mouths together, trapping me in a violent kiss that undoes me in moments. He breaks the kiss and pushes me down until I'm on my knees, looking up at him with lust and fury.

"Crawl to the bed. Take off your clothes. Bend over."

I nod, and do as he says. When I'm naked, I lay myself over the bed, pressing my face into the comforter and spread my legs apart. Owen comes up behind me and massages my ass cheeks, and I wait for the satisfying sizzle of his hand smacking my skin. He draws it out, making me aroused and needy, until I'm whimpering.

"Owen."

The word is barely out of my mouth before the first smack comes, and he keeps going until my ass cheeks burn in the most satisfying way. I hear him move behind me and jolt and then groan when he sinks his teeth into my abused cheek. He keeps sucking and biting my ass cheeks as he slides his hand along my slit, teasing my clit with all the wetness pooling there.

"You're going to do everything I tell you when we go. The obedience you show me in this room is going to extend outside of it. If you put yourself in danger, if you are hurt in any way, the moment you are healed there will be no mercy. If you thought I punished you before, wife, you have no idea."

He pinches my clit and as my orgasm unexpectedly blasts through me, I bury my face in the comforter to scream. It's not even over when Owen slides inside me, bending over me to torture the sensitive skin of my breasts and play with my nipples as he fucks me. I lay there and take it, loving the feeling of him owning me.

As another orgasm starts to build, he pulls out and flips me over. Owen slides his hand to the back of my neck, bowing my body and making me watch as he slides back inside me. I can't look away, and the position puts pressure on my g-spot in a way that makes me want to close my eyes in pleasure.

"I love you," I whimper as I spread my legs wider and rest my heels on his back.

"I love you beyond words and reason, Anora." His voice is deep and raspy, and I look away from our joining to meet his eyes. The love and obsession inside them makes a shiver run through me, and he speeds up his thrusts. I moan as I start to orgasm, the pleasure rippling through my body and causing all of me to tense.

I'm mesmerized watching Owen as he tips over the edge into his own release and fills me the way he was meant to, then yanks me to him. He stands next to the bed with my body wrapped around him, his cock still inside me, and our racing hearts thumping against one another.

I know he's scared to lose me again. I'm scared too. But I also know that this is the end we've been searching for. This is closure. We have to lay this past to rest in order to build our future.

42

Anora

This time it's family only. Alonzo is waiting with me in the woods as Owen, Gailen, Aster, Isaac, Harp, and Aro approach the cabin. If you'd told me a year ago that Aro would be this much of a badass, I would've laughed so hard. Now I look at my baby sister, scarred but unbroken, and I'm so proud of how far she's come and how much she's overcome to get there.

Gailen insisted on coming even though he's barely out of the cast for his broken arm.

I tried to tell him that he doesn't have anything to prove but he waved me off.

The group fans out and approaches the cabin. There's a front and back door, and it's kind of a sprawling ranch house out in the woods. Even from this distance, I can see Elton pacing in the great room of the house as it's nothing but windows.

I thought I'd feel afraid, but all I feel is angry.

I can't see Aspen anywhere.

They get closer when a loud siren echoes through the air.

"Fuck," Alonzo says. "This place has proximity alarms. He got smart."

I watch as Elton stops his pacing and picks up a gun. The group keeps going, and I hold my breath as I wait for them to enter. As I wait for anything to happen. Elton starts heading toward the front door, and as he opens it, Aro rushes in and takes him down.

I can't see anything then, they're out of sight of the windows as I assume everyone rushes inside. From here we can here thumps and crashing, even under the sound of the proximity alarm. I jolt when I hear the first gunshots, and then there's shouting, more shooting, and I am barely holding myself back from racing into the cabin.

"What's going on?"

"We have to wait, Anora."

"I know," I snap. Anxiety is racing along my veins and I start to shake with it.

A sharp, loud blast booms through the clearing. For a second, everything is silent. Then it's like sound comes back with a vengeance, and a wave of fire blasts through the great room. I can't see anyone inside, and no one is coming out.

Before Alonzo can stop me, I run toward the house because I have to get them out.

When I step inside, I nearly trip over Isaac. I squint my eyes and try to see through the smoke and heat. My family is laying on the floor, knocked out from whatever the fuck that firebomb was.

I grab Isaac by the protective vest around his shoulders and start dragging him out. Alonzo catches up to me and takes over.

"We have to get them out," I yell, and run back into the house. Aster is next, and she's easy to move given that she's tiny. Alonzo charges past me and grabs the next body. It's Owen, thank god. I step back inside to find Harp or Gailen.

The smoke is thick and it's getting hot, but the fire is mostly in the great room right now. We're near the kitchen and a hallway into the rest of the house. Aspen will be there. When I get them out, I can find her.

I take a step deeper, looking at the ground. A heavy body slams into me, tackling me to the ground. Immediately, I fight and squirm away, struggling out from underneath the weight.

"You came back to me," a voice whispers and a mouth is mashed up against my cheek. "I knew you would."

Elton straddles me and has his whole body weight holding me down. I don't stop fighting, and I try to smash my head into his. He laughs.

"We're going to stay right here. The last of our family. Me and you will go down together, my cupcake, my love." He sounds unhinged. "Aspen will burn with us. This is how it has to end or they'll stop us from being together. I thought I'd lost you, but now I get to die with you. Burn with me."

He presses me into the floor and I scream, trying to get anyone to hear me.

Elton is yanked off of me and thrown away. I look up to see Gailen over me, offering a hand to help me up. I stand quickly and Elton is behind him, gun aimed at his back.

"No," I yell, distracting him and pushing Gailen away. Elton looks to me and I run toward him, arms up and open as if I'm waiting for him to embrace me. The gun lowers and Elton opens his arms to me. I crouch slightly lower as I run, and dive my shoulder into his stomach.

Elton stumbles back and falls into a chair that's on fire. It consumes him immediately, racing along his clothes and engulfing his chest in flames. His screams haunt me for a moment, but when I turn away, I see Harp. He's too big for me to drag on my own. Gailen runs to me and we start pulling his body as the fire starts spreading, the heat pounding, and the wood crackling violently.

We're almost to the hall when Alonzo comes back.

"I need to find Aspen."

"Get out," Gailen yells, "I'll find her."

He moves away before I can stop him, and I help Alonzo get Harp onto the lawn. The house is burning, the flames licking through the roof. I wait and wait.

"Where is he?"

The others are waking up, and Alonzo says he called emergency services. I can already hear the sirens because we aren't too far from a city. Probably one of the reasons the family has the cabin.

Owen coughs and I look down at him, leaning over to look into his face.

"You good?" my voice is almost a whimper.

"Good enough."

"I need to go back in."

"No," Owen groans even though he sits up quickly and grabs me.

"Aspen is in there," I whimper. "I have to get her."

The words are barely out of my mouth when a man on fire comes charging out the door, a tiny body in his arms. For a second, I'm afraid that it's Elton, but I know he was more burned than this. I did it myself, and there was no coming out of that. It has to be Gailen.

We all run to him as he falls back onto the grass. I try and get Aspen out of his arms as the others pat him down and roll him around, putting out the flames. His face looks unharmed, the fire was confined to the back of him.

Finally, he loses consciousness and lets go of Aspen. I yank her into my lap, checking her for injuries. She's unconscious and definitely hurt, but she's breathing.

Elton is dead. I have Aspen.

My family is safe.

The glare Owen gives me when I tell the EMT that I ran into the burning cabin to save them is definitely going to earn me a punishment later. He's wearing an oxygen mask which should make him appear less threatening, but it's a look so powerful it overpowers even that.

I give him a shrug.

I'd do it again, no matter what punishment I earn.

After giving me an oxygen mask too, I move to sit next to Owen.

"I told you to stay."

"We never had a plan for if things went wrong."

"I told you to stay," he repeats, his growl sounding funny behind the mask.

"I couldn't lose you," I say as I lean my head on his shoulder. Owen sighs, and I know I won the argument, because it's the truth. If Alonzo and I hadn't run in there and dragged them out, there's a chance they could all be dead.

Gailen and Aspen were taken by ambulance immediately, their gurneys side by side. There was a burn on her face that looked painful, and I need to know if Elton did anything else to her. Where he kept her, what he did, why it took Gailen so long to get her out.

I can't believe he did that.

"What happened?" he asks me quietly.

"Elton attacked me. He said we were going to burn together. Gailen pulled him off." I take a deep breath because if he was mad about me dragging them out, he's really going to pissed off about the next part. "He was going to shoot Gailen, so I made him believe I was coming to him and I...I shoved him into the fire."

Owen is dead silent, and when I look over I don't see anger, I see shock.

"You pushed him into the fire."

"Yeah. Then we got Harp and Gailen went after Aspen. Then you woke up."

"Anora," Owen starts, but I shake my head.

"I heard him scream, and I didn't feel anything. I know I killed him, but honestly, I'm fine."

"If that's ever not the case, you come to me. You tell me right away."

We sit in silence as chaos continues around us.

"Do you think…Aspen will be upset with me?"

Owen stares down at his hands. "I doubt it. But if she is, we'll deal with it. We have her. She's safe now."

"Right." Tears finally fall as the truth of what happened hits me. Owen holds me as we breathe in the fresh oxygen, together and alive.

43

Owen

We are once again sitting in a hospital waiting room. This time, it's a much more broken and bedraggled group than the one that waited for the announcement of Wyn's birth. All of us were treated for minor burns and some cuts, but nothing overly serious.

I hope that puts karma on our side as we wait to hear about Gailen and Aspen. He came out of that house with his back on fire. There's a chance he won't survive. With Aspen there's a significant burn on her arm, as well as the damage the flash might have done to her eyesight, not to mention whatever the fuck that monster did to her while on the run. She couldn't save herself because she couldn't walk. It could be injury or malnutrition, and we can only wait and hope for them both.

I've never doubted Gailen's loyalty, even when I did question his judgment, but knowing he walked into that fire to rescue a girl he didn't even know was beyond what I would have asked of any of our staff. He risked his life for her. When he came out and collapsed, when we quickly snuffed out the flames, he never let her go.

We had to move his arms so that Anora could take Aspen, and then he finally collapsed into unconsciousness. I've never seen anything more brave, or more reckless. I'll pay whatever it takes, find whatever treatment he might need, and it still won't be enough.

Anora sits in her chair, soot on her face, and messages Alina on her phone. The groupchat has been working overtime as everyone gets updated, as the other members of our family deal with the fallout of everything that happened.

I was on the phone with my attorney the second I could breathe more freely. He's finding the records of Aspen's birth. If Don Sorrelle isn't listed as the father, he's got my permission to do whatever is necessary to get us granted guardianship of her until we can prove her relation to the Sorrelles via DNA. Harp is researching treatment options for what she's been through, both residential and outpatient, and he and Aro are going to assess what might be best to help Aspen recover.

When my parents died, I was barely older than her. Even though my home life had been hell, I'd at least had school and my weekends to escape and carve out some life for myself. I'd been able to get moments of relief and I think that saved me. Aspen never had that. She was a prisoner in her own home from the moment she was born, and I want nothing more than to help her figure out what her freedom looks like.

Anora will want to keep her close, and I understand why, but I also know that when you have been under someone's thumb for so long, never able to truly rest or have peace, sometimes that's not what you need. Whatever Aspen says she wants or needs, I'll try to convince Anora to go along with it for Aspen's best interest.

She might be a 15 year old girl, but she was never allowed to be a child. I'm going to trust her judgment of herself as best we can, as long as she's not hurting herself.

A nurse walks into the room and we all sit at attention. I stand and approach her, appointing myself as the person in charge of this motley brigade because in almost every sense, I am.

"Owen Carver?"

I wince. I'm making that name change official when we get home. I nod and she talks quietly.

"I have an update about Mr. Burke, and currently I can't speak to you about Ms. Forrester." My stomach churns at calling Aspen that. She doesn't belong to them. She's ours.

"A notice of guardianship should be coming shortly." My voice is more clipped than I mean it to be, and I give her a tight smile asking for pity, given our situations.

She nods. "Mr. Burke suffered third degree burns on his back as well as significant smoke inhalation that's straining his lungs. He's currently heavily sedated and will be for some time. The good news is that the damage was a smaller area than anticipated when he was brought in, but it's still serious. The doctor will want to meet with you, likely tomorrow, to discuss treatment options for the burns. Right now we're making sure the wound is clear and clean, and that should give some idea of what might be the best next step."

"Whatever it takes. Please let me know when the paperwork comes through and we can talk about Aspen."

The nurse gives me a sad smile and leaves the room. When I turn around, the troops have circled, and I fill them in on Gailen's injury. In a way, it's better than I expected. He's going to be in a fuck-ton of pain, but the nurse made it sound like we had options to help, and that he was out of the woods in terms of if he was going to make it or not. A new fight begins now to get him healed.

After everyone gets updated, we resume sitting and waiting. I get a text from my attorney that Don was listed as Aspen's father on her birth certificate, and since three of us in this room are legally related to him, they should be able to talk to us as the family of a minor.

Hours pass before a different nurse returns. It must have been a shift change.

"Mrs. Sorrelle?"

Anora stands and I follow, approaching the nurse together. I've never been this tired in my life, but this is where we need to be.

"Is this your husband?" The nurse asks. Anora nods and tries to offer a smile.

"Aspen has a third degree burn on her arm, and likely temporary vision damage in her left eye. We suspect there's also a tear in her right knee from a fall, and we'll do imaging within the next few hours to confirm now that the more acute issues are being handled."

We nod, demonstrating that we understand, and the nurse hesitates.

"She's quite emotional and afraid. I don't know what the situation was that you rescued her from, but we may need to sedate her."

"Okay," Anora agrees. "Can I see her? Does she know we're here?"

"She does, and she wanted to see you. She also asked after Mr. Burke but we can't disclose his condition."

"We can, thank you."

"This way." The nurse steps out of the room and Anora turns back to the group, murmuring that we're going to see Aspen and will be back soon. The rest of them are eager to meet her I know, but that time will come.

The small girl from the cabin seems even smaller in the bed, a single light shining down on her. There's a bandage over her left eye and the skin of her face is red and angry like a sunburn. When she hears our footsteps she jerks awake and then groans in pain. Her eye finds Anora, and then me. It rests on me with suspicion and mistrust, but I charge ahead. I don't think any of them will understand a part of her the way that I do, and I want to make sure she knows.

Anora runs right to Aspen and takes her undamaged hand. "I'm sorry we couldn't find you faster."

Aspen shakes her head. "It was less than 24 hours between my message and you showing up. I think you did okay."

Anora laughs, and Aspen turns her hand so that she's grasping Anora in return.

"This is Owen," Anora introduces me. "He's making sure they can't take you away from us. That we can take care of you and bring you home."

Uncertainty drops over Aspen's face, and she looks from Anora to me and then back again.

"You want me to come home with you?"

"Of course. Everyone wants to meet you."

"They do?" Aspen looks so skeptical I can't keep a smirk off my face.

"They do," I answer. "No one blames you for anything that Elton did, even if you helped him do it. You didn't have a choice."

"But your dad..." Aspen points to herself.

"Our dad," Anora corrects, "found comfort in another person after a heartbreaking loss. If he'd known, he would've claimed you. Being in our home is your right, and it's where you belong. Please, Aspen. It's not too late for you to have a life."

Aspen nods slowly but I don't think she believes Anora. If anything, she looks nervous, like the very idea of something approaching normalcy is too much for her. She's led such a dark, but also oddly sheltered life. I can understand why it all scares her.

"When can we go?"

"They haven't told us yet, but I would guess soon. They want to do some imaging on your leg, and when they know what's going on that will decide it. We can take you home to Chicago for treatment too."

Aspen nods and then yawns. "Who wants to meet me?"

"Everyone but Alina and Derick are here. Aster is especially excited."

The look Aspen gives us is so wary that I laugh out loud. "Do you want to meet them?"

After a long moment where Aspen looks down at her hands, she nods. I tell Anora I'll get them and leave the two of them alone. Even though Aspen is a wild card, I don't think she'd ever hurt Anora and I can feel it to my core that she didn't want to do any of this. She was under her brother's thumb, and he warped her into something she didn't want to be. Hopefully we can help her choose her path forward.

I get to the waiting room and tiredly wave my arm, calling up the crew to follow me to Aspen's room. When we all shuffle in her eye gets big, going from person to person. I have no doubt that she knows who everyone is and has been talked at about them frequently. Her gaze lingers on Aster, but then jumps around until she's taken all of us in.

"I'm Aro," she darts forward to introduce herself and then steps back. "This is Harp, he doesn't say much." Aro fondly smacks his chest and he smiles at her, and then at Aspen.

"This is Aster, and I'm Isaac." He introduces them while Aster stares, arms crossed, assessing.

"We're your family. We can do a video call with Alina soon," Anora reassures her.

Aspen stares at them all and I can almost feel the questions and doubts racing through her mind. The idea that she's getting absorbed into this family with no questions, without reservation, can be intimidating as hell.

"It'll be nice not being the youngest anymore," Aster drawls. "I have so much to teach you," she grins after, and it's the right mix of mischief and evil. Those two as allies is going to be formidable, given the skills Aspen already possesses.

"Can we do anything for you?" Aro asks. "Is there anything you need? Books, movies, whatever?"

"I don't know. A phone would be nice?" Aspen braces herself and we all see it. I know what it's like to be afraid that every time you ask for something you're going to get punished for it. She's bracing herself because she thinks we're going to be mad at her, or accuse her of asking for too much.

"Of course," Anora assures her. "We'll get you something."

"They also said I could wear regular clothes until I'm released." Aspen makes it a statement instead of a question because she's still afraid to ask.

"Done. Do you want me to stay with you?" Anora asks. The war on Aspen's face wages between wanting to push them away and desperately wanting to belong. That same war waged in me when I first got to live with the Sorrelles. It's hard not to want to be part of them but it's so easy to think you don't deserve it.

"Yes," Aspen finally answers, very quietly.

"We'll get the clothes," Aro volunteers her and Harp.

"I'll get the phone," Aster adds. They give her various goodbyes and shuffle back out of the room. Anora is twitching in her seat.

"Go to the bathroom, I'm here," I tease her. Anora laughs at me and then checks with Aspen, who snorts at her.

"Go, I'm fine."

Anora hustles out of the room to find the bathroom, and I take her seat next to Aspen. We stare at each other for a moment, and I let her see me. The wall comes down because Aspen needs to know she's not alone in this world. That she won't be ever again.

"How much do you know about me?"

"I know your parents were murdered and you've been the Sorrelle's ward since you were 16. I know you and Anora were a thing even when he didn't notice it." Aspen doesn't say her brother's name and I understand.

"The people who gave birth to me were monsters. They were never my family. You don't treat family the way they treated me."

Aspen and I stare at each other, and I let what I said sink in with her.

"I'm sorry."

I nod, knowing there isn't much else to say to that kind of confession.

"The Sorrelles are my family. They were before I ever knew or accepted it. I'm still not sure I accept it, but I try. I know right now you think you don't deserve them. That you fear at some point their love will be conditional. I get why you feel that way. All I'm asking is that you give them a chance to prove you wrong."

She swallows thickly and looks away from me as a single tear falls down her cheek. Aspen sniffles and takes a few deep breaths before turning back to me.

"Trying is the best I can do."

"That's enough for now." I offer her my hand to shake and she takes it. "Our stories are different, but I'm here if you need to talk. Anora will listen, of course, but it's not the same as someone who...knows."

Before Aspen can say anything else, Anora returns and I move from the chair. We share a look and she gives me a small nod, acknowledging that she understands my offer.

44

Anora

Three days later, we get cleared to take Aspen home. All of the paperwork is in order that she's legally ours, and we have flights booked to get her back to Chicago. Gailen is going to be here awhile. They still haven't really let him wake up, although they did decide to do a skin graft on part of his burn because it went deep.

Aster and Isaac agreed to stay in New York and coordinate his care. The doctors are hopeful about Gailen's healing, and his lungs are already cleared. They think he'll be fully mobile within 6 months, and I hope that's true.

The night before we leave, Aspen asks to see him.

He's on his stomach in the bed, his head turned toward us. In this position and asleep, he looks so young and innocent. Gailen is Aro's age, and I am struck again by how much he sacrificed for our family. Gailen didn't owe us this, not even after what happened to dad.

I wait by the door as she approaches the bed and looks down at him. She's nearly shaking with emotion, but we're not in a place yet where I could go comfort her. Aspen leans over and I see her mouth moving as she whispers something into his ear. The nurses have told us that unconscious patients can sometimes perceive what's happening around them, so we've tried to talk to him or read to him while we sit at his side.

Aspen's lips briefly brush over his cheek, and then she turns and walks to me without looking back. I get her to her room and tuck her back into bed, giving her the rundown for tomorrow morning when we'll pick her up and the itinerary for our flights.

Before leaving, I lean over and kiss her forehead.

"Goodnight, sweetie. Text me if you need anything."

Aspen grabs my hand before I can pull away. They removed the cover on her eye and the damage wasn't as bad as they feared. It's currently red and angry, and her eyelid is likely permanently damaged, but her vision should return to almost full capacity.

"Thank you."

"For what?"

"Never holding anything against me. For coming for me."

I take a risk and press forward to hug her. She's still so small. It makes my heart clench when she hugs me back. We stay like that for a long time, and I hope she feels how much I love her. Aspen was my lifeline at the scariest moment of my life, and I want to be the same for her.

"I couldn't stop him," she whispers.

"You're a kid, Aspen. I know it doesn't feel like that, but you are." I pull back but keep my hands on her shoulders so she looks at me. "Your only job was keeping yourself alive. You were supposed to have adults to take care of you, and they didn't. Let us take care of you."

Aspen nods and I squeeze her again before leaving the room. I look back at her before stepping out, and she's staring off out the window, lost in thought. It's going to be so much better when we have her home where she can be safe, comfortable, and have things and space of her own. When I can get her into therapy and help her find a sense of safety again.

Owen and I are wrapped up in each other, deep asleep, when someone pounds on our hotel room door. Someone is yelling my name and before I can second guess it I stumble to the door and open it, glad I'm in at least a t-shirt after the sexual gymnastics Owen and I engaged in before bed. There's always something extra kinky about hotel sex, especially when he finally punished me for running into the burning house.

Alonzo is there looking haggard. "She ran."

Owen steps up behind me and opens the door further. "How do you know?"

"One of the nurses I bribed called me because they're all freaking out. They'll be calling you any second."

"What's going on?" It's taking me too long to compute, and the only thought that occurs to me I immediately reject.

"Aspen is gone."

"No." I freeze. "She wouldn't do that."

Alonzo and Owen share a look.

"What?"

"There's a reason I paid people to watch her when we weren't allowed to keep a guard or staff there. She was a flight risk."

"Fuck," Owen swears. "Get everyone up. Meet here."

I let go of the door and it falls closed. I feel...shattered. We saved her only for her to run away again. She's a kid, on her own. A smarter kid than most, and one with access to money at least, but a kid nonetheless. The next call I'm going to get about her is that she's been hurt or killed.

I failed. Again.

Owen's there to catch me before my knees can hit the ground, and he wraps me in his arms. I bury my face in his neck and cry.

"This is not your fault," he assures me. "I won't disagree it's our job to take care of her, but with everything she's been through...running is what she needs. I think she's wrong, but you can't imagine..." He trails off.

"Imagine what?"

"The only family she knew until now abused and manipulated her. Made her do things she didn't want to do, and hurt people she didn't want to hurt. We're offering her a dream, and she's not ready."

"So she runs away?" I sit up, indignant.

"Yes. Sometimes we have to run away in order to come home."

I think about that. Owen and I both ran away from our home at some point. When he left early for college to get away from me, and when I fled to the East Coast to stop being haunted by him. We avoided our issues until we were in a different place to process them. I get it, but that doesn't mean I don't hate it.

Owen hugs me when I sink into him, defeated.

"Get dressed. She might need to run, doesn't mean we aren't going to try and find her."

I throw some clothes on just in time as the door rattles from another knock. Everyone piles inside. The tension is ugly.

"She left a message," Aster snarls. "It was embedded in a worm." She hands me her tablet and I see the short sentences in between lines of code.

"Let me go. I don't deserve you. I'm sorry," I read out loud. My heart breaks for her.

"Not a fucking chance," Aster snaps in response. "We're going to find her."

"Yeah we are," Aro agrees silently, leaning on Harp. Both of them spent the last few days getting to know her, playing endless card games and watching movies. Alina called her every day, and they had a video call where Aspen got to see Wyn. When Alina called her "auntie Aspen" I had to hold it together when Aspen almost cried. She was finding her place with us.

Part of me understands. Most of me is heartbroken.

"I just want to lay it out there, totally clear, that we are not going to stop until we find her and bring her home. Right?" Aro asks softly.

"Even if it's not until we're old and gray," Owen promises. It's like he knows I'm incapable of forming words right now as I use all of my energy to process and control my feelings. We stand in a circle, looking at each other, experiencing this together.

It's hard enough without Alina, but it already feels like space where Aspen should be is conspicuously empty. When she would let down her guard, it was obvious how much she fit with us. She looked like me, but her personality was more similar to Aster. The two of them could snark at each other without hurting a feeling.

Aspen wanted to be loved, and we gave that to her.

She deserves it.

"So what now?" I ask, my voice raspy.

We make a plan.

45

Owen

Aspen might be better than us.

At first, it was a flood of information. We knew she got out a fuck-ton of cash, everything liquid she had access to from the Forrester accounts. Aster hacked her ass off and tracked Aspen leaving the hospital through CCTV and traffic cameras, but at some point Aspen got a computer and started covering her tracks. It was once again the war of the hackers but it's a lot easier to hide than it is to hunt.

Aspen made herself disappear and there was fuck all that we could do.

We tried to go back to normal life, and we watched the days slip away until nearly 6 months had passed. Aster and Isaac were home, Gailen was nearly recovered, and we were no closer to finding Aspen than we had been when we left New York.

We hired professionals. We spent a heap of money on people who were supposed to be experts at tracking people down and while there were hints here and there, nothing panned out. The last we could confirm was that she had gone south, and the last camera-confirmed sighting of her was in North Carolina.

After that, not a peep. That was two months ago.

We were all back at work, trying to keep our lives going while also having the search exist in the back of our minds at all times. Designation was doing well, and I felt like I was protecting our families legacies as best I could. Anora was doing charity work again, and raising an astronomical amount of money.

Aro and Harp had returned to their cabin in the woods, which they now shared the location of with us. They went out on jobs together and used local contacts to put the word out about Aspen. There was a reward for any information about her whereabouts, but despite the enticing amount, not a single credible piece of information had made its way to us. If I ever see Aspen again, I'm going to tell her she's a genius.

Wherever she is, I hope she's safe. I hope she's taking care of herself.

We're eating a subdued dinner together. The last call from the last investigator we hired came through a few hours ago with us ending the call telling him we were done with his services. We had no next steps.

Anora pushes the meat around her plate. It's the only thing left on the plate.

"What now?" Aster asks. Isaac reaches over and puts his hand on her thigh.

"I don't know," I answer honestly. "We keep putting it out there that we're looking."

"I'll look for her."

We turn toward the new voice in the conversation. Gailen moves slowly into the living room. He moves more carefully than he did before, but the doctor said that will fade with time and deeper healing of his burn.

"I can't..." he looks away from us in shame, and I watch his jaw work. "I can't protect you anymore. I'm not fit. But I can hunt for her."

"Gailen, no," Anora starts. "You've given enough for this family."

"I don't have anything else." His voice is hollow. "Please."

I glance at Isaac, then Aster. He nods, and she gives me a small shrug.

"I won't give up. I saved her once. I'll do it again."

"Alright," I say quietly. Anora snaps her head to me. "If this is what you want, then yes. We can talk tomorrow."

Gailen nods and then moves out of the room. He knows he's welcome at these dinners, but chooses to eat alone. Fair enough. My gut tells me this is the right thing to do.

Dinner ends shortly after that, and I hear and feel Anora stomping after me to our room.

"This is a bad idea," she hisses at me.

I whirl on her and back her into our bedroom door. "It's up to me. He needs this."

Anora huffs and glares at me. It frustrates her when I'm unruffled, and I keep my face as careful and neutral as possible.

"I'm worried about him too."

The admission softens her, and I know I've won. I slide her pants over her cute, tight ass and let them drop to the floor. She's not wearing any panties, so I give her a short smack before sliding my hand between her legs. Anora is already wet for me, and I play with her until she's squirming and seeking more.

"Knees," I command. Anora slides down the door, and I gather her hair in my hand. "Take my cock out. I'm going to fuck your face and I want to watch you get yourself off as I do it. I want to hear that wet pussy as you finger fuck yourself, loving the way I use your mouth."

"Yes," she whispers, and frees me from my pants. I shift my grip on her hair and then watch as her mouth drops open and she sticks out her tongue. It's perfectly warm and wet when I slide my cock along her mouth. I work in and out slowly, going deeper with each stroke, giving her time to relax before I start moving faster.

"Let me hear that pussy, Button," I encourage her, and remind her

THE FEEL OF YOU

that she needs to work. Anora groans around my cock and I love the vibration. I work her mouth, thrusting into her throat, listening to the wet sounds of her as I own her body.

"Good girl," I praise. "I'm using your mouth and you love it. Come for me." I move faster, torturing her with the quick movements and my punishing grip on her hair. Anora practically vibrates under my hands and then moans around my cock as she comes.

I pop out of her mouth and look down at her. Her lips are swollen and she's almost breathless, her chest heaving as she recovers.

Anora's deep brown eyes open, glistening with unshed tears as she looks up at me.

"I'm pregnant."

The world drops out from below my feet and I drop to my knees in front of her.

"What?"

A hint of a smile flashes across her face. "You heard me."

"Are you sure?"

She nods, and the first tear drops before a smile takes over her face. "I didn't even realize...I took a test before dinner."

"Anora." It's all I can say. The amazement, the love, the reverence I feel in this moment is indescribable. When I pull her into my arms it takes a second for me to realize that I'm crying too. This is more than I ever imagined or believed I deserved. To be making a family of my own and having no fear that I'll ever hurt them the way my family hurt me.

"Thank you," I finally manage to get out. She laughs against my shoulder.

"For what?"

"Letting me love you." I pull back and take her face in my hands. "We've fucked up so much along the way, but this is all I've ever wanted. You, a family of our own, a chance. You are my soul, and I can't..."

I break, crying and pressing my forehead to hers.

"I love you," she says softly. "I don't live without you. You are the spark. The joy. The beat of my heart." Anora presses our hands to her stomach. "We made magic."

46

Epilogue - Anora

4 Years Later

The house is chaos, and I wouldn't have it any other way. The entire extended Sorrelle clan is home to celebrate Wyn's 5th birthday. Everyone and their families are back in their old rooms, the staff area is stuffed with extra security, and the caterers have made the kitchen a disaster area but are keeping us well fed.

I'm happy, but I'm sad.

When we told Aster and Isaac I was pregnant, they started renovations on the guest house and moved in. Aster feels safer on the compound, and like they have a better chance of keeping us safe. Plus, once she got promoted, the proximity to her boss helped when a crisis went down at work. Owen and Aster could deal with it together at home instead of having to go into work.

We've grown so much. Alina, to everyone's surprise, can't stop having babies. After Wyn, she had her first girl, Siobhan, who just turned three, and little Bran is only 6 months old. He looks like her, and I can't stop pinching his cheeks. I've been there for every one of her births, and her for mine.

When Rianna came, she almost didn't make it to the hospital because of a freak thunderstorm, but she got there just in time to promise me I could do this, and hold my leg like I did hers. Owen was a rock, but I needed a woman who knew me to reassure me. Now, Wyn and Rianna are sitting in a chair together watching something on their tablet, laughing together. Even separated by a country, they're best friends.

Our twins were a much more organized birth since I had to be induced. We still don't know how I had them since it doesn't run in anyone's family, but Malcolm and Adelaide completed us. They're currently napping, excited about the big party when they get up. It's already been a year since I had them.

We know we're done having babies, but I already miss their tiny infant stage. Despite the lack of sleep.

Aro and Harp were the last to arrive. Like the true mountain woman she's become, Aro had a home birth. Harp delivered Henry himself, in their living room, and it went amazing. They'd spent the entire year reading about it and preparing themselves. I wish I could have been with her, but when I see how they are with each other, I know it was something just for them. A thing they needed to do together. Henry is already 2, and already talking, although his favorite thing in the world is to whisper like his daddy.

The first thing Aro asked when she arrived: "Aster, when are you having babies?"

"NEVER!" Aster and Isaac responded at the same time.

"There are seven children in this family. We don't need any more!" Aster shouted.

She's right, and she's wrong. Aster never needs to have kids, but there could be more.

We still haven't found Aspen. She's 19 now. Does she look the same?

Did she ever get taller? How did her scars heal? Is she happy? I want to know if she ever fell in love, if she goes to college, if she has a favorite dessert, what kind of music she listens to these days. I want to know what she had for breakfast and her favorite pair of pajamas to relax in. I want to know if she has any pets. What kind of car she drives.

I want to know if she's still afraid, and if she dreams about Elton. Sometimes I do.

Dr. Landry said the nightmares might never go away, but I always have Owen to turn to when they wake me. They come less and less with each year. I'm afraid that's not the same for Aspen. I'm afraid she never got the help she needed.

I feel like if she had, she would have come back to us.

Aspen teases us. Gives us just enough to know she's still alive. I'm grateful for it, even though it breaks my heart again every single time we get an alert.

Gailen has never given up.

He's followed her across the country, catching her breadcrumbs, almost finding her. Aspen is always one step ahead, and I hope she knows we'll never stop. I think she does. I think that's the reason she started leaving the signs behind. Hoping that if she gave us a little bit, we would let it go.

Never.

The babies are all doing their things, or with their dads, and I've pulled my sisters into the library. We started using it again a year ago, although we did some major redecorating so it feels like a new space. The colors are lighter, the furniture is big and soft, and one corner of it - where dad's desk used to be - is a play area for the kids.

I sit with them in this room for hours every day. Rianna is old enough to start asking about her grandparents, and I love telling her about dad in a space that he spent so much time. Even if it's also the space we lost him. I'm reclaiming his ghost as a guardian angel for all of them.

"Why do I live so far away?" Alina groans, flopping onto a beanbag. She's kept her fighting figure, and I'm jealous of the lean muscle of her arms and belly. I let myself get soft, and most of the time I don't mind. Owen loves it. He can't stop touching the soft stretch of my belly that's left from having the twins.

"Make Derick move Venture here," Aster suggests.

Alina laughs. "Sure. It's the travel though, ugh."

"Okay miss private jet," Aro retorts. "How about hours in the car with a 2 year old?"

"I'll trade you," Alina answers. "Car over plane any day."

"Road trip it next time," I suggest. "And you can't be that mad, Wyn is so happy."

Her face softens and she smiles. "Yeah. But next visit you all come to us."

Aster, Aro, and I all exchange a glance. "Fine," I sigh.

There's some commotion in the hall, and in mom and protective mode we all immediately get up to go see what's going on. Owen and Harp are standing at attention, and when I look toward the door I see a battered but energized Gailen. He's breathing hard, he needs a shave, and his hair is a touch too long.

He meets my eyes.

"I found her."

Playlist

The Last of the Real Ones - Fallout Boy

Wild Heart - the Vamps

No More Sad Songs - Little Mix, Machine Gun Kelly

Golden - Cannons

Ghost - Justin Bieber

Forget Me - Lewis Capaldi

Clarity - Zedd, Foxes

Set on Fire - MAGIC GIANT

Crash My Car - COIN

You Belong to Me - Jason Wade

Acknowledgments

Sorry not sorry about that cliffhanger. When I first started plotting this series, I didn't even know Aspen existed. Don't worry, she'll get her happily ever after, too. Thanks for reading Anora and Owen's story. I would keep writing without readers but talking about something you made with other people is so much more fun and I appreciate all of the support.

Husband. It's not publicly appropriate what I have to thank you for in regard to this book but you know. Thank you for letting me talk to you, for taking care of me and our girls, for being tech support at all times.

When I was 3, I saw the Little Mermaid and vowed that I was never getting married. The parents were talking about this in front of my bestie, and he then declared that I was going to marry him. I agreed. While we are now both married to other people, our families did maintain a friendship for quite some time and it was one of the tiny nuggets that formed this story. So thanks to our parents for thinking that was hilarious.

Rachel, you killed it with this cover, especially since I seem to get more vague with each one. Thank you for understanding the vibe of this series so well and giving me covers I love using excessively on social media. Your work is gorgeous.

Cati, you are a champion. Thank you thank you thank you. I decided to hyphenate fuck-ton, so we remember this moving forward.

Annie-la. Kim, Viktoriah, Brittany, Jenn M, Jenn S, Sydnie, Anya, Keira, and anyone else who has said nice things to me about what I'm doing. I am a baby author in so many ways and the temptation to give up is so high. Thank you for making me feel like I'm not wasting my time.

My mom and my MIL for being so supportive and making people read my books.

Also by Ashley Mack

The Senses
The Sight of You (Alina and Derick)
The Taste of You (Aster and Freelancer)
The Sound of You (Aro and Harp)
The Feel of You (Anora and Owen)
The Scent of You (April 2023)

Companion Novellas
Look at Me (Kade and Cara)
Savor Me (Dominic and Cleo)
Silence Me (Rebecca, Shane, and Connor)

Elmwood College Tales
Offerings (Colin and Elise)
Preservation (Rome and Cyn)
Transfigured (Tate and Halle)
Beguiled (March 2023)
Constraint (May 2023)

About the Author

Ash lives in the Midwest with her husband, two girls, a dog, and a cat. She reads during every spare moment. She hopes that her characters go in new directions with terrifying, strong women who go feral for their men, and that sometimes the men are the damsels in distress who need saving. Connect on Instagram and Tiktok at @totalsassreads

You can connect with me on:

🌐 http://www.ashleymackauthor.com

Subscribe to my newsletter:

✉ http://www.ashleymackauthor.com/contact